AUREUS

JOAN CATHCART

DORRANCE
PUBLISHING CO
EST. 1920
PITTSBURGH, PENNSYLVANIA 15238

Dorrance Publishing Co
585 Alpha Drive
Pittsburgh, PA 15238
Visit our website at *www.dorrancebookstore.com*

ISBN: 978-1-6393-7007-8
ESIBN: 978-1-6393-7795-4

This book honors my parents,
Harry and Mary Lou Lindhorst,
who sent me on life's journey
with love, encouragement,
and a strong belief in education.

The Plantagenet Empire
at its 12th century peak

SCOTLAND

IRISH KINGDOMS

DUBLIN ●

ENGLAND

WALES

● NORTHAMPTON

NORTH SEA

LONDON ●
CANTERBURY ●
DOVER ●

● CALAIS

THE HOLY ROMAN EMPIRE

THE ENGLISH CHANNEL

NORMANDY

● PARIS
● FONTAINEBLEAU

ATLANTIC OCEAN

BRITTANY

MAINE

ANJOU TOURAINE

FRANCE

LANDS UNDER DIRECT RULE OF HENRY II

AQUITAINE

SPANISH KINGDOMS

FRANCE

CHAPTER ONE

1157 A.D.

THE SHOUTING SOARS UP THE Ardley castle parapets. It's the clatter and chirping of young voices. Boys attired for battle, brandishing sticks for swords, are engaged in maneuvers on a grassy play area. Four girls wearing pretty dresses stand on the periphery. They applaud the warriors while setting child-sized tables with cups and pitchers.

"Charge, infantry! Onward brave knights!" Richard's stubby young legs propel him in several directions to face the enemy. The boys flail their fake swords at invisible foes. Ten-year-old Jerrard shouts out his success. "I've run him through. He's done!" Planting one foot atop the unseen vanquished warrior, he raises his mighty saber to the heavens. Then he turns and runs the length of the castle courtyard, seeking other enemies to slay.

"Who are we beating today?" Gregory, still hopping up and down, always has to have the facts. "The Scots or the French?"

"In honor of the king, we should clobber the French today." Harold is an eight-year-old diplomat in-the-making. "You see, I know something you don't know." He waits for the desired attention. Then he continues. "King Henry is coming here, so we should present him with a victory over the French. That's why you're all visiting us, to dine with the king."

The young earls and their maidens stare. The king is coming. That is news.

"How do you know?" asks Emma.

"First I would like some mead." Harold points to the pitcher of water. "Then when I have rested and fed my horse, I will tell you."

Giggles from the girls. "Your horse, Lord Harold, has run away. Here's your mead." The cup of water is presented, with a gracious curtsy, to the aspiring soldier.

"Thank you." The bearer of exciting news pauses, then raises his cup for effect. "Well, now, my parents were talking, and I was listening. They don't know that I can hear them when they talk in the cloister. And don't tell. Anyway, my sister Lillian is going to be promised to the Count of Anjou, and the count is one of the king's favorite cousins. So, the king is coming here to look at her. He will see that she is pretty, so she will be betrothed before he leaves. My parents are sure of that. Then, King Henry will get another ally, my father, in his fight with the French king, my family will get another estate with hundreds of workers, and I will get to lead an army. But that will be later. The marriage won't be for a few years, you know, until Lillian is a woman." Harold nods knowingly.

"That's a lot to happen. You're sure?" Gregory is unconvinced. "I have two sisters. They're not betrothed, and one is sixteen...I think."

"That is so old. When I am sixteen, I shall be a countess somewhere, with babies. And a manor to oversee." Fiona peers past the castle's grey walls into a rosy future. "I wonder if King Henry has other cousins across the water."

❀

"LONG LIVE THE KING! Long live King Henry!" Holding goblets high, the gathered noblemen shout the phrase again and again. They wear fine velvets. Many are red, a color denoting high rank; the dye is costly. These well-dressed aristocrats are seated at a long polished wooden table, headed by a young man whose attire is modest by comparison to the other diners. He is King Henry, known to be less flashy in dress but more flamboyant in manner.

Wives, children, attendants, retainers and some palace stragglers stand at the periphery. Only the men are eating now. The king speaks with a French accent. "My lords, your fine families and others, I am delighted to be dining at the Ardley Castle, sharing the fine food and wine provided by my excellent host, Lord Clarence." He pauses, allowing a ripple of applause for the smiling earl. "As I travel throughout my land," he allows another break before speaking the next six words slowly, for emphasis, "and it is my land…now," a royal nod and smile create the vacuum to be filled by more polite clapping, "I have delighted in the hospitality of my new countrymen. Though I was born to the Anjou House of Plantagenet, on the other side of the water, I consider England to be my permanent home, as well as my consecrated duty. I am traveling the length and width of this kingdom to meet my subjects and establish royal courts throughout, but here, at Ardley Castle, I have also a more personal reason to visit. The Earl of Ardley and I are pleased to announce the betrothal of his charming daughter Lillian to my cousin the Count of Anjou."

"Here, here." Goblets are raised along with voices. King Henry drinks, then waves his hand downward. The cheering stops. Henry stands and sweeps the hall with a beaming face. "Ladies, my Queen Eleanor sends her regards and wishes she could have joined me." His goblet follows his gaze. He has captivated his audience.

Emma is standing with her mother, whose crimson dress billows in the drafty hall. "Mother," she whispers, "Is it true that Queen Eleanor is over ten years older than the king?"

"Shhh. Do not embarrass your father."

"The king is talking. He can't hear me. Is it true?"

Emma's mother leans over and speaks into her ear. "She is in her thirties. Countess Richmond saw her. In her thirties, can you imagine?"

Emma can only shake her head. The handsome young monarch in front of her has an old queen. She must find out why he chose her. But not here. Not now.

❀

LATE THE FOLLOWING MORNING, Ardley Castle is a flurry of activity. Carriages assemble in the general courtyard. The castle gates are open, and children run out into the surrounding fields to play while their parents bid farewell to the Earl and Countess of Ardley.

"My dear," Emma's mother reaches out to Lady Ardley. "Your charming hospitality is made even more gracious by your splendid location in the beautiful countryside. You are the essence of English womanhood." She performs a pretty curtsy.

"Thank you, but the queen wears the crown."

"The queen is from across the water. She speaks French. I stay with my opinion." A practiced smile parts her lips. Then a frown appears. "Emma, where are you going? We're leaving shortly."

"Mother, the kids are going to the fields. The boys are going to show off their military skills. They want an audience."

"Don't go far." She returns her attention to the countess. "When did the king leave?"

"Oh, madam, he was gone at sunrise. He wastes no time in establishing his sovereignty throughout the land. Such a busy man. By the time he arrives in London, his English will be perfect."

The field outside the castle is a picture of children at play. Emma spies a beautiful patch of blue flowers. She kneels down to pick them as a gift for her mother. She does not see the boy soldier running through the field. As she stands, he gallops into her. The flowers scatter, landing on the ground.

"Oh, oh," Jerrard stops, flustered. "Uh, are you okay? I am sorry. We were conducting battle games."

"I guess your horse didn't see me."

4

A bashful grin spreads across Jerrard's face. "Uh, no, he is a blind horse. What's your name? Wait, are you Lillian?"

"No, I am Emma."

"I'm Jerrard. I heard Lillian is very pretty. So I thought you were Lillian." He has also heard that flattering ladies on their beauty can be beneficial, though he is not sure exactly why.

"I am only eight and a half. She is older than that. In a few years she will go away and live her life across the water. But now, your blind horse made me drop all my flowers. Would a fine swordsman help pick them up?"

"Sure." As Emma brushes off her dress, Jerrard gathers the bouquet. "Here."

"Then, here's one for you. A knight should have a flower from a lady."

"Thank you."

A distant mother's voice calls. "Jerrard, are you out there? We are leaving."

The young knight bows and runs to where his mother stands, near their coach. She stamps a shiny leather boot in irritation. "Don't tell me you were picking flowers. Is there something I need to know about my warrior son?"

"Oh, no, mother. A pretty maiden gave this to me."

The mother shakes her head, eyes beseeching the skies. "Of course, just like your father."

CHAPTER TWO

Five years later, 1162 A.D.

THE HALL IN KING HENRY'S palace is afire with burning torches along the walls. Candles illuminate the furnishings. It is a bright afternoon outside, but sunlight is a stranger to the monarch's great room. Clad in hunting gear, Henry sits on a small throne, deep in royal thought. His friend Thomas Becket, resplendent in a fine robe, paces near him. The king has many advisors, but only one friend, Thomas, whose counsel he considers to be first-rate. Henry has told Thomas many times that he does not trust the nobility, who are always jockeying around for status and royal favors while conspiring to increase their power at the expense of his own. Likewise, he distrusts the lesser squires, who collect the local taxes throughout the realm. Henry is sure, he confides to Thomas, that they are skimming precious coinage off the top before delivering the annual levy to the royal coffers. A plan to remove these middlemen is stewing in his brain. But right now, the king needs money.

Henry leans forward. "I've been thinking about the crown's expenses, my dear chancellor, and there is a solution that is so obvious that I don't know why I didn't think of it before." He regards his friend with hard eyes and pursed lips.

"I am afraid to ask, Your Highness." Thomas has grown accustomed to the tossed idea followed by silence.

"Well, you should be. You see, if I had the money that you spend, out of your royal stipend, courtesy of me, on your splendid outfits," Henry points, with a flourish, at the chancellor's robe, "I would have no more financial worries."

"And embarrass my friend, protector and monarch by wearing rags?" Chancellor Becket delights in this brand of banter with his pal and mentor, the king. "I couldn't diminish your reputation by doing that. Much better to tax the barons. They dress well, but they also have what I don't: big estates, armies, serfs, daughters to marry, sons to fight, just for starters."

"The nobility, my dear Thomas, are a thorn in my side, if I may use one of your favorite English phrases. I need fighting men to confront King Louis of France. I am technically his vassal, but we know that's for show. So, the English nobility must supply troops from their estates so that I can make war. And they are *my* vassals, and that, too, is often for show. The system is fraught with uncertainty, and uncertainty is an undesirable commodity when waging war. What I need is more money to hire a large private army, a full-time fighting force under my command. That's a new idea. And a good one, because it's my idea. Now I am thinking of appointing you as Archbishop of Canterbury. That way more of the church's money can come to me, don't you see? I know you'll have to make it right with the Pope, but he's in Rome, and we are here, far away. What do you say?"

"My king and my friend, it is difficult to serve two masters."

"You will figure it out. Think of it this way. Should a king really have to beg the Great Council for money to expand the greatness of the realm? Shameful."

"Can't you arrange any more marriages? You've done that very well, and you've created some powerful alliances. And allies have armies."

"Yes, Thomas, yes, but here's the thing that bothers me. Because of my matchmaking, families on both sides of the water are more interconnected and wealthier. They owe me." He shakes a knowing head. "Yes, they owe me, but they don't always pay up. Now, be my archbishop, and the English monarchy will be independently wealthy."

THE FOREST CLEARING IS DAMP from a season of rains. Trees laden with saturated branches hover over two ragged men, kneeling over wet earth. Mud covers their bodies. They don't seem to notice; they are busy with the forgiving soil.

"This will be a nice crop of carrots, John, if you can keep the location to yourself. Give me your promise one more time."

"If you ask me one more time, I will piss on all these new plantings. Ahhh." John stands up and stretches. He is a hairy, husky man, still bent over as he raises his head. "I see the forest fairies in the trees, and they tell me it is time for beer. Where is the jug?"

"I hid it, you arse, so you would plant until we are finished. We still have to put in the lavender, or all our work will be become deer food in two weeks. Think about that."

"You may be my brother, but you are not my jailer. I think I'll look for the beer." John lifts his legs over the upturned dirt, mud flapping from the laced goatskins that cover his feet. "Yes, a walk in the woods is a fine bit of exercise for a planting man." Bits of soil fly through the air, striking the brother whose name is Alger.

"God, man, you are sloppy even when you are taking a stroll." Alger watches John plunge into a thicket. "Hey! Hey! Stop! Where are you going?"

"I told you. For a drink. Maybe you don't like the direction I am taking? Ha!" His voice becomes more distant. "That tells me. The jug is this way. See, you talk too much. Just like your big brother, the man who tells carrot secrets. Ah ha. I see it."

Alger tries to run in his brother's direction, but his limp forces him into an unsteady walk over the vines and branches strewn on the forest floor. When he reaches a small opening, his brother is taking the cork out of the jug.

"I told Matilda I would bring you back sober. Stop."

"Matilda, another jailer. Here's to both of my would-be jailers." John tilts his head back and raises the jug.

"Damn you!" Alger pushes off with his good leg and tackles John. They roll through the thick growth. Curses and grunts echo in the forest air. Spewing its contents, the jug rolls into a knot of vines. A cavern of greens swallows the brothers who are, once again, settling a sibling feud.

"Ow! Ow! That's not fair!" Alger's voice shouts pain and outrage.

"What? What did I do?"

"You stuck a pike in my back, that's what. Like you didn't know. Coward."

"Alger, whatever it is, I didn't do it." John rolls away, his voice wounded. "I have no pike. If I did, I wouldn't stick your back with it. I'd stick it up your arse. Ha. Now get up. Let me look." The bushes rustle as the two bodies hoist themselves up. John turns his brother around.

"Oh, the saints! You are bloody. Let me see." John lifts Alger's shirt, revealing a nasty gash near his right shoulder blade; it is bleeding.

"It hurts. Really hurts. You say you didn't do it?"

"Of course not. I can beat you any time without poking a hole in your back. Where's the jug? I will wash it with beer, though it will be a sad waste of a good drink." John steps back into the small open area. The jug is on its side; liquid drips from its opening. He lifts it up and shakes it, nodding. "Ah, good, there is some left. Okay little brother, bend over."

Alger shoots him a sly smirk. "You bugger." He complies. The beer splashes over his wound. "Ow, ow, ow. Hey, wait a minute."

"Don't interrupt me. I'm inflicting pain."

"Stop! There's a stake sticking out of the ground. That's what I fell on. Someone has put it there. See. Look there." Forgetting his wound,

Alger grabs his brother's left arm, pulls him forward and points to a crafted piece of wood emerging many inches from the ground. It is old and black; the sides are sleek, as if a fine artisan had polished it for use as a small spear. The tip is red from Alger's blood.

"What?" John just stares. "What?"

"Listen, we need some digging tools, you know, better than what we use for the carrots and lavender. I think there is something down there worth digging for. I think the spirits of the forest wanted us to find this. That's why they made you thirsty. Let's cover it up and come back. Okay?"

"Okay."

IT IS DARK NOW. The daytime forest, filled with chirping birds, rustling animals and wind in the trees, is now a sea of black silence. Alger and John, aided by a small torch, grope through the green and brown tangle. They are still wearing the morning's dirt, though Alger has changed his shirt. He is wearing the only other one he owns.

"I see our carrot patch, just over here." John's stride follows his finger. He examines his handiwork, patting down the newly planted soil with the top of his foot. "Wouldn't his lordship have a bloody fit if he knew we were planting carrots in his private woodland?"

"No, he wouldn't," replies Alger. "He would just eat them all and then cut off your head for fun."

John gets his bearings. "Let's see. I went this way." Holding the small torch in front of his chest, he charges through the brush.

"Hey, John, careful. Don't burn down the forest. Can you hear me?"

The response is jubilant. "I found it. I tell you, I'm a natural tracker."

Alger picks his way through the blackness, tripping over vines. "Damn forest!" Ahead, John is barely illuminated by the puny torch. He pushes back a fortress of greens and waves the flame over the ground.

"Can't see it. Guess I'll do this." Down on one knee, he waves one hand back and forth over the top of the soil. "C'mon, you sweet pain in my brother's back, present yourself. Alger, hold these branches back. There. There we are. I found you, you little dagger. C'mon. Let's dig."

❧

AS SLIVERS OF GREY tint a corner of the forest sky, the nightlong cadence of grunts suddenly stops. The two forest men, now much dirtier than when planting carrots, hover above a two-foot hole. The sharp stake lies to one side.

"Hey."

"Yeah, there's something hard down here. A box maybe. Something that someone wanted to hide for a long time." John wipes his dirty brow. "Dig. Dig. Dig."

The grey streak gives way to pink; then a pale yellow announces the approaching dawn. No longer really speaking, the two men utter noises like oxen pulling a cart. Suddenly they toss aside their crude shovels. Only their hands are digging. Dirt flies in all directions.

"I feel something. It's round. Do you feel it?" John is a burrowing animal, covered in grime.

"Yeah, yeah," Alger pants.

The brothers, heads bumping, cry out their discovery. "It's real! A treasure, for sure! Just a few more scoops! Got it! Got it!" Mud drips from their noses, mouths, chins.

"Okay, we'll get our fingers under the bottom, like this." Alger cups his hands, catching his breath. "You get right opposite me. Yeah, like that. Now, on three, we pull up."

"One.... Two.... Three." The brothers bellow and pull. The container is heavy, but slowly it emerges from the hole. John grunts an order. "Down, over here."

The prize is round, the size of a man's belly, with a flat bottom. It is black as its resting place. It feels like pottery. Bumpy. The wide opening at the top is covered by thick leather, held in place by a strap wound round and round the container's neck.

John draws a short knife and saws through the brittle layers of leather. "Ah, I'm through this thick stuff. Reach in, little brother. I'll give you the honor." Alger reaches out, then hesitates at the jagged opening. "I can't. It could be a wicked forest spirit."

"All right, little brother, I must do this for you, but I get to keep what I bring up."

"We are partners, remember."

"Oh, sure," John promises, as he plunges his hand into the opening. His arm jiggles around. His lips part in a victorious beam. He pulls his hand out. His fingers are curled around a golden coin.

"We are partners with all the rest of this booty, but this one is mine."

Dawn breaks over the brothers, clasping hands in triumph. The forest becomes lighter, outlining two men replacing their treasure and covering it with dirt and vines.

CHAPTER THREE

THE IMPOSING BOULTON CASTLE looms into view. Ornate carriages approach on different roads. Retainers ride alongside the lumbering conveyances. Banners and baronial flags flutter in the afternoon sun. Arms wave in distant hellos. Voices hail greetings. The mood is merry. At last, after many years of war against the French king, there is going to be an extended party.

Emma, new to being a teenager, peers out her carriage window. She has acquired a young woman's grace, but a child's playfulness still dances in her eyes. This gathering will be her introduction to society. Because of the rigors of travel, she has been to only a few of the smaller aristocratic celebrations, where she dressed in her finest gowns and learned to dance the carol. It's important to have her fun now because, who knows, her father may have already begun negotiations for her betrothal. The memory of her older sister's departure is fresh. Catherine was barely a teen, just learning the womanly arts, when she was whisked away to wed one of Queen Eleanor's relatives in the Aquitaine, across the water. Rumor was that he was even older than the queen. Poor Catherine, with a husband who probably had no interest in dancing, just producing heirs and listening day after day to stories of war and intrigue. Well, she, Emma, will dance the carol until the candles flicker out. She will taste freedom and frivolity before her body seals an alliance somewhere in England or across the water.

A galloping horse momentarily blocks her view of the landscape. The rider is young. He holds the reins in his left hand and waves wildly with his right. "Welcome, one and all. Boulton welcomes you. We have mead and venison. We have music and dancing." The horseman circles Emma's carriage, riding close to the window. "Hello, fair lady, welcome to our festival. Please make our very humble castle your home." A smile. A wave. And he is gone.

Emma is elated. The rider is familiar. He is the son of Boulton. And handsome. Perhaps he will dance with her. She will have fun...while she can.

The carriage passes through the castle gates and into a throng of horsemen, wagons, retainers pulling garment-laden trunks, chattering guests and other coaches disgorging their passengers. The young rider strides across the parade ground, the site of long-ago jousting contests. He has given his horse to one of the stable boys, and now he is embracing his peers, sons who will inherit, make war, and support the king, if that is the current strategy. Tall and ruddy from practicing outdoor skills, Jerrard welcomes with arms that display the tendons of an accomplished archer.

Emma's father assists her mother in exiting the carriage, but Emma remains, awaiting aid in her dismount from the confines of the coach. Castle couriers, sweating and swearing in their own jargon, haul handsome valises off the jitney attached to the carriage back. A stool appears, thrust at the open door by a teenage hand.

"For you, young maiden." The next Earl of Boulton has learned his manners well. "Hello again."

❊

THE FEAST IS NEARLY FINISHED. Long tables feature the remains of a fine venison, courtesy of the earl's deer forest. A goose carcass occupies an ornate platter, now strewn with bones. Bits of bread remain uneaten; the revelers shout their appreciation for the fine Boulton wine. Lord William, Earl of Boulton, raises his glass.

"First, to His Majesty King Henry. To the king's health and victory on the battlefield."

"Here, here!" The diners raise their glasses. Emma joins her parents in toasting the king. She also enjoys the wine, which she is permitted to drink on special occasions.

"And now, my esteemed friends, we will dance."

The glossy guests abandon their seats. Kitchen workers and castle servants dash into the hall, pulling stools and tables off to the side. Hungry fingers pull stray morsels from the plates and platters on their way to the scullery room to be washed. A circular table holding the Boulton arms appears in the center of the great room.

"And for your listening pleasure," the earl pauses to allow his phrase to settle on his guests' ears, "For your listening pleasure, we will dance the carol to the mellow tones of a flute and a lute. Ah, tonight I am a poet. And a dancer. Come, my dear, let us begin."

The sounds of the stringed lute and woodwind beckon the dancers. Formed from segments of two or three people, a hand-holding circle grows into one huge circumference around the table in the middle. Children join in with their parents. With a kick, step, step, step, the dancers move slowly to the left, some singing to the familiar melody. Plentiful wine has improved the leg motions of some, while others are stumbling to keep the pace

Then the music changes. The tempo becomes livelier, faster. Children topple and are quickly righted by their parents' sure grip. One dancer falls, to the amusement of his partners to the right and left. The circle hops up and down in one place while the slightly inebriated old lord resumes his place.

Emma is transported. Her laughter seems at one with the music. Dancing between her father and mother, she kicks, hops and jumps, all to the tune of a familiar folk song. Suddenly she feels her right hand being parted from her mother's grasp. She had been looking left, in the direction the circle was going. Her head turns. There is Jerrard, dancing between her and her mother. He is laughing and singing simultaneously. His strident young voice attracts her father's attention. Jerrard nods a greeting.

That hand. It is tempting, to Emma, to peek at the source of the strong hold on her fingers. But she must look left. That's where all the dancers are looking. If you dance left, then you look left. But when dancing, she has always held her parents' hands, or those of her sisters and brothers, or other children of the court. This is different. It feels different. Emma wishes Jerrard had entered the circle on her left side where she could examine his young hand more easily. But then he would be next to her father, who is frowning at the intruder. Emma is quite aware of her father's protectiveness toward his daughters. He often speaks of their virtue as a commodity, reminding them that their value in marriage negotiations depends on more than just his estates, his position in the king's court and, of course, their dowry; it also depends on betrothing a daughter who is an untouched maiden, not used goods. Shaking off these sober thoughts, Emma kicks and steps, always looking left.

The room is loud now, with much off-key singing. An increasing tempo produces a hodgepodge of kicks, steps and other footwork. The earl's entertainment is a success, and he is delighting in the carol as much as his guests. With his wife dancing on his right, the earl suddenly loosens his left hand from its grasp and pats his other partner's bottom. The startled lady jumps, loses her rhythm, scowls, then laughs as she regains her step. "My dear lord, you are a bear."

"Grrrrr. Let me show you my paws." He, too, is laughing, but the countess, Jerrard's mother, is not amused.

A kitchen boy appears, out of breath, tugging at the earl's elegant coat. "Sir, sir, you must come at once. Very important, says your steward. He is just outside."

Stepping out of the circle, Lord William passes his wife's hand to the laughing lady. "My wife is not a bear, but rather a raging tiger. So you are no safer."

The earl's steward, Sir Ralph, is standing outside the kitchen entry, beyond the light. His brown leggings and cape make him nearly invisible. William steps into the darkness, adjusting his vision to the color of night.

"Here, sir," the steward reaches for William's arm and pulls him further into the misty blackness. "Come here." He is panting, out of breath. They step near an arched entry looming out of the shadows. No one is near.

"Well what is it that brings you to my party, dragging me away from dancing the carol and swatting the bum of a pretty woman?"

"You know that I would only take you away from pleasure if it were truly important." The words tumble out of Sir Ralph's agitated lips. "It's a secret, but not anymore, that is, it won't be. Everyone will be trying to find it. You must come now."

"The secret is still a secret to me. Out with it."

"Right, right. You know perhaps the man called Tanner. He lives in the settlement by the river. He has made saddles for you. I think some fine deerskin cloaks. Other things, I can't remember."

"Oh, I see," the earl interrupts with sarcasm, "he has made a cloak for me, and you have dashed here to give it to me. Fine. It's cold out here. Good God, man, what is the secret?"

"Tanner says he will make you richer than the Pope. He only hopes that you will be generous with your reward for his humble person. That's how he put it. Tanner. But I, too, look forward to your generosity."

"Sir Ralph, if the secret does not find its way to my ears forthwith, your head will adorn the center of my table, and my guests will note your frozen smile, saying that you must have gone to your untimely end knowing a fine secret." Lord William's festive personality has disappeared into the night. Something savage lurks at the corners of his mouth. His right hand rests on his scabbard, which encompasses a small sword, always sharpened.

Mouth agape, the steward looks like he has been slapped.

"I see I have your attention. Now, what is *it*?"

"There are two men in the settlement. Brothers. Sometimes they plant in your forest. That's what they were doing when they found the container. Buried. They dug it up. It's full of Roman coins. All gold. There's a name for it. I don't know. It's reburied now, but John kept one coin. He was drinking beer tonight. Too much beer. He was shouting that he was rich. Alger, too. Nobody believed him, so he went into his hut and came out with the coin. Tanner saw it. He touched it. He says it's beautiful, unlike any coin he's ever seen. And the brothers say the container is full of coins like that. It's in your forest. It's yours." Sir Ralph's voice is heavy with an awful reality. "You're a fine gentleman, so you can spend it without fear. Do whatever you like with it. Alger and John can't. Neither can Tanner. Neither can I, quite honestly." There is a bitter tone in these last words. Sir Ralph doesn't have to explain further. This fabulous treasure, if it exists, has no value to a man who does not have the noble credentials to spend it. To try would mean having one's head displayed on a pike.

"So, your lordship, Tanner came to me, hoping for your generosity if he could lead you to the brothers. I share his hope."

"The Aureus."

"What?"

"A treasure. From long ago. Yes, our Roman forbearers minted very fine coins. Gold. I have heard that they left some here, in their haste to retreat." The earl refashions his demeanor. "Sir Ralph, you were right to come to me. Tell no one else. You will be rewarded. Tanner, too. Good night."

❄

IT IS STILL NIGHTTIME. The same night. The same castle. The same yard beyond the door to the kitchen scullery, where the clatter of dishes being washed, dried and put away still floats out into the quiet courtyard. A lone figure stands off to one side in the tall shadowy arched entry. He wears a monk's brown tunic, bound by a waist cord around his generous midsection. His face beams as he sips fine wine from a goblet. At his feet there is a jug, holding more wine, that he has pilfered from an overburdened kitchen shelf. He did not dance or sing earlier, for such frivolities are not permitted to one who has dedicated a life to poverty and prayer. No, he was just finishing the wine that was on the shelf, left for the taking. God must have wanted him to have it, or else He would not have put it there, unattended. His smiling lips form one word. "Aureus."

THE FOLLOWING DAY UNFOLDS on preparations for an outdoor entertainment at Boulton Castle. Stools are assembled on a lawn beyond the palace gardens, now brilliant in their summer colors. Festive tables are laden with meats, cheeses, breads and sweets. The guests circulate, catching up on family news or matters of estate management or, the men's favorite, war with the French king. There is always much to share. These gatherings are infrequent; overland travel is difficult when you must transport a family and chests of finery. Young attendees, friends since childhood, have changed much since the last baronial festival. Some of the boys are now strapping teens: riders, archers, hunters and inheritors of the land. The little girls have become young maidens, all clad in finery befitting daughters of the nobility. They are a pretty lot, soon to be the glue that seals treaties, alliances and families.

Four of these young ladies, childhood friends who seldom see one another, drift apart for some long-awaited teen talk.

"Gweneth, are you betrothed yet?" It is a question often asked.

"I think my parents are negotiating right now. They aren't outside, so I think they are talking to Lord William."

"No! Are you to marry Jerrard? You lucky girl."

"Oh, I don't think that's the case. And Jerrard is very, um, nice. No, the earl is arranging an alliance between us, Boulton and Westland. It's very complicated, and no one is explaining it to me."

"Well, then, it would seem that you are to marry the Earl of Westland or one of his sons. Which is it?"

"I don't know, but a son would be better. Our children would be safer. You know how it is. If I marry the old earl, our children would be second in line, behind all the children he has now, and I do happen to know that he has three sons and two daughters. See, I do know something."

"Which son would you marry, if it is the son? The oldest, I hope."

Heads nod at this comment. It's usually better to marry the first heir, unless he is raving mad or physically deformed.

Gweneth shrugs and shakes her head. She doesn't know the answer to that question either.

Emma offers her view. "If I were betrothed to someone in Normandy or Anjou, or better yet, the Aquitaine, then I could see my sister Catherine now and then, so I hope I cross the water as a bride. Of course, there are some suitable young men on this side." She remembers the firm hand that held hers last night.

Beatrice jumps into the conversation with an announcement. "I am betrothed. Since February. I might get married as early as next year. It could be five years as far as I'm concerned. Scotland is so far away, and I'm afraid I won't see my family for a long time after I go to Prince Robert's palace."

The girls cluster around her. They giggle with excitement. Beatrice is the first to be pledged in marriage. "Why didn't you tell us? We've been here for a whole day." Another voice chimes in. "No fair keeping secrets."

"I feel like, if I don't talk about it, maybe it won't happen, at least not soon. Do you understand what I mean?"

"Not really. It will happen when your father and the prince decide, whether you talk about it or not. Do you know anything about Prince Robert?" Gweneth, the realist, is always so matter-of-fact.

"More than you know about the Westlands, whether you are going to marry the father or a son," Beatrice retorts, then permits a tiny grin. "Prince Robert, I am told, carries a handsome face, and he is a fine horseman. And hunter. He will be an attentive father, too, because he is generous with his bastard son, whose mother is a washer woman." A moment of silence, then a giggle. "I'm not supposed to know that last thing, but my governess often has tea with my mother. Sometimes they drink wine instead, and that's when they discuss certain...ah... grownup subjects."

"So what else do they talk about?" Shy Caroline's curiosity has been awakened.

"Well, they talk about the king, our king, Henry. Interesting things." She nods, waiting, savoring the pleasure of knowing something juicy about the most powerful man in the kingdom. The girls are clamoring, "C'mon, c'mon, tell us."

"Alright, I won't torment you, because you would never guess what I'm about to say. You just can't make this up. But you also can't say that you heard it from me. The king, I hear, has a mean temper, and he would not likely be averse to cutting off my head if I displeased him."

There is much crossing of hearts and promises. Fingers are pressed to lips, forever sealed.

"When Henry was nineteen, he traveled from Anjou to Paris – it's a short trip, my governess says, though she has never been across the water, but anyway, he traveled to Paris to present himself to King Louis. It was a matter of protocol, and appearances, to maintain the pretense that the King of France was somehow his superior. Everybody following?" The circle nods in unison.

"This is the first surprise. At that time, King Louis VII was married to...**ta da**...Queen Eleanor."

The response is a jumble of voices. "No. Our Queen Eleanor? You mean another Queen Eleanor. No? You're confusing us. Go on! Go on!"

"King Louis was married to Queen Eleanor, now our Queen Eleanor, but at that time she was Queen Eleanor of France."

Silence now, as the crowd processes the news, the impossible news.

"And King Louis and Queen Eleanor had children, daughters. Anyway, King Louis was, and still is, very pious, unlike Henry, who made a big impression on the French queen, who was not attracted to her husband's piety, shall we say." Beatrice beams. The story is going very well. She had asked her governess to repeat it twice, so that she would be able to retell it in full and accurate detail.

"Here's my second surprise. Queen Eleanor sent her bishop to Rome to secure a divorce from King Louis."

"Divorce?" The word erupts from the assembled mouths, simultaneously. "That is not even possible," whispers Caroline.

"Well, it *is* possible, because it happened. And here's how it happened, in case you ever need to rid yourself of a husband. Well, on second thought, you probably would have to be a queen to be able to get away with *that*. Of course any one of us could be a queen, or maybe an empress. But I'm digressing here. My governess tells me that I must stick to my subject when engaging in a conversation."

"Oh, I wish your governess were my governess. Mine never tells me anything. Go on, what did the queen get away with?" asks Emma.

"Queen Eleanor petitioned the Holy Father to grant a divorce on the grounds of consanguinity. Con-san-guin-i-ty." Beatrice had practiced this word until it rolled off her tongue like sweet sap from a forest tree.

"What? What is that word?"

"It means that she and the king were related by blood, so they shouldn't be married."

Caroline shakes her head in confusion. "Didn't she know they were related when they got married?"

"You would think so. You would certainly think so. Which is why you can't say it was I who told you this story. They say that King Henry gets very, very angry if anyone asks what you just asked. And there is still more."

There is a chorus of "Oh, no!"

"Yes, three more things, exactly." She waves three fingers on her right hand, then letting two of them drop. "First, two months after Eleanor received her divorce, she married Henry. Everyone was shocked." Beatrice raises the second finger. "At the same time, the Duchy of Aquitaine, Eleanor's province, made a huge donation to the Church. That's the second thing. My governess calls it a, mm, a…" Beatrice slows down to get her words right, "an 'agreeable and profitable coincidence.' The third thing you may already know, but at the time of her marriage to Henry, Queen Eleanor was thirty, or around there."

"And Henry was nineteen, you said." Emma adds.

"And now he's, what, mid-twenties?" Caroline must offer up something.

"He must be," Beatrice goes on, "which means his queen is…" She shakes her head. "But she has given Henry sons."

Emma nods. "I knew she was old, even when I was just a young girl. But, wow, that's quite a story. I'm sure glad you came to the festival, Beatrice. The Boulton entertainment is nothing compared to yours. But I am thinking of something my father talks about, a lot, when the king asks him for soldiers during the planting season, which makes my father very angry. He says King Henry and Queen Eleanor own more land together than the King of France. Yet we still make war on the French, which my father always seems to understand. Now I understand, too." She permits a dramatic pause to allow her audience to catch up. "No wonder our king is so aggressive on the other side of the water. He has taken the French King's wife. Why not take his land? No wonder King Louis fights back so hard. He has been humiliated."

The girls stand in silence, absorbing the observation. They may, in a short time, be betrothed and shipped off to live in the midst of this turbulence on the other side of the water.

❋

THE MUSICIANS ARE ASSEMBLING in the afternoon light. Many of the guests are now seated on stools, picking bits of food off of their plates which had been piled high with meats freshly hunted in the Boulton forests. Tankards of wine and mead adorn the tables, an essential at all gatherings where the host must pour his finest for the assembled baronial families of the realm. A clatter of hoofs arises from a distance, the sound growing louder, until the pounding is reinforced by dust and shouts from three young riders as they burst onto the castle grounds. Jumping from their steeds and throwing the reins to stable children, who materialize whenever horses appear, the riders bellow "hallo, hallo," to the assembly.

Jerrard half runs and half jumps to where his mother stands, surrounded by guests. "Hi, mama. Hi everyone." He bows and tosses off a showy salute, receiving warm nods from the powdered ladies. Only mama looks at him with disapproval. Holding his upper arm, she guides him out of the chatting circle.

"You are late. The guests are here, assembled, and you, our eldest, should be here to greet them."

"Well, where is father?"

She lowers her voice to a soft hiss. "Where he usually is. Rolling on a bale of hay with the milk maid. Or the scullery girl. Or, who knows? You've no time to change your clothes, so you must work your charm dressed like one of our peasants. Oh, well." She turns and re-enters the coterie of revelers.

Jerrard continues his journey through assorted knots of merry-makers, now listening to the play of minstrels. The party is picking up its pace. Some guests are dancing in tiny circles; others laugh, eat, flirt, and sing. A few party goers are doing all at the same time. Children play hide-and-seek behind the billowing dresses of their mothers. It is a fine festival, and Jerrard walks through it, the self-assured son of the host who is not there. Off to one side he spies a small group of girls, giggling as if they have just shared a very amusing secret. He recognizes one of them, the one he is looking for.

"Hello ladies," Jerrard announces his presence. "Are you having fun this afternoon?"

Not waiting for an answer, he continues. "We have a lot of food for you. Be sure to try the swan with the berry sauce. Miss Emma, do you have a flower for me?"

A memory of another party, perhaps five years ago, jumps into Emma's brain. So this is the boy swordsman who vanquished the imaginary warrior, who helped her pick up her scattered flowers, blue flowers she remembers. He is last night's circle dance intruder, the young earl. He is, she thinks, the embodiment of her mother's favorite descriptive word for a healthy male adolescent; he is robust. Emma hopes the figure in front of her does not notice her red cheeks. They must at least be pink, she thinks, because they feel quite hot.

"I would have picked one for you, but I do not see any growing in your castle yard." Inside, Emma is proud of herself. She has found a suitable retort for the unexpected question.

"Come with me. I'll take you to the flowers if you promise to pick one for me." Ever so lightly, he steers her elbow away from the girls. "The flower garden is just past the stables. That way we always have a fresh supply of fertilizer close by." Jerrard laughs, an easy laugh, which softens his reference to the use of manure. "Our gardeners need the fragrance of flowers to mask the odor of their trade. They grow our vegetables over there. The ones on our tables today." He points to a well-tended field of green leaves and stalks. "We have fields of wheat outside the walls. Of course, we must grow barley, oats and rye for our workers. Oh, I do apologize; I am giving you so much information about our farming, and you likely are not interested in what our peasants eat." Jerrard slows his pace, realizing that his stride is forcing Emma into a semi-trot.

"Do you let your workers have any of the flowers? My father says their dark homes offend flowers."

"That I don't know. My mother could answer your question."

They are rounding the stables. Emma walks more carefully now. Her delicate shoes pick their way around familiar clumps. Jerrard, in his riding boots, does not notice. He is concentrating on what is around the corner. "There, look there, so many nice flowers, even though quite a few were cut for today's celebration. I think you'll still find enough to choose from." Ahead there is a blaze of color. Flowers of all descriptions waft in the light breeze.

"Wait, I am picking a flower for you. So, you must tell me your favorite color."

"Mmm. A good question. Let's see." Jerrard scratches his head. He is searching for a particular mental image, and he finds it. "Blue."

They walk through a sea of yellow and white daisies, then on through red and pink geraniums. Orange poppies give way to lavender, then violets. There is another sweep of yellow buttercups and daffodils. In a far corner, there are bluebells and forget-me-nots. Jerrard stops.

"These look familiar. A girl gave one to me once. I thought her name was Lillian, but it was Emma." He points to a blue forget-me-not. "That one."

"You sure. That very one?"

"I am sure. In fact, you can pick a whole bouquet, and I will have a maid set them on my table."

Emma leans in and tugs on a few blue flowers, but they are tenacious and don't want to leave the garden. She frowns. "They are stubborn."

"I have what you need." He draws a small dagger from a leather sheath hanging from his belt. "I could help, so that you don't get dirty."

"Alright. That clump there." The dagger does its work quickly. "I think your bouquet should be large. Those two clumps there." The blade, fashioned for more demanding chores, severs the stems in swift clean cuts.

"Here," Emma reaches for the blue cluster, "let me put them all together. Yes, a very nice bouquet for a gentleman. And one for me."

Slender fingers push the stem of a single flower into her long chestnut curls, just above her right ear. "Shall I carry them or you?"

"You know, you can take pleasure in them now, and I will enjoy them later." He turns to begin retracing their steps. "Now tell me, what were you and the other girls laughing about?"

"We were talking about matters of statecraft, actually."

"Really. You girls were discussing matters of state...and laughing?"

"You see, we started talking, just in general, about being betrothed and then, surprise, Beatrice told us she is already betrothed."

"Beatrice?"

"Right, Prince Robert of Scotland. Actually I thought we were fighting the Scots again, but maybe this will end it for a while. Anyhow, Gweneth might be marrying one of the Westlands. We don't know which. And Beatrice told us all about King Henry and King Louis and Queen Eleanor and divorce and remarriage and paying the Pope and age. I mean the age of *someone*. Someone important. That's why we were laughing."

They are past the stables now. The sounds of merriment and music draw nearer. Jerrard slows the pace, frowning. "Listen, you're no longer a child who can be forgiven for foolish talk. You should take care when discussing His Majesty's personal life. He can be mean. Yes, he isn't known for beheading women, but he has other punishments. Understand?"

"Like what?"

"Your father could lose his considerable influence at court. There's one. Or he could insist that you marry a small boy who is simple minded. That's another. Should I keep going?"

They are on the fringe of the partiers. Emma stops, curtsies and presents the bouquet to the young host. There is applause from the onlookers, who are, at this point, easily entertained.

"Nonsense. I shall be betrothed to someone across the water, so that I can visit my sister Catherine. I just know it."

"Oh." Jerrard retreats with his forget-me-nots.

CHAPTER FOUR

THE SCREAMS ARE FROM the innermost part of the forest, but those huddled over their fires in the settlement can still hear the agony. It's not the first time that the inhabitants have been a distant audience to the sounds of torture, but it has been a while since the pain in the night air was so piercing. The rack had been removed from the castle over one hundred years before; the occupants disliked mixing fine dining with the audible shrieks from the bowels of the dungeon. Now this ugly instrument resides in a crude building constructed in a forest clearing. The Earl of Boulton has not used it for a while; he fancies himself to be a civilized man, at least on the outside, where appearances count. He wears red velvets and polished leather boots. His wines, from across the water, are first-rate. The art in his castle has been chosen with taste. His preference in women is likewise refined, in spite of his wife's references to an occasional dalliance with someone from a lower social order. After all, he muses, when the apparel is removed, whether frilly or ragged, what is underneath is quite the same.

But occasionally the hut must be used to address a wrongdoing. Theft by the castle staff was not unknown. Lowly peasants, arrogant on a jug of strong beer, might forget their place. Certainly they should not cheat when delivering the required annual levy of barley or potatoes. As the ultimate overseer, he, the landowner, can do the math, and his stewards know how much produce his villages must deliver. Oh, yes, he is aware that some of the peasants plant in his forest. Their tiny harvests, often carrots, parsnips or turnips, are consumed by the families living on his estate. Lord William ignores these childish transgressions, boasting a patrician pride in overlooking the small sins committed by his underclass tenants.

These screams, however, are not the result of a small carrot sin. Two brothers have found something on his property, his baronial forest, and therefore it is rightly his. It also happens to be quite valuable, and these two foolish men refuse to divulge its location. Well, not for long, for the rack is as good as ever. In using it, he must don his other personhood, one that sometimes gives him pleasure. But that's only for him to know.

The earl stands outside the hut at the edge of the clearing, aglow with the pigments of early autumn. Screams and another kind of sound rend the evening air. All else is silent. The forest bows to anguish, the anguish of two men, one howling in pain and the other begging for mercy.

The screams stop. A door opens. Into the silence lurches a burly man covered with blood and vomit. He pulls a flask from his vest, tosses his head back and gurgles as the tawny liquid pours down his throat.

"Hard work, eh Gillem?"

"Yes, your lordship. Alger, the skinny one, is no good for the rack. He's a screamer, for sure, but then he keeps passing out every time we give it a good pull. Brittle bones. He's no fun, but he sure makes a mess." Gillem brushes his soiled garment. "Ugh."

"I thought his brother would confess to help him out, but I was wrong. Put the big one on the rack and let the gimpy one watch."

Gillem tosses down one more swig and returns to his calling. The door remains open so the earl can view one body, still unconscious, being unstrapped and carried to a corner. Three men must subdue John, who keeps muttering, "It's mine. It's mine."

"Not for long." Lord William of Boulton leans against a tree to listen to the resurgent sounds of agony.

❀

KING HENRY II TRAVELS LIGHT. His stocky frame rides a horse with ease. With his sandy hair blowing in the breeze, he might be mistaken for one of the knights who accompany him. His mode of operation is to cover distances quickly; hence, clothing-laden carriages and elegant courtiers are absent from his travels. In Henry's mind, they are an impractical extravagance. It's more agreeable, and safer, to ride in his daily hunting attire with his loyal men from Normandy, the Aquitaine and Anjou. What is important to this monarch is securing domination of his realm and expanding the crown's administration of England. Henry is fluent in several languages, and all that he has read tells him that a unitary system of government is better, much better for the king, than a decentralized system where everybody is doing things differently. It's a simple matter of control.

"How far away do you estimate is the earl's castle, young Edwin?" The king throws his head back to check the position of the sun. The small company is picking its way along a wide path through the Boulton forestland. He estimates that it is midday. "Check your map, if you will."

The horses halt, snorting as if this unexpected stop is unwelcome. The king and his men, of course, ride the finest steeds in England. They are built for speed and endurance and, most of all, for battle. It appears that they cannot be still, bumping and pushing against one another, like young boys at play in a castle yard. Their riders pat them with affection, while Edwin studies his drawing, which contains some annotations.

"I would say that we have come three quarters of the way from the monastery because we veered southward about an hour ago, so we should be here." Edwin holds up the map, jabbing his index finger at their presumed location. "We should intersect the main road in yet another hour, and after that, our trip will be a breeze."

"Very good. I am looking forward to the earl's fine dining hall. And I am thirsty for some of his well-known wines, since they are known to come from Anjou." Henry kisses his fingertips. "Ah, the delectable nectar of one's homeland. Now, lads, don't tell the English barons I said that. They order wines from across the water by the boatload, then boast of their own shriveled grapes."

The men are accustomed to their king's jesting. Most have been with Henry since his first tangle with the French army in Normandy. He is one of them.

"Let's ride." Henry turns his horse. The men follow. The restless horses are happy to resume their outing. The knight known only as Neville resumes his forward position, riding with the royal banner. He is first around another southward turn in the trail.

"Stop! Stop!" Neville pulls up his horse and turns back to face the company. "There is a man ahead on the trail. He appears to be injured, but let's take care that it's not a trap. I'll ride up to him. If it's robbers or worse, they will see your banner and know they had better not mess with the king."

"Go!" Henry turns. "Swords out. We wait." The men follow Henry's example and unsheathe their weapons. After several seconds, they hear Neville speaking in the distance, but his words are too faint to discern. The horses are very still. They know the difference between a short respite, where they can be playful, and the quiet moments before battle, where they summon strength for the charge.

The forest silence is broken by the sound of Neville's voice, growing nearer, and the soft trot of his horse. Then he is around the bend in the trail. His face tells the story. There is no danger.

"There's a peasant on the trail. He's been crawling for two days, he says. I'd wager he's about dead. One leg is broken in several places. All cut up. A sorry sight, Your Majesty. Not what you would expect in a woodland belonging to the Earl of Boulton. What do you want to do?"

"Let's go to him. Jerome, you have a bible, right? We can help him leave this life by hearing of the next. Get out some mead. On, lads."

The horses proceed, but not quickly. There is a wariness, borne of warfare, in the approach to the crumpled man on the trail. When the men stop, they do not immediately dismount. Cautious eyes scan the surrounding woods. The horses are motionless, noiseless. Only their noses twitch, then relax. This is a good sign. The man lying on the trail watches, saying nothing.

Henry orders, "Dismount. Swords at ready."

As the men follow orders, the bloody figure on the trail reaches up with one hand. "The royal banner. I think the king is here. Do my eyes lie to me?" The words are just above a whisper, with pain seeping through each syllable.

"I am your king. Here, drink this." Henry holds the small jug to parched lips.

"Thank you, sire." He sips. Coughs.

"What has happened to you? Where is your family, someone to help you?"

"Don't know. Tortured. I was tortured. For a secret. Then my brother John. He's dead." Alger gasps, his voice growing fainter. "John told them where it was. He had to. His bones were all broken. They brought me out here, into the forest, to die. And I will." Alger's head sinks into his chest.

"Why was this done to you? And your brother?" Henry is curious. These Englanders and their racks. Breaking peasant bones. Barbaric.

"We had a jug of gold coins. Tanner told them, I'm sure. The Earl of Boulton wanted it. Now he's got it. It was ours."

Henry kneels next to the pitiful form on the path. "Yours? The gold belonged to you? A peasant? Don't tell false stories to the king. I don't like it. Do you want to die even sooner?"

"Found it. Buried. Here's one. It was my brother's souvenir, and it killed him. And me." Alger's arm slowly pulls a gleaming gold coin from inside his bloody shirt. It is his final move. The coin falls from a limp hand.

"Move him off the trail. Cover him. Then say a prayer." Henry picks up the coin, turning it over several times, studying the delicate engravings. The silence is broken only by the sound of a body being dragged over dirt and vines. Henry's long gaze finally abandons the small treasure and settles on the forest backdrop; then, nodding, he looks beyond the trees, far away to the English shore and farther away across the water. A plan is taking shape in his mind, commencing with short-term gamesmanship and ending with a long-term solution to a pressing monarchical problem. He allows himself a vision of riding at the head of a well-fed, well-paid permanent royal army, chewing up poor Louis's French forces. The idea generates a heave of satisfaction, interrupted by his words: "The Aureus."

IN HIS PRIVATE STUDY, the Archbishop of Canterbury is busy with correspondence. He has spent nearly two weeks trying to organize the vast amount of paperwork that he has inherited from Theobald, his predecessor. Even with the piles of work strewn around, the chamber exudes a sense of history, power and purpose. The Pope's primary representative in England lives in a splendid miniature palace adjacent to the Canterbury Cathedral. Thomas is only now settling in while attending to his numerous duties to the Papacy, and to his King.

There is a small rap on the door. Thomas, immersed in writing, does not hear it. Another rap. This time it is louder. Annoyed, the busy Archbishop glares at the door. "Who is it?"

"Your Grace," the aged female voice is barely audible, "many apologies, but there is a holy man from the countryside wanting to see you. He says he has traveled far with important information meant only for you."

Thomas has heard about this. The supplicants arriving from all corners of England. Theobald had complained about the unending line of scruffy petitioners, always needy, always with some righteous angle to their particular story. Well, at least he had been spared for two weeks. He should be grateful for that. "Send him in. And thank you."

He can hear murmured voices in the passageway, then his study door opens to reveal a rotund monk clad in a brown tunic typical of the ones worn in south England monasteries.

"Well, come in, please. Yes, sit there. Would you like tea? I can ring for it."

"No thank you, Your Grace. I came only to tell you of something that will increase the blessed church's wealth tenfold, enabling it to do so much more of God's work. It is a miracle that I am privileged to be the bearer of this wonderful news, and I thank Our Father for that. Hopefully you will thank me, too, and will enable me to live out my meagre life of prayer and toil with a gift, if you will, of a certain Anjou wine to comfort me at the end of each day. You see...."

"Hold on, friar uh, what's your name anyway?"

"Friar Merlin."

"Friar Merlin. You are asking me for a lifetime supply of fine wine without telling me how you are to earn such a bonus. Please." Thomas drags out this last word.

The friar inhales. As long as he owns his secret, he has leverage, if he is believed. But how does a lowly man of the cloth negotiate with the most powerful religious figure in England? Merlin can see the impatience on the Archbishop's face. He might as well take a chance. Else he will find himself sleeping on a rough pew in the cathedral before returning to the monastery empty handed.

"Your Grace, please forgive the sin of self-indulgence in this humble man of God." Merlin glances at Thomas, whose face reveals nothing.

He takes the plunge. "You know of the Aureus, Your Grace?"

"Of course. Are you going to tell me that you have it?"

"Oh, no, but I know who does." This time Thomas reacts with a swift turn in his seat.

"Oh, my. Really. Really." The words ring with surprise, followed by disbelief, ending with a tinge of curiosity

"Yes, Your Grace, I was an accidental party to a conversation about it, about who had it at that time."

"You were snooping?"

"Oh, no, it was nighttime, outdoors, after a grand party. I was partaking of a, uh," he stops to choose his words, "leftover beverage behind an archway. The owner of the castle was talking with his steward, who had learned that two peasants living on his estate had found it. They drank too much beer. Bragged about it. Flashed one of the coins. I know that the men, two brothers, no longer possess it because we buried one of them in our monastery cemetery. He had been tortured."

"Manner of torture?"

"Looked like the rack. All those broken bones. Death was a blessing for the poor man."

Thomas leans forward, his expression suggesting an amiable country priest about to dispense a sacred sacrament. "Friar Merlin, it appears that I have forgotten my good manners. I should, of course, know which monastery you are from, so that I may convey my good wishes to your abbot who, I suspect, does not know the nature of your visit to me."

"Wilshire Abbey, Your Grace, built hundreds of years ago. Abbot Eldred does not even know I am here, I regret to say. I requested permission to leave for the purpose of purging my worldly sins by spreading the gospel in the poor estate settlements. You understand."

The Archbishop is not listening. He is rapidly leafing through a thick book whose parchment pages are yellowed and creased. He slows down when he nears the back of the book; the monasteries are listed alphabetically. A single page describes Wilshire Abbey, an ancient, crumbling jumble of buildings in southern England. He marks the place with the nearest quill and turns to a second thick book lying atop a tall stack next to his richly carved lindenwood desk. "I've kept this volume close for many years. It has the most useful information in the realm."

Friar Merlin watches the pages turn. His right hand strokes the glossy top of his tonsured head. It is a nervous gesture that he had displayed even as a boy, before his crown was shaved. His hand rubs, then scratches, trying to activate his nearby brain. He senses that he has lost his information edge.

"Ah, here, this is what I want." The congenial priest has evaporated. In his place sits a prince of the church wearing a hard, superior expression. "The Wilshire Abbey is located on the edge of, ah, yes, I know him, Lord William, yes, on the edge of the Boulton estate. A very distinguished manor. And man. Is this who has the Aureus, Friar Merlin?"

"Yes."

"But it belongs to the holy Church. You know that, don't you?"

Merlin's eyes erupt in a fit of blinking. He can't seem to catch up with the archbishop. The scratching is feverish now, as if motion would conjure up a worthy answer. Instead he replies, "No. Wait. Yes."

"Yes, indeed, and you were so right, so insightful, to come to me rather than the king, who is, after all, your master in all things nonspiritual. And you would be forgiven for thinking that gold coins are not spiritual, not godly, and therefore, the property of the crown. You would definitely be forgiven by me for thinking that."

"Thank you." Merlin had not been thinking that. In fact, the ancient homily about rendering to Caesar what is Caesar's and to God what is God's had not surfaced when preparing his presentation to the archbishop. There is an instant but dim realization that years in a monastic backwater have eroded whatever sharpness he once had. The Archbishop, on the other hand, is a scholar, a man of the world, exceling in statecraft and now theological intellectualism. He, a lowly friar, can only wonder where this is going.

"Tell me Merlin, in your ecclesiastical studies, did you read much about Pope Gregory I?"

"Probably, Your Grace, a long time ago. Did he know about the Aureus?"

"Not specifically, but he issued papal decrees on the subject of Roman wealth left in England, which, in his day, was turning up now and then. He decreed that such wealth, if transportable, should be rendered to its rightful place in Rome, once the seat of the Roman Empire and now the seat of the Universal Catholic Church. Some jugs of coins were retrieved and shipped to Rome, but many more were hidden, the Aureus being one. Today we must rejoice and give our eternal thanks to Saint Gregory, whose wisdom will render this treasure to God. Now, tell me," good will spreads across the Archbishop's face, "what Anjou wines give you special pleasure?"

CHAPTER FIVE

THE GRAND HALL OF BOULTON CASTLE IS, once again, the scene of a lavish party. William, Earl of Boulton, deserves his reputation as an excellent host. His vast forestlands are home to several species of deer, all welcome on his banquet tables. The Boulton archers are renowned for their long bows, both in the woodlands and on the battlefields. The wild boars inhabiting his estate can feed a whole festival, with plenty left over for the kitchen workers, who are much more portly, on the average, than their counterparts who work the fields. The estate falconers, wrists wrapped in leather, guide their trained killers to bring in ducks, geese and pheasants. These executioners, with their lethal talons, are rewarded with the entrails. Later, partygoers savor the prepared fowl served with excellent sauces. Tonight, all of these dishes adorn tables where the earl, his family, baronial guests and the king are dining.

The invitations, so soon after the summer festival, have been issued with care toward family ties, long friendships and politics. Arthur, the Earl of Cambridge, his wife, daughter Emma and her siblings are among the guests. The two nobles are not related and are not friends. Intrigue binds them. They, with their kindred lords of the land, are united in their belief that a strong monarchy will nibble away at their baronial power while increasing their mandated annual contribution to the crown. And Henry is gaining a reputation as the most able administrator in the realm. Therefore, if the king is a guest, those who oppose him will also be seated at the banquet tables.

The Countess of Cambridge hurries her children through the maze of castle corridors. Her husband has preceded his family, hoping to have a few private words with the king. The earl has been chosen by his peers to suggest a different approach to increasing the royal treasury. Of course, protocol must be observed. He will approach the subject delicately. Lord Arthur begins by complimenting Henry on his excellent horsemanship.

"Your Majesty, you could make your steed dance the carol. Such control. I envy you."

"My esteemed Arthur, your talents at court are the envy of your peers. That's why I seek you out, even if you are of that pesky baronial class. You are a masterful diplomat. So persuasive. My horse would play a flute if you administered his oats."

"Ha, that's a good image. I shall get my stable boy to bring your horse some prime oats immediately after dinner so that we can hear a thoroughbred concert, but before we sit down, there is an idea that I want to suggest to you." He leans forward, picking up the pace of his conversation. "We have so little time. Here is the basic plan. I…" Lord Arthur sees that Henry is looking elsewhere. In fact, the king is motioning toward Arthur's approaching family. Of all times for them to be prompt for dinner. His presentation will have to wait until the following morning when Henry is, once again, prepared for serious business. He hopes the king will appear at breakfast.

"My dear Countess, you are lovelier each time we meet." Henry exudes the charm for which he is famous, the charisma that won over the Queen of France. "And the children, they are ruddy and strong, and this one is the lovely Lady Emma, yes?"

The proud parents nod.

"A beautiful likeness of her mother. Do you have plans for her?"

Emma feigns ignorance of the implied question, staring at the piles of food being transported to the tables. It's the suitable thing to do.

Her father answers: "Not yet."

HENRY AND HIS KNIGHTS occupy a table laden with a cornucopia of colorful foods, scented venison and sugary pastries. The king, who has been hailed the required number of times, raises his goblet to each noble family. For his final toast, he faces the Earl of Boulton. "My dear Lord William, heir to a fine name, fortune and estate. I drink to your health and continued prosperity. And to your son, the young earl." The royal glass moves slightly in the direction of Jerrard. "He is a mirror of your fine face, your Boulton countenance. I see your greatness in his features."

Glasses throughout the hall are raised to honor the evening's host and heir. The earl beams a thank you that disguises his distain. Royal blood may course through Henry's veins on his mother's side, but his family name, Plantagenet, is not even a generation old. The story, and William wonders if it's true, is that Henry's father, Count Geoffrey of Anjou, wore a sprig of the broom plant in his riding hat. Somehow the Latin name for this yellow-flowered shrub, the planta genesta, became Geoffrey's nickname. Now his son has turned the nickname into a royal house with a fancy French-sounding title. What nerve. What absolute brazenness. His own lineage, the House of Boulton, goes back several centuries. And yet this upstart, Henry of the House of Plantagenet, is king of England, a monarch to whom he, Lord William, owes fealty. The irony is enough to kill one's appetite.

The king raises his glass a second time. The earl's face continues to radiate good fellowship. The immense room once again echoes the swilling and swallowing that follows.

Henry continues addressing his host. "Permit me, Lord William, a stroll, after dinner, through your well-stocked wine cellar. I must follow your fine example in selecting my own stock. You can give me some pointers." Henry's tablemates do not attempt to disguise their amused glances. The earl's ego is well known. He will not notice.

Indeed, William's face evolves into a picture of triumph. In addition to his contempt for the Plantagenet pretentions, he views the young monarch through the prism of middle age. Probably Henry never had the time to develop an appreciation of exquisite wines and life's other refinements. Likely he was too busy acquiring an ambitious wife, then consolidating his power on the other side of the water, followed by more war with France. The earl suspects that Henry prefers to drink mead with his young cronies. Still, as a good host, he will parade him through the corridors which embrace his vast collection of vintage reds and whites. This will be amusing. "Your Majesty, any time after dessert."

❀

LORD WILLIAM AND KING HENRY each carry a torch. There is no other illumination in the network of passageways that are home to a vast collection of Boulton wines. Built as tunnels for hiding in some earlier century, these corridors retain the rough stone walls and uneven flooring that generations of owners have chosen to keep in this antiquated state. The earl is deep into a discussion of his Bordeaux clarets, stacked in floor-to-ceiling barrels, when Henry interjects. "Stop now."

William stops, of course. But he is flustered. His dissertation on the clarets had been, in his opinion, well organized and filled with obscure details that were sure to impress any listener.

"Your Majesty," he stammers, "what is wrong? Do you prefer to view other parts of my collection?"

The torches reflect the disappointed surprise in one set of eyes and the hard stare in the other.

"Here's how it stands, Lord William. I would like the Aureus. As your king, I demand it, and you, my loyal subject, must give it to me. Is it down here among your clarets and other reds?"

The earl blinks. Disappointment evaporates from the look of surprise. It is replaced by a twinkle of amusement. "Perhaps you consumed too much of my fine wines tonight, Your Majesty. I would not blame you."

"You are entertaining, as always. Now, here's the way it stands. We found one of the brothers before he died. He gave me this." Henry reaches into a leather pouch at his waist and produces the coin. "I am an impatient man, an impatient king. Don't depend on my remaining your gracious guest."

There is silence. The twinkle of amusement is gone. The two men stand in the dank corridor, doing battle without moving.

THE PARTY IN THE GREAT HALL has moved into adjoining rooms. The guests roam about, seeking old friends to greet or new faces to impress. Many were here at the summer festival. The reminiscing, often covering years of social separation, is focused on the activities of just the past few months. The ladies recall the carol being danced in the nearby hall. Although soft music emanates from a corner, there will be no carol tonight. A pity. This is a working party.

Emma is seated with her peers, watching the grownups converse. She is expected to learn from these occasions. The flicker of a fan. The curtsy, perfectly executed. A kiss blown, just so. She does not see Jerrard approach until he takes a chair and places it next to hers, on the right.

"I did not think we would see you so soon again. My father makes decisions about these meetings so quickly."

"Yes, we didn't have time to organize our wardrobes." Emma nods. "I guess it's a short visit."

"Likely so, which means that tomorrow I shall take you to the garden again. Mother tells me that the fall flowers are in bloom, and you can pick another bouquet for me. The other has wilted." Jerrard leans back, pleased with his cleverness.

"I'm not sure." Emma is torn. The young man is nice. And handsome. And being in his company gives her an unfamiliar pleasure. But would her father approve? On the other hand, the men will likely continue their conclave tomorrow, and she would like to see the garden. "Are your fall flowers blue?"

"I don't know. I think we will just have to go and pick some. And, of course, one to go right here." His hand brushes her long locks, which frame her oval face in reddish-brown ringlets. "I think most colors would look very nice with your hair."

The gesture is not quick. Emma absorbs the touch on her flowing hair. There is a tingle near her right ear, as if a feather had tickled it. But there is no feather, only an agreeable awareness of the young man next to her. What should she say next?

"You know, Jerrard, I have only visited parts of your castle. Our chambers, of course, and they are quite lovely. And the great hall, and now these entertainment rooms." Emma has amazed herself with her bold words, but she keeps going. "I would like a tour, if you can arrange that for tomorrow as well."

"Let's start now. Some parts of the castle are more interesting after dark. Like the dungeons. They are inhabited by ghosts. Don't worry. Friendly ghosts. In any case, I will protect you."

Jerrard, who has received excellent instruction in courtly etiquette, rises and takes Emma's arm. They are a couple, walking past their elders, some of whom beam at the youthful pair. A few of the men wink and refer to the apple not falling far from the tree. Most of the guests are too engrossed in conversation or too addled by wine to notice two adolescents. A handful of furtive paramours are whispering plans about meeting later. The castle is conveniently filled with chambers designed for adulterous assignations.

Large doors open to an outer balcony that narrows into a hall embracing the length of the curved castle walls. This citadel is a home, a fortress and a small city, with a bit of country within its enclosure. The autumn evening is clear, chilly and brimming with the lights of small fires in the many courtyards below. The sounds of life, a different kind of life, drift up through the night air: stable whinnies, children chattering, women cooking, men murmuring. It is the distant drone of a hereditary subsistence existence, interrupted by an occasional burst of merriment. It is also the engine that drives the house of Boulton, making this fine gala a reality. Emma sees, hears and smells it, and she shivers.

"Just a minute. I'll get a wrap for you."

Jerrard returns with a delicate pastel shawl, one of the many that his mother makes available for guests who wish to get some fresh air. He puts it around Emma's shoulders, carefully adjusting it at her neck and upper arms. Her eyes follow his gestures. The shawl gives off an instant warmth. Jerrard lifts her chin, and her gaze follows to his eyes. Emma feels like she is standing in a glow. This is different. Jerrard's smile is tentative, as if his lips have other plans. She hopes so.

"Jerrard!" A voice pierces the soft night. The open doorway is occupied by Sir Ralph, the earl's trusted steward. "Young sir, I beg your pardon. Your father must see you immediately. Go to him in the wine cellar. The first corridor of the clarets." And he is gone.

The enchantment likewise evaporates. The eyes disengage. Suddenly the evening is much colder.

"Damn." Jerrard steps back. "I must go. I don't want to. Sorry. I will see you early tomorrow."

AT BREAKFAST, Emma and her family learn that the king has already departed. Lord Arthur was afraid that would happen. Henry is known for his early departures in his mission to visit all corners of England. The Earl of Boulton and his family are not in attendance either. That is strange. One purpose of this conclave, unspoken by the attendees at this gathering, is to solidify a united front to the power of the crown. Another subject on the agenda is the immense wealth of the nation's largest landowner, the Catholic Church. These noblemen reason that since Thomas Becket, the new Archbishop of Canterbury, is a close friend of Henry's, perhaps the king can persuade him to send less of its sacred wealth to Rome and more into coffers of England's treasury. That would surely take some of the pressure off of the baronial class. Emma's father comments that he never had a chance to describe this plan to Henry before his morning exit.

"We come all this way for a first-rate meal and a few toasts, and off he goes," he grumbles.

Emma's mind is elsewhere, reliving the previous evening. She is standing on a balcony. Strong, sure hands are adjusting the beautiful shawl. His lips are leaving a smile and preparing for something else. Oh, that would have been nice. More than nice. What kind of emergency, or whatever it was, would require Jerrard's presence? Maybe she should just look forward to the immediate future, like this morning's visit to a flower garden, now abloom with crocus. Or perhaps lilies, just like at home. She wouldn't have to be guessing if Jerrard would only appear. Then they could continue their tour, and she could gather real flowers for a bouquet. He would help cut them with his knife, and she would put one in her hair. Emma is summoned from her imaginary garden with a reality that is not welcome.

"Good morning Lord, Countess, Lady Emma. My apologies. There is unexpected family business. My presence is required." Jerrard hesitates. "It would have been very nice to spend more time in your company," he bows to Emma, "but circumstances make that impossible. Another time. Good bye." A second bow and he leaves.

CHAPTER SIX

HENRY AND THOMAS ARE SEATED at a table in a small room in the royal hunting lodge outside London. The king often comes here for a respite from the necessary duties that fill his days at Westminster Palace in the city. This is a male habitat. His wife Eleanor and her fine ladies know that the lodge is off limits. It is not a retreat for pleasure, usually. The king formulates strategy and executes statecraft within its homey walls, decorated with the heads of unlucky deer and other inhabitants of the king's forest. It's where he can throw out ideas and get feed-back, but he does this only with Thomas, who has been less accessible since becoming Archbishop. Now, Thomas sits across from him, savoring a wine from Henry's home province of Anjou.

"It's been a while, Thomas. How are you adjusting to your new position? I mean, being God's primary representative in England. My, I should be kissing your ring." Henry tries joking because Thomas's demeanor is unusually stern.

"It is a formidable task, being Archbishop. Much to do."

"That's all you have to say? Much to do. Where did my companionable advisor go? Have your church duties taken away your sense of humor? And, by the way, what's with the drab priestly garb? Can't the Holy Roman Church put you in more fashionable clothes?"

"I dress for the seriousness of my sacred trust, the well-being of the Mother Church."

"You were more fun as chancellor. Don't make me regret appointing you Archbishop."

"Oh, no, just tired after a long day of my new duties. But enough about me. Tell me of your recent sojourn across our fair land. Didn't you visit Boulton?"

"I did. Among many places."

"And how did Boulton go?"

"You know, the usual banquet and toasts. Good food. Fine wine. Beautiful women. What sacrifices I make for England." Henry laughs and pours more wine into his goblet.

"And that was all?" The question hangs as Thomas refills his wine.

"Is that not enough for any man?"

Thomas inclines his head. His sigh suggests fatigue, but his brain is racing the breadth of England for a solution to a particular dilemma. The Earl of Boulton, unlike Friar Merlin, would be less intimidated when reminded of Pope Gregory's decree. William is a lord of the realm with his own army. Would the threat of excommunication separate him from the Aureus? Thomas hopes, but wonders. An obvious answer is to obtain Henry's help in retrieving the treasure. But the king has money issues of his own. He would want his share, or maybe all of it, if they could somehow wrest the coins from Boulton. Thomas does not want to prolong the silence, but he cannot think of anything to say.

The stillness within the room, within Thomas, is not lost on the king. Why, he asks himself, is Thomas acting like this? His query about the Boulton visit could be just small talk, but Thomas is not himself. Perhaps it is the considerable weight of his new responsibilities. It would be a bit of bad luck if *his man*, his appointee, suddenly became a dedicated prince of the Church. Then he would not be able to tell him about the Aureus. The king is well read. He knows about Pope Gregory's decree.

Henry hesitates, choosing his words carefully. "There is more, but it's between you and me. It's something that you and I must undertake together. It will be to our mutual enrichment, you will definitely agree."

Hearing these words, Thomas is buoyed by a small surge of hopeful anticipation. Perhaps Henry knows more than he is revealing. Could he possibly know that Boulton has the Aureus? If so, is he going to suggest a mutual undertaking to recover it? What if the king would take a modest share? He surely knows that, by papal decree, the Church is entitled to all of it. But Thomas, in his role as friend, could grant the monarchy a portion of this fortune as thanks for the royal assistance in retrieving it. Yes, this could work out well for all concerned, if the king does indeed know about the treasure. Thomas's face, so somber just seconds ago, radiates a sudden cheerfulness. The corners of his mouth tilt upward. Henry observes this transformation. He is intrigued.

"Thomas, my favorite and only Archbishop, I see that the mention of enrichment has elevated your spirits. I must use that word more often with you. Yes, we can share the work, and we can share the riches. It will be a holy and profitable alliance. We will be on top of all Europe."

Under his brown cassock, Thomas is trembling. Is the king suggesting a shared war, a shared victory and a shared Aureus? He must treat this delicately, not giving up anything. Is it better to slowly flush out what the king knows or wants, or should he lead from the strength of his position as Archbishop?

"Are you talking about a partnership? To acquire something valuable? I don't know. This business about sharing. I have the papacy to consider."

"I'm talking about joining forces. It's all about mutual prosperity." Henry tosses a casual glance at Thomas, a man who heretofore always understood alliances made in the interest of keeping and increasing wealth.

"But, the papacy. I must think about it."

Henry studies his friend, his advisor and now the high priest of an order that is a counterweight to his own power. He is sorting out

Thomas's replies. Is it possible that the Archbishop knows something? All this blather about sharing and the Papacy. But how could that be? Two dead peasant brothers. The Archbishop of Canterbury does not ride the countryside checking on baronial treatment of serfs. His communications to the church hierarchy throughout England consist of letters to the bishops, his lieutenants in the front line of church administration. It is doubtful that the Earl of Boulton has confided in his local bishop about the treasure. This whole conversation is troubling. Change the subject.

"Absolutely. Oh, before I forget, I have another mission entirely. The brother of King Louis. Isn't he shopping around for a wife?"

"Henry, don't change the subject. What is this thing that we must undertake together for our mutual benefit, or enrichment, as you term it?"

"Oh, that. Lord William has all the barons on board, obviously easy to do, to pressure me into raising the taxes on church properties throughout England, thereby reducing the financial pressure on them to support the government. They were going to present the idea to me at the Boulton gathering, but I left before they had a chance. My spies are very useful." Henry watches Thomas, his eyes, his mouth, his facial expression. He sees only a quick blink.

"I see. That's the plan you were referring to?"

"Of course. What else would I be referring to?" Henry permits himself a slight hesitation to gauge the attitude of the Archbishop, who is sitting quietly. "And here is *my* plan. And fortunately, we have some time to develop it because the barons don't know that I know their plan." Thomas continues to look past the king, tightlipped. "Just follow. It's complicated, but you'll agree that your monarch is, in matters nonspiritual, a genius."

"Yes, I do see that." The air in the room seems heavier.

"Okay, back to Louis's brother. Prince Arnaud. We find him a highborn English wife with an immense dowry. I have someone in mind. Result: The prince is no longer feeding at the financial trough of the

French king, who then is happy. And indebted to me. We call a truce for an indefinite period of time, releasing my troops across the water to come over here and administer a slap on the hands of Boulton and any of his allies."

"You wish to make war on your own nobility?"

"Happens all the time. You know that. I've been reading about English history ever since I became king. Our nation's chronicle is a tale of one civil war after another, often in the manner of parents punishing errant children. And my nobles are misbehaving children, especially Boulton, the instigator. So, when we have administered the strap and sent them to bed without supper," Henry looks to Thomas for appreciation of his metaphor, "when we have done that, and maybe chopped off a few heads, there will be peace and discipline in the realm. And, by the way, they will pay reparations for the cost of this war. Well, it won't really be a war. More a short military operation. Also, the taxes on church lands will not increase. Maybe go down. You will help me raise an additional army on this side of the water, right? That will make it our mutual undertaking."

"The Holy Church is blessed by your protection of our worldly possessions." Thomas's voice is flat. The room is darker. Two candles have burned out. Then he speaks in a lighter voice. "Who do you have in mind to betroth to Prince Arnaud?"

"Ha, I can't give away all my secrets now, can I?" Henry ends the conversation.

JERRARD AND HIS RETAINERS have ridden for three days, stopping only to sleep or to restock their provisions at monasteries and friendly estates. They have been preceded by faster riders who have already contracted with the boatmen at the Southampton harbor. A fine oaken cog, the single-mast, flat-bottom craft favored for small numbers of men, has been chosen to transport them across the channel. After their arrival on the continent, they will acquire more horses and journey to the court of Normandy, where Jerrard will pay a baronial visit and await a hoped-for summons from the French king. By the time Henry learns of this expedition, the heir to the Boulton earldom will have completed his mission and returned home.

Five days before Jerrard's arrival at the coast, a single man had made the same crossing and was now hopefully on his way to the French court in Paris. This was a dangerous mission in many ways. King Henry controlled Normandy, facing the channel, but this involved a longer boat trip than crossing directly to France. The waters were often rough and the winds unpredictable. Once he arrived, this brave man had to obtain a steed and provisions to take him to the French border, where English and French troops were presently at a stand-off. What was needed was a very plausible reason for an Englishman to ride through Normandy on his way to see King Louis of France. He might ride the entire distance unimpeded, or he might be stopped by soldiers and taken to the Duke of Normandy's castle for questioning. Putting all this together had preoccupied the Earl of Boulton from the time he had the unnerving conversation with King Henry in his wine cellar. His only confidant had been his son Jerrard.

The single man was his steward, Sir Ralph, who was provided with all the requisites to make this journey a success. He carried money to pay the shore sentries for a horse and food. Inside his leather bag, he transported a letter written by the Earl of Boulton to the duke, who was related to Henry by blood and marriage. This letter, Sir Ralph was instructed, should be delivered only if the duke was too curious about his mission or reluctant to allow safe passage to the French border. Even better, the steward should endeavor to avoid Norman troops, hence any contact with the duke. Sir Ralph also carried another letter penned for King Louis VII. Lord William had long labored over the wording of both documents. Sir Ralph's life depended on their acceptance.

The "Dear Duke" missive was, in William's mind, a work of genius. He bade good health to his contemporary, saying that the tie that bound them, their equal station in the court of Henry II, dictated some kind of consistent communication. "In the year 1162," he went on, "we cannot be isolated simply because we are separated by water. If we are to be at the front of modernity, we should share ideas, knowing that our pooled knowledge is far more helpful to King Henry than our separate, sometimes conflicting, strategies." The earl had been amused by this part. As if he really wanted to hear any addled Norman ideas. To him, Henry's continental pals and cousins were only good for supplying well-trained armies.

The real challenge in the "Duke" letter was presenting a convincing reason for Sir Ralph's continuance to France and the court of King Louis. The search for this rationale had occupied his time for several days. The elusiveness of an answer had been dispiriting. Then, one afternoon, when gazing out the window of his study, he hit on an idea. The solution to his problem was his daughter Aldreda, now a shy fourteen-year-old and already an integral part of his larger plan. Why not also use her as the missing piece in this convoluted blend of untruths? He would reveal, with some embarrassment, that his present financial circumstances prevented him from betrothing her with a suitable dowry, as was expected of someone in his position. He had no choice but to consign her to a convent, but as a doting father, he had naturally asked her where she would like to spend the rest of her cloistered life. She had read of a beautiful convent near Paris, and she wanted to go there. He simply was going to ask a favor of the French king, who also had daughters and would surely understand. He prayed that the duke would allow the Boulton emissary safe passage to ask a parental favor from the French king.

The earl allowed himself a solid guffaw. It was possible that this missive could eventually find its way to Henry who, when all Lord William's excellent schemes worked out, would see how he had been outwitted and beaten in the political arena, because the earl's letter to King Louis presented an enormously different scenario. Writing it was pure pleasure.

Knowing that King Louis had a reputation for intense piety, he opened by begging the monarch's acceptance of a visit by his son Jerrard, a devout Catholic who wished to pray with the Church's most powerful defender in France. To that end, he had engaged Friar Merlin, from the monastery on his estate, to resume Jerrard's religious studies, long ago abandoned due to disinterest. The friar enthusiastically volunteered for this task when the abbot had called for a religious instructor to be assigned to the young earl-to-be. William's goal was that his son would absorb enough spiritual fervor to be convincing at the French court. The portly friar always joined him in conversation at the conclusion of his son's lessons. He seemed to favor the Boulton clarets.

The letter continued, suggesting that Jerrard would like to travel on to Rome to meet Pope Alexander and receive his blessing. Perhaps King Louis would consider accompanying him and taking him under his spiritual wing. The Earl of Boulton hoped that true men of God could communicate on a higher level, in spite of the English monarch's insistence on making war with France. At that point, William insinuated, only slightly, that these continued conflicts interfered with the primary mission of the Mother Church: the protection and spread of Christianity.

Having commenced with the *soft touch*, Lord William veered to his proposal, based on his knowledge of a certain difficulty within the French royal family. King Louis's brother, Prince Arnaud, was widely known to be seeking a wife, preferably one from a noble family who could betroth her with a very generous dowry. Presently the French king was paying for his brother's lavish lifestyle, and he was very unhappy with this arrangement. Trying to remain humble, the earl simply stated, "In deference to Your Majesty's benevolent Christian rule of the French nation, I offer my beautiful daughter Aldreda, with a dowry given her by loving parents, to become the wife of your fine brother, Prince Arnaud." William reread his offer, permitting himself a congratulatory smirk. Once the dowry was paid to Prince Arnaud, an untold amount of French francs would be freed from sibling support and switched to a vastly increased financial support for the French army. Henry would then have a real continental war on his hands, and he would lack the necessary military power to wrest the Aureus from Lord William. The royal boot would be off of the barons' necks for a very long time. The letter concluded: "My son Jerrard is presently visiting the Duke of Normandy. He awaits your reply to this letter, hoping that you will receive him at your court. He will discuss the dowry in detail, and I am certain that you will be pleased by its considerable size."

There is always a downside to such matters, William reflected. His wife would likely be displeased to have her favorite daughter shipped off to France, but sometimes, in matters of money and war, a brilliant betrothal is the only solution. The Earl of Boulton rewarded himself with a short trip to his wine cellar.

KING HENRY IS ATTIRED in monarchical splendor. His fine ermine robe sweeps the floor. He is actually wearing a crown. All of this pomp, unnecessary in his opinion, is for a formal meeting with his chancellor, Thomas's successor.

"Chancellor Geoffrey, I bid you good morning." Henry's meetings with Geoffrey Ridel are infrequent. The man is quiet, industrious and certainly capable, but he lacks the manner and wit that so endeared Chancellor Thomas Becket to the king. Henry wastes no time in stating the reason for the meeting.

"I wish you to go to the court of King Louis."

Geoffrey's mouth drops. "We are at war, sire."

Henry leans forward in his ornate royal chair. The Chancellor's earnest nature is tiresome. "You may be surprised, but I know that. You will get a safe passage. Here is a very important letter from me to King Louis. You must hand it to him and no one else. Please return to me with a favorable answer to my proposal. Oh, and give him my best. You know all the right things to say. Now, prepare to depart at once."

CHAPTER SEVEN

IT IS LATE AUTUMN IN NORMANDY. The channel winds scatter flurries of an early snowfall. Peasants trudge out of the woods, bearing bales of twigs on their backs, the fuel for warmth in the coming months. The milky sky provides a backdrop for a fine castle, home of the Duke of Normandy, located near the city of Rouen on the river Seine. Hills roll right up to the ancient castle moat, now devoid of water and mainly a repository for garbage and human waste. An abandoned canal, linking the moat to the river, is filled with an accumulation of nature's castoffs over many decades. The duke, like his father and grandfather before him, has always wanted to dig another moat, transforming this fetid perimeter into a waterpark for his grandchildren. Clearance of the canal is another vision, so that a miniature dock could be constructed at the terminus of this narrow waterway, giving him easy access by small boat to his larger one moored on the banks of the Seine. If only there was a respite from the incessant wars between the duchies, his included, and France. And now that Henry, who counts Normandy as one of his many continental possessions, is England's king, things are only worse. The duke dotes on his distant cousin Henry, but it seems that a state of war will be a perennial fixture on the landscape. And so, too, his moat and canal are doomed to be a perennial dream.

There is a quiet knock on the door of the duke's study. It is followed by a low voice. "Good morning, sir. I have come to say goodbye and to give you my thanks for your excellent hospitality." It is Jerrard. Based on his conversations with his host, he assumes that his father's letter to the duke did not have to be delivered. That is a relief. He didn't wish to be a pitied guest, even if the cause for pity was a total fabrication. That means Sir Ralph took a more roundabout route to reach Paris. But he did arrive, because Jerrard has received an invitation, conveyed by a courier from the Norman border garrison, to visit, at once, King Louis of France.

"Yes, yes, come in. We certainly have taken pleasure in your company and that of your companions. It's refreshing to entertain rather than spend endless days fighting for inches of territory on the plains of Normandy. Perhaps a time will come, in some future century, when battles on these fields will be more decisive, hence shorter. Or not at all." The duke shakes his head. "I must be getting old. There was a time when the taste of blood in battle was sweeter than a kiss stolen from a scullery maid. Or whatever it was that I stole from the scullery maid. Oh, I am definitely getting old."

Jerrard offers an insincere smile. If his mission on behalf of his father is successful, the duke will be fighting until the end of his days. The time spent here has been most agreeable though, and he must convey his appreciation for that. King Louis has penned a lengthy letter, commending Jerrard on his life of devoutness, noting that young barons do not often display zealous piety. He regrets being unable to accompany the next Earl of Boulton to Rome, but looks forward to his coming visit when they can discuss the Church and its mission. He concludes wishing him a safe journey from Normandy. There is a short postscript, noting that France will joyfully welcome Aldreda. He hopes that will be soon. A separate safe passage document is included in the royal invitation.

❉

AUREUS

THE COURT OF KING LOUIS VII of France is nestled comfortably in the Chateau de Fontainebleau, constructed nearly thirty years before to be a hunting lodge and royal retreat. Since then, it has been evolving into a singular wonder of the world. It is the inspiration for the word *Grandeur*. There is nothing like it elsewhere on earth in the year 1162. It is true that the opulence displayed by the Holy Roman Emperor's retinue inspires awe when he sweeps across the center and south of Europe. But he cannot boast of a single royal home that shimmers with the brilliance of this majestic chateau, south of Paris. Likewise, the Great Palace of Byzantium, a labyrinth of imperial residences, dominates the entire city of Constantinople. It can certainly claim first place for longevity; some of its foundations date back to the fourth century. But it cannot begin to match the expanding splendor of the golden halls of Fontainebleau. Yet, to visit the French monarch in his magnificent residence is unthinkable by most of his subjects. On a late November afternoon, Jerrard, a citizen of England, presently at war with France, rides through its gates with his entourage.

King Louis's welcoming letter is specific. His visitor must present himself precisely at full nightfall on the day of his arrival. At that time, the King greets invited guests in an ornate receiving hall. Thereafter, the monarch attends evening vespers, usually alone. Jerrard's invitation, however, specifically bids him to join the king in prayer. In preparation for this opening volley of phony spirituality, he has been reciting biblical passages and other Catholic litanies during the journey from Normandy to Fontainebleau. His companions, long his compatriots in riding, archery and other masculine pastimes, have begun to call him Father Jerrard. They assume that some political mischief is afoot. It is not their business. Their only duty is to protect the adolescent master of the Boulton earldom.

Jerrard has borne the good natured jibes from his escorts. Occasionally he raises his hands in a priestly blessing or asks to hear their confessions. "Come, unburden yourselves to Father Jerrard so that I can absolve you of your transgressions. You are sinners, all." The horsemen are entertained, and the journey is less boring.

A lifetime of preparation precedes this diplomatic mission to the French court. The eldest son of Boulton has been raised to be his father's successor in administration, battle and the art of intrigue. Power politics has been his major course of study. He will need all of his considerable training to seal an alliance with King Louis, always pious but sometimes petulant and cunning. He must not lose sight of his father's singular goal: secure possession of the cache of golden coins. However, he is confident. His previous assignments on behalf of the mighty baronial House of Boulton have been successful. Protection of the Aureus, however, is the first where he must weaponize his faith and barter his younger sister. This has been troubling, but, he tells himself, he will get over these temporary jabs at something…he can't quite describe what…at something in his core that doesn't quite feel right.

KING LOUIS'S PRIVATE CHAPEL is dark, somber. The golden richness of the small altar is barely visible in the waning candlelight. Two men are kneeling, intoning a Latin prayer. One wears a crown.

"My son, Jerrard, you know the scriptures. I commend your father on your training."

"Thank you, Your Majesty. I am privileged to pray with you."

The king stands and makes the sign of the cross. Jerrard follows his example. Exiting the rich oaken pew, each man genuflects. Their movements are slow, almost lethargic, as if leaving the sanctuary is a burden. The king bows his head, staring at the fine carpet which softens each measured royal step. His prayers tonight have been directed to a compassionate Heavenly Father: Please bless the covenant which he will make with the House of Boulton to rid him of the insufferable burden of brotherly support. He promises an early pilgrimage to the Holy See in Rome. Perhaps the young earl would consider postponing his upcoming trip to Rome and accompany him in the following year.

Jerrard's gait must match that of King Louis. It would be bad form to be in a hurry to exit this hallowed space. He, too, prays for a happy outcome for his visit. Then he thinks, what can go wrong? This is a win–win situation.

❊

THE ROYAL DINING ROOM is resplendent with tapestries and swaying candelabras. Louis's Fontainebleau lacks the customary great room, which can be used to dine, hold dances or conduct ceremonies. When the chateau was in its design phase, the idea of a multi-purpose hall had offended the king's architectural concept of gracious dining in a country lodge setting. As the lodge grew to be a palace, he retained the concept of elegance joined with intimacy in many rooms, including this one, which exudes a kind of cozy opulence. Tonight five diners savor the royal chef's creations. The carved mahogany table groans under piles of delicacies. The men, engorged with the creations from the royal kitchen, lean back in their chairs. Two teenage princesses, sitting on each side of the king, arise and caress his shoulders.

"Papa, we bid you good night. You have much to discuss, and we must be prepared for our lessons tomorrow. Good night, Uncle Arnaud and Lord Boulton. We so enjoyed meeting you and look forward to seeing you." Princess Marie kisses her father's cheek. Her sister Princess Alix, the playful one, plucks her father's crown from his head and plants a quick peck on his thinning hair, returning the crown somewhat askew.

"Good night. Say your prayers." As they exit, King Louis beams at his brother and guest. "They enchant my life. Their little sisters do as well. I cannot imagine being without them. And yet, perhaps not so far from now, each will leave me to live in another palace, in another land, with another man – a husband. Even though it pains me, I have already made some inquiries. Of course, their well-being is uppermost in my mind, as, I am sure, the well-being of your sister was critical in your father's offer to betroth her to my brother. Am I right, Jerrard?"

"Absolutely, Your Majesty." Jerrard turns to Prince Arnaud. "My father had heard about your many excellent qualities. He has said, so often, that he will die a happy man knowing that my sister is entrusted to the care of a royal gentleman."

The prince, still attacking a sugary morsel, emits a small burp. "Ah."

"As king as well as older brother, I must give my permission, you know. So I would say that we should cover the details, get them out of the way, before toasting the upcoming nuptials. First, the marriage should take place here in France." Silence. "Fine, that is settled."

"The dowry?" Prince Arnaud enters the discourse. A speck of pastry dots his chin.

"Allow me to conduct this discussion." There is a tiny edge to the king's voice. He stops long enough to inhale. His cheerful tone returns. "Well, now that you have brought it up, yes, we might as well just sketch out the dowry, as in how and when it will be delivered, and, let's see, oh, of course, the form of it and the value. Then we will have all the specifics out of the way." The king leans back in his regal wing chair. He is in control, as it should be.

"I agree." Jerrard's instructions are to let the monarch guide the be-trothal conversation.

"What does she look like?" Prince Arnaud pours another glass of wine, some of which has already spotted the front of his elegant vest.

"Stop interrupting!" King Louis's fist thumps the fine mahogany. The plate closest to him quivers.

Arnaud persists. "I know it doesn't matter, but I'm curious. Her brother certainly knows what she looks like. Let's just say that he can prepare me."

The king's skin tone deepens from pink to crimson to a tinge of purple. His lips, tight and thin, move. Harsh words are forming.

"Prince Arnaud," Jerrard amends his directive and enters the crumbling discourse, "I'm delighted to paint a word picture of my sweet sister, Aldreda." He glances at Louis, who appears to welcome this short recess from sibling confrontation. Returning to his topic, he feels a momentary twinge. He is sealing his sister's fate. On the other hand, he can't unseal it. Anyway, the truth is that Aldreda is pretty. His hunting friends have told him that she, accompanied by a generous dowry, will be the catch of 1163. He begins. "The young barons who have seen her are all smitten. Of course, she is so fine in manner and beauty that my father decided long ago that her destiny was to adorn a royal household. My prince, when you first see her, you will think that you are beholding an angel. Yes, an angel alighting in your presence with a gift of worldly wealth." Jerrard stops, checking his audience for a reaction.

The king continues to glare at his brother, but his tense demeanor is softening; his normal color is returning. Prince Arnaud's mouth hangs open in a goofy grin. Along with the dowry, Aldreda is a prize.

"Well, Arnaud, it's all you could hope for. Jerrard, thank you for your introduction to your sister. And you have a talent for words. As we join our families, it is my hope that you will grace our court from time to time. We not only share a deep devotion to Almighty God, but I think we may also appreciate engaging conversations on other subjects of interest. But first, let's tend to the necessary particulars of the dowry. Where were we? Had we discussed its form and when it would be delivered? No, I don't think so." The king, ever so casual, has returned the conversation to where it was a few minutes ago.

There is a small ado in the arched entry to the dining room. A courier is arguing with Louis's man-in-waiting, who is trying to prevent him from entering the king's presence.

"I say, Bernard, what's going on? Can't I have a meal with guests without an interruption?"

"Your Majesty, this man says he is announcing the visit of the Chancellor of England, who has arrived with a safe passage from King Henry. He is in your greeting hall."

"The Chancellor of England is in my greeting hall? Now?"

The courier drops to one knee. "Sire, we have come a long way. I ask your forgiveness for this intrusion. My mission is to deliver the Chancellor to your Royal Highness."

King Louis, ready to nail down the specifics of the dowry, pounds the table in irritation. First the interferences from his lamebrain brother. Now a totally unexpected visit from the English chancellor, of all people. It will be past midnight when he finds out the actual substance of the dowry. He will likely spend all night considering it, possibly negotiating with a teenager. What good is a wondrous dinner if the dessert course is followed by nonsense and a surprise emissary from an enemy king? Oh, well, a monarch must shoulder whatever burdens God sends his way.

"Tell the Chancellor we will meet now in my private chamber."

"Thank you, Your Majesty."

THE MAHOGANY TABLE has been cleared by silent servants. Prince Arnaud, still seated, is snoring. His hands are folded over his ample belly. The room is darker. Candles that flickered out have not been relit. Jerrard wanders the room. He is tired from riding since dawn and now regrets consuming such large quantities of food. Suddenly footsteps lightly punctuate Arnaud's steady drone. They are closer. King Louis bursts into the room, followed by his man-in-waiting.

"More light. We need to light all the candles. Arnaud, wake up. Wake up! We, uh, we have a situation." Louis waves a document clearly marked with King Henry's sizeable royal imprint. "A very interesting situation. Arnaud! Open your eyes!" The king's eyes, on the other hand, are wide with excitement and a hint of avarice.

"I don't wish to intrude on a family matter. It would be my pleasure to meet with Your Majesty tomorrow or whenever it's convenient for you." Jerrard bows and is backing toward the darkened arch.

"No, no. You must stay. Arnaud, wake up, I said." Arnaud shifts in his chair. "And sit up straight. Now, sit here. No, Arnaud, stay where you are. I mean Jerrard. Yes, here, close to me so you can see what your king has written."

"Arnaud! Oh, Lord give me strength, he's asleep again." The king motions to his man-in-waiting. "Shake him."

Two firm hands grasp the caped, fleshy shoulders.

"Okay, I'm awake. No need. It's past my bedtime. I do need a good night's rest, as you know."

"You will go nighty night after we have conducted business. And there are new circumstances regarding you. Your betrothal. The dowry. So stay focused."

"Okay. You have my attention." Arnaud turns to Louis's servant. "More wine, fast."

King Louis clears his throat as he waves the parchment over the table. "This is a very interesting development, for all of us. That's why you must stay." The parchment waves back and forth in front of Jerrard. The king's voice is picking up resonance.

"Chancellor Ridel has come as an ambassador from King Henry. Your king." He nods at his guest, now sitting to his right. "His proposal to me is most intriguing. Brother Arnaud, the English are obviously concerned over your continued bachelorhood. First the House of Boulton offers the fair Aldreda to be your wife. Now, no less than the King of England, a man who has greatly troubled the French nation, but nonetheless...the King of England has taken a personal interest in your matrimonial future."

"What?" Prince Arnaud is the picture of puzzlement.

"King Henry II of England has combed the land and found, in his opinion, the ideal bride for you."

"I always liked Henry. How is Eleanor?"

Jerrard does not move, not even his eyes. He concentrates on being motionless while absorbing this unexpected royal ruse by his sovereign.

"I'm sure Eleanor is fine. Now, back to his offer. He proposes this: a wife of noble caste and an immense dowry from her father, supplemented by the royal treasury. Mmm. That is nice. Here's the other part. Henry offers us a truce as a personal wedding present."

Jerrard's head snaps, ever so slightly.

"Who is the girl?" Arnaud is staring at Henry's letter.

"I was coming to that. She is Lady Emma, daughter of the Earl of Cambridge, one of the most powerful men in England."

Jerrard cannot contain himself. He turns in his chair, directly facing the king. "Your Majesty, surely there is some kind of joke going on here. Are you having fun at my expense?"

"In my wildest dreams, I couldn't have conjured up this scenario. Two daughters tendered to my bachelor brother. Two huge dowries. I guess yours is huge. We never got that far in the conversation. One offer of a truce. The other offer. Let's see, Jerrard. Can your father offer a truce? Does your father even want a truce?"

"Does the king's letter say what this Emma girl looks like?" Arnaud's curiosity offers Jerrard an opportunity to dodge the question.

"Prince Arnaud, I know this girl. She is maybe twelve, if that. Rather chubby. There is a certain malformation of her left leg. I think from a childhood disease. Her face is, well, uh, round. Eyes are a little bulgy. There is the beginning of a wart, right about here." He taps the edge of his chin. "She doesn't talk much, but that's okay because she has an unpleasant lisp." He shakes his head. "Sad."

Louis's head begins nodding, at first imperceptibly, then graduating to an overdone gesture. His eyes twinkle. His lips curve upward, then part to reveal a royal set of teeth. It does not often happen, but at this moment the French king is close to outright laughter. He looks at his brother to see if he is likewise entertained. No, Arnaud is not sharing the moment. Hardly. He is frowning. He has just heard bad news. Up until now, the evening had been going well for him, first with a betrothal to Aldreda of Boulton, then an additional girl, the Cambridge one, thrown in. Both with the requisite dowry. The first one is pretty.

It would have been most agreeable if the second contender had also been fair of face. Then, either one would have been fine. Of course, his brother would make the decision, and he knows that the king bases his decisions on factors that generally don't interest Arnaud. In contrast to the king, his facial expression is one of uneasy anticipation. Jerrard is staring at a far-off candle.

"Well done, Jerrard. You are very convincing. Look at my brother. He believes your every word."

Arnaud blinks. What is his brother implying? Jerrard has just said that he knows the girl Emma. That's highly likely since their families travel in the same social circles. Just because he is king, it doesn't mean that Louis has a special talent for distinguishing truth from falsehood. He, Arnaud, knows better than that.

"See. I mean it. He believes you. It's written on his sweet gullible face."

Jerrard rises, placing both hands flat on the table. "I tell the truth, Your Majesty."

"Oh, please. You want your sister to be my brother's bride. Obviously. Maybe you have never even seen Emma. But regardless, you are putting your thumb on the scale of choice. The choice that I must make. As Louis VII of France, I consider it to be a very serious offense against my person to fabricate evidence in our betrothal negotiations. You have a safe conduct passage to visit my court, but you do not have a guaranty of your safety if you lie to me."

The dining room is very still.

"Is there a bible in here?" Jerrard's gesture sweeps around the room.

"There is a bible in every room when I am in residence."

"Please give it to me."

The king's personal servant brings a bible from a side shelf and places it on the table next to Jerrard, who drops to one knee. He faces King Louis, bows his head and closes his eyes. Having shut the room from his view, he is transported to a special niche in his memory, a

69

garden filled with flowers. A girl is picking a blue forget-me-not. She gives it to him. Her hand is soft. He remembers cutting the flowers for a full bouquet, a present for him. The daydream shifts to a balcony. He is adjusting a shawl around the same girl's shoulders. She is nearly a young woman. He touches her arms and neck, then lifts her chin. The cold night is becoming warm. He is warm. The vision freezes momentarily, then fades. The warmth fades. Returning to the dining room, he places his right palm on the gilded holy book and speaks: "With my hand on this bible and in the presence of King Louis VII of France, defender of the faith, and in the presence of God, I swear that my description of Emma of Cambridge is in no way, I repeat no way, related to the offer, made by the House of Boulton, of my sister Aldreda to be betrothed to Prince Arnaud of France. I solemnly swear."

Stillness returns to the dining room tableau.

"With Your Majesty's leave, I will retire to my chamber now and await your summons tomorrow." Jerrard bows and exits. King Louis and Prince Arnaud sit silently, both absorbing the events of the evening.

In the depth of the silent, semi-dark halls, Jerrard stops and whispers, "Forgive me, Aldreda."

KING LOUIS IS ALONE in his chapel. He kneels at the altar and commences his dialog with God. "Oh, Lord, Protector of my Domain, I beg your guidance on an important matter of state. My course of action was easy when there was only one offer, Aldreda of Boulton, to be my brother's bride. Now King Henry has sent his offer, Emma of Cambridge. Both have dowries, though the amount is a question mark on both sides. I must nail that down with Jerrard tomorrow. Then I can give Henry a chance to do better." The king shakes his head. He is praying and plotting simultaneously, and he knows that is wrong.

"Lord, I humbly beseech your forgiveness for mixing statecraft with prayer." The king endeavors to assemble his thoughts in a way that will please the Almighty, but his mind persists in wandering. Really, he grumbles, his brother has a disturbing way of interjecting his idiotic concerns into a sensitive discussion. Who cares what the girls look like? It's not as if Arnaud is seeking a seductive mistress. But Jerrard swore the Cambridge girl is ugly. Swore on a bible. Well, wait. No, he didn't actually swear that she was ugly. Let's see. He swore his description was unrelated to his father's offer of his sister. Never mind. Louis chides himself for over-thinking this matter. Young Boulton swore on a bible. That's all that counts.

King Louis buries his head in his hands. He feels an obligation to lay out all the facts, all the options to God, who, he is certain, already knows these things. Perhaps God is walking him through the process, leading him to a logical solution of his dilemma. It would be natural for the All-Wise to choose this form of revelation to a righteous follower. The king's spirits are lifted. His communication resumes: "My duty is to France, so I must look to the consequences of my choice. Henry proposes peace, at least a temporary one, as a wedding present. A respite in our war could be a very pleasant interlude. On the other hand, a mere nobleman, like the Earl of Boulton, lacks the power to offer a truce, and, perhaps it would not be to his advantage to have King Henry unencumbered by war with France. In either choice, I will enrich the royal treasury by discontinuing my support of brother Arnaud. How will I spend this unexpected fortune? On war or other ventures? It is my devout entreaty, dear Lord, that you will guide me to an answer."

He remains kneeling, bent over in supplication. Then, slowly, he raises his head to behold the golden statuary populating the front of the altar. "Thank you." Standing, his lips curve slightly upward. "Yes. No need to discuss the dowries tomorrow. Yes. Yes. And, who knows, this might create a bit of mischief in England. Perfect."

❋

SHAFTS OF MORNING LIGHT illuminate the royal receiving room in the Chateau de Fontainebleau. The king is seated on a lush settee. His grey robe suggests austerity and the extreme burden carried by God's Protector of France. A jeweled diadem rests on his head. Prince Arnaud lounges nearby on a tapestried chaise. He is yawning.

Jerrard and Chancellor Ridel have made their expected deferential bows. Both stand silently, awaiting the monarch's words.

The king beckons a servant. He is in no hurry. There is something rather amusing about the tension in the room. For as long as he has occupied the throne, he has derived pleasure from the nervous anticipation of his petitioners.

"Bring me my bible."

The servant has heard this command regularly. A bible appears immediately and is placed in Louis's hands.

"I trust you slept well. Our country air is quite wholesome."

Agreeable murmurs punctuate the edgy atmosphere. Prince Arnaud's eyes are closed.

"I have been praying over this matter. Passages from the bible have guided me as well." The king gently pats the heavy book resting on his lap.

"Chancellor Ridel, please convey to my dear King Henry that I accept his betrothal offer of Lady Emma, daughter of the Earl of Cambridge, to my brother Prince Arnaud and the generous double dowry and peace between our two countries. You will stay to execute this agreement with my personal secretary."

Jerrard does not move. He cannot. He is frozen by disbelief.

"Brother dear, did you choose the ugly one for me?" Arnaud's eyes are now open.

"I did. Chancellor, perhaps this respite from war will afford our two countries an opportunity to further the work of our Mother Church. Please convey that message to King Henry and the Archbishop."

"Of course, and thank you, Your Majesty, on behalf of King Henry II."

"Young Boulton, I regret having to make this choice, because your father's offer of your sister Aldreda was, I'm sure, made with only the best of intentions for our mutual prosperity and good relations. I wish I had yet another brother to betroth. Then we would all be delighted."

"I wish I were the other brother," Arnaud grumbles.

The king ignores this interjection. "Because we will no longer be at war, I extend an invitation to your family to visit us at your earliest convenience. And I will do all I can to send you on to Rome in style. I wish I could go myself, but royal duties at this time of year prevent me from accompanying you. I do so envy your journey to see the Holy Father."

Jerrard seeks the words that will camouflage his astonishment, disappointment and something else, an inner twinge of pain. "I think I will cancel my planned trip to Rome. My father would want to learn of your decision as quickly as possible." He hesitates, staring at his boots, then remembers his manners. "Thank you for your offer to assist my entourage in preparing for our planned journey south, but now, all I will require is a safe passage document to return the way I came."

The king continues his patter of small talk while his brother peers through the window at the winter sun. Geoffrey Ridel, elated by his coup, is happy to stand and listen to the monarchical ramblings. Jerrard suppresses a desire to abruptly end this audience, but he knows that he must not act the vanquished warrior. What he really wants to know is this: why is peace so attractive to the French king, who delights in battling the English, especially the English king who took his wife? What does he hope to attain by giving the English army a respite? Jerrard needs his father's sage counsel to understand the motives of both kings. And what about Arnaud? Did he not have even a tiny vote on who would be his wife? Wait until he sees Emma. He will be ecstatic, unlike Jerrard who is experiencing a sadness that is unfamiliar. And when King Louis beholds the fair Emma, will he recall Jerrard's unfavorable description of her and his oath on the bible? Hopefully the king will remember exactly what was sworn to, but he can't count on that. Obviously, it would not be advisable for his family to accept the king's invitation to visit France. In fact, Jerrard cannot wait to gather his men and flee the country for the safety and comfort of England and the Boulton estate.

CHAPTER EIGHT

"I BID YOU A FINE NEW YEAR, Thomas. Let 1163 bring prosperity to the crown and more souls to the church." The king raises his glass toward the Archbishop. "The Christmas season was less jolly because of your absence. My boys miss their pal. Young Henry especially. You have been part of his life for so many years."

"Yes, I know. I miss them, too. Princess Mathilda always wanted a story from me. She knew how to coax one out of me, even after a heavy dinner. Now I am quite overwhelmed by my duties. I hope you have explained that to the children. I wouldn't want them to think that I've lost my affection for them."

"I think you should take young Henry under your archbishopric wing and supervise his preparation for the monarchy. It's time he began a more formal education. His tutors are fine, but your influence as a teacher, leader of the church and your special relationship with your king, me," Henry's fingertips tap his chest, "make you, and only you, the person to mold the character of the future king of England. Say yes. Eleanor says that I cannot accept any other answer from you."

"Well, why didn't you say that the queen wanted me to supervise young Henry's upbringing? My answer now can only be *yes*."

"Very good. Thank you, Thomas. Now we must catch up on other matters. Here's one for starters. Are you ready for a surprise?"

"Henry, nothing you do surprises me anymore, but go ahead and try."

"Alright. Chancellor Ridel has just returned from the French court, where he presented to King Louis my proposal to betroth Emma, daughter of the Earl of Cambridge, to Prince Arnaud. I offered to augment the dowry with an appropriate amount from the royal treasury. And I threw in an additional offer of peace. Well, a truce, anyway."

"This is no surprise. You told me you were going to offer up somebody's daughter. You just didn't tell me it was Cambridge. Remember, you said you couldn't give away all your secrets. From the way you are acting, I presume Louis accepted."

"He did. There's more. That's the surprise. When Geoffrey arrived, there was already another offer on the table. Want to guess who...no wait, want to guess which English baron had already served up his daughter, like a confection, to be nibbled on by that piece of blubber Arnaud?"

"You mean like you served up Emma?"

"A king's prerogative. So, guess."

Thomas hesitates. This began as a characteristically Henry-like gambit. But why? Why take Arnaud off the royal dole? Why offer peace? And there was a second English offer. Thomas does not like where this is going. Which English nobleman would want to do a financial favor for King Louis? There is a tiny sensation in the pit of his stomach that he might know who it is.

"Who presented this other offer?"

"Jerrard of Boulton, the earl's son. See, I really wasn't going to make you keep guessing."

Boulton would have been Thomas's first answer.

"Jerrard stayed at my cousin's place in Normandy awaiting a summons from the French king; someone trusted by the earl went to the French court first to get an invitation and safe passage. So I've known that Boulton had some kind of plan regarding the French. I just didn't know what it was until Geoffrey returned. Now, what do you think of all of this, Thomas?"

"I think the Earl of Boulton wanted King Louis to have more money to fight the English. A nice Boulton dowry to Arnaud would have taken care of that. So the question is, why would Boulton aid the French king, who is fighting against you?"

"My question exactly." The answer is so clear to Henry.

The Archbishop clasps his hands together, resting his forehead against his fingers. His posture is prayerful, but his mind is assembling the facts. The Canterbury ecclesiastical library, the finest collection of manuscripts in all King Henry's vast lands, holds many learned books on Roman law. He has read in depth about the crime of treason. It could be argued, in a round-about way, that the actions of the Earl of Boulton fit the definition of this capital crime. Boulton has, in effect, aided a wartime enemy of the crown before knowing of Henry's offer of a truce. Why would he do that? It would seem that there can only be one answer. Henry knows that Boulton has the Aureus, and Boulton knows he knows. That's why Henry proposed the war on the nobility, the punishment of errant children. He's going after Boulton's treasure. And now he has Roman law to back him up. What a gift to Henry. With any luck, the rest of the nobility will stay out of it when they learn that Boulton went to King Louis with a financial deal that would benefit the French army. They may oppose the ambitious king, but the stain of treason is always to be avoided.

"Thomas, what are you thinking?"

"Your Majesty," Thomas emits a long sigh worthy of an archbishop. "I am beseeching the Lord for guidance in this matter, so that I can advise you the best way I can."

"In that case, take your time."

Thomas wonders: Did the nobility really ever intend to ask Henry to increase the taxes on church land? Possibly. It certainly makes sense. Or did Henry make that up to get Thomas's sympathy and aid in his war on Boulton, the "errant" child? No matter. He must determine how to maximize the Church's influence in this contest of wills; the goal is to get the lion's share of the Aureus if Henry prevails.

"Your Majesty," the tone is deferential, "We may have a meeting of the minds on this matter, so we must be honest with one another. Why is Boulton your enemy? Does he, perhaps, have something you want?"

"Maybe I just don't like the turn of his mustache."

"Ha, ha. I ask again. Does he have something that you want? Something of great value? Something you believe you are entitled to?"

It is Henry's turn to deliberate. He admonishes himself for his waste of time in trying to figure out how his friend could know about the Aureus. Because Thomas does know. It's obvious. And he's going to bring up Pope Gregory's papal decree. That's for certain. Bloody church. His great-grandfather William had kept the ecclesiastics in their place. Likewise his grandfather Henry. It's all the fault of his predecessor, weak Uncle Stephen, who conceded too much power to Archbishop Theobald. He, Henry, will get it back; that's his next project. But now he must concentrate on Thomas; he needs to offer him something to secure his aid in wresting the Roman coins from the Boulton grasp.

"Henry, or rather Your Majesty, are you daydreaming?"

"No, I am admiring your splendid intellect. How do you know about the Aureus?"

"Well now, that's a new topic. Do you want to expand on it?"

"Don't answer a question with a question. Weren't you taught that it is an unacceptable conversational ploy to do that?"

"You will notice that you just answered my question with a question. To quote Your Majesty, that is an unacceptable conversational ploy."

"In my reading of English history, I do not recall a monarch ever ordering the death of an Archbishop of Canterbury. Oh, well, there's always a first time. Sarcasm being a very serious crime against the crown. Like treason."

"I am quivering with fear." Thomas always relished these exchanges with Henry. It has been a long time since they engaged in repartee. He is having fun, even if the subject is fraught with danger to his goal.

"I can see that. But you have nothing to ever fear from me. I would never let harm come to you. And since you now understand that I am not only your king, but your protector, be so kind to tell me how you know about the Aureus."

"The villagers who unearthed it got drunk. They were bragging and displayed one of the coins. Someone reported it to Boulton. The conversation was overheard by one of my distant friars, and he told me."

"He journeyed all the way to Canterbury to tell you that? My, he takes his vows seriously."

"He wanted a reward."

"What kind of a reward?"

"A lifetime supply of fine wines."

"This tale is being fueled by a lot of alcohol consumption. Is that a problem here in England? I had not noticed. Maybe it's the weather. Damp. Foggy. Not like the crisp clear air of my birthplace in Anjou. Was it wine from Anjou, by the way, that your friar preferred?" Henry, like Thomas, feels liberated by the subject being out in the open. But liberated only for a brief moment. He produces a gold coin from his vest.

"This brought two villagers to their untimely end. They were brothers."

Thomas peers at the glimmering coin. But he sees more, a pot of gold for the church.

"Yes, I believe Anjou wines were his preference. And now, it's my turn to ask. How did you acquire this Roman jewel?"

"Of course, one revelation deserves another. When traveling to visit Boulton last year, we encountered a man, nearly dead, in the forest. He was one of the men who dug up the Aureus. The last thing he did before he died was to give me this. You see, even in his final moments, he knew that this was the property of the king. Good man."

There it is. The gauntlet thrown. Thomas considers invoking the papal decree, but decides to keep it in his arsenal, temporarily. Let's see what the king wants.

"So you are going to beat up on Boulton until he gives it to you, right? And since you are no longer at war with France, all your homeland troops plus your considerable continental armies will be quite a formidable force. Throw in treason and maybe, just maybe, Boulton won't even have any allies. Well, good luck. You'll do just fine. Now, this has been fun, but I must return to my many duties."

"Hold on, Thomas. Your newly acquired religiosity hangs heavily in the air. Where do you see the Church in this conflict?"

"Your Majesty, you speak of war. We will be busy praying for the thousands of souls that might be lost in this conflict."

"Oh, please spare me all this praying. You and I have always worked well with one another. Except in the last year or so, after I gave you a new job. Join forces with me. Your church lands can feed a vast army, and you can throw in a considerable amount of money from your treasury. If you recall, I was prepared to disregard the barons' idea of increasing taxes on papal lands and decreasing taxes on theirs. If you think this is just a monarchical fabrication, ask the Earl of Cambridge. He was going to broach the subject with me, but a bit of luck enabled me to avoid the conversation." Henry stops to allow his listener time to absorb all of this information.

"However, I have always had an excellent relationship with Cambridge, so I made a deal with him: I would lower his taxes, but only his taxes, if I could do a bit of continental matchmaking with the lovely Emma. He hated the idea of shipping her off to France and goofy Arnaud, but he eventually came around when we did the mathematics." The recitation is once again suspended. Thomas's mouth is set in a stern grimace, but his eyes flit around, following each new revelation as if it were a bird leaping from branch to branch.

Henry resumes. "Now, you are wondering, what's in it for me, or the Church actually? Well, obviously the Aureus is the prize we are both seeking. Right?"

Thomas hesitates. The answer is certainly yes, but somehow to admit it seems like he is giving up some negotiating power. The question dangles between them.

"Let me put it another way. I am seeking the prize. Are you not likewise interested in it? For the papacy? Aren't you going to invoke Pope Gregory? I have been waiting for that, and I'm becoming impatient."

"I had thought of bringing it up, but I preferred you to do it. And you have, thereby acknowledging the authority of the decree."

"I acknowledge nothing. In matters of power, prestige and wealth, everything is negotiable. Everything is on the table. Shall we commence a discussion of this matter?" Henry's manner is impersonal, businesslike.

"I was prepared to reward the crown for its assistance in recovering this treasure belonging to the church. I was ready to bend papal rules to thank you for your help, and you want to discuss it?" In contrast to the king, Thomas is speaking in a voice rising with indignation.

"Absolutely. You're my man. You're lucky I'm willing to bargain with you."

"I'm not your man. I am the Church personified in England. The Church does not bargain."

"Listen, Thomas, you're Archbishop because I made you the Archbishop. You owe me. Now let's make a deal."

"You want to negotiate the terms of a papal decree made by a pope, now also a saint? Is that really what you want to do?" Thomas's questions ring with astonishment and outrage.

"Yes."

THE CATHEDRAL OF NOTRE DAME is the newest sensation in Paris. Part is still under construction, but it is clear to all Parisians that this will be the crown jewel of their city. The spires reach toward the heavens, invoking an almighty blessing on this earthly palace of worship. Inside, the scaffolds have been removed for the first major event to take place in Our Lady's sanctuary. There are no seats yet. Europe's richly clad royalty and nobility mill around, as much spectators as invitees to a wedding. They marvel at the golden altar and statuary, while assessing the finery worn by their contemporaries.

Two trumpets sound an attention-getting clarion. The crowd turns toward the magnificent arched entry to the cathedral, where a red-vested herald is waving the French king's ensign. He is aided by royal guards who are motioning for the jumbled throng to stand to the right or the left. As the throng parts, a second herald strides down the newly created aisle and cries, "His Majesty, Louis VII, King of France." As one, all heads bow while the king, followed by his couriers, makes his purposeful walk to the altar and drops to his knees in prayer. The corseted and perfumed guests try to emulate the king, but the absence of kneelers produces a scene of toppling bodies and noisy complaints. King Louis does not notice. He is thanking God for the Earl of Cambridge, and he is even thanking God for King Henry II.

The trumpets blast once more, and the guests restore their standing positions and their regal dignity. Prince Arnaud, followed by his men-in-waiting, waddles down the aisle. He embraces his brother, who is his official witness.

A third round of trumpets resounds in the vast interior of the cathedral. At the door, glimmering in an ivory gown and heavy veil, Emma clutches her father's hand. During the arduous winter journey to Paris, he has told his daughter how much he will miss her daily kiss on his forehead. He has almost apologized for sending her away, but that would only make her sadder. And she is sad, but she has been raised to do her female duty as a member of a noble class. Perhaps she will see her parents again, and her sister Catherine, if the current peace prevails, but one can never be sure what will set off the two warring monarchs again. So Lord Arthur holds Emma's hand tight and walks her down the aisle.

Prince Arnaud watches, with curiosity, as his bride approaches. He wonders if a round face is all that bad. But bulging eyes? Better not to think about that. Perhaps the newly forming wart on her chin could be removed. Then there is that speech impediment. Well, he doesn't really have to talk to her. Just concentrate on the dowry.

Emma stands before him now. King Louis, on one side, is beaming with brotherly happiness. Lord Arthur, on his other side, places Emma's hand in Arnaud's pudgy paw. He raises her veil to give her a fatherly kiss. Arnaud gasps. "Oh, my!"

❈

THOMAS CONTINUES TO REGARD HENRY with stunned silence. His jaw has dropped, leaving his mouth agape. He is shaking his head. His hands open in a plea for reason. Finally he speaks. "You would defy Saint Gregory's decree?"

"Your performance of outrage is excellent. Well, maybe a little heavy on the melodrama. If you join forces with me, you get a portion of the Aureus when I wrest it from the earl's hands. And notice that it is I who will be doing the hard work here. By that, I mean waging war. While you get to sit in your hair shirt, hands nice and clean, and talk to God. Or did you intend to send your friar to ask Lord William to give it to you?"

"I have a weapon that you don't have."

"And it is?"

"Excommunication. For the entire Boulton clan. No sacraments. No last rites. No Christian burial. Eternal damnation. You see, Henry, my sword is stronger than your sword."

Henry leans forward. A smirk appears at the edge of his lips. "Nice try. Speaking of damnation, you know that the earl doesn't give a damn about excommunication. You can't scare him out of a fortune. Once you revoke his church membership, he will likely make a sizeable contribution to the Holy Father in Rome and get reinstated in the faith before you can deny him one Sunday communion. His steward rides a very swift horse. Think over my offer. You are dismissed."

CHAPTER NINE

CHANCELLOR RIDEL IS SEATED at a writing table. The king is standing. And pacing. They are in the royal study. It is the chancellor's first visit to this room. His meetings with King Henry are still formal and infrequent. In this modest work area, the chancellor sees Henry in another dimension. The décor is masculine, spare, with a few embellishments likely contributed by Queen Eleanor. Obviously this is where the intellectual work of the monarchy takes place. The walls are lined with books written in Latin, French and English. One book is on the table, a marker jutting out of its midsection.

"There is what you need to be my scribe." Henry points to the parchment and quill pen next to the book. "I had the pen made especially for you from a royal goose feather. This is a momentous occasion. Only you should write the formal charge of treason."

The chancellor looks up. "Treason? Who?"

"You are being disingenuous, my dear Geoffrey. You were the first to know, even before me, that the Earl of Boulton was offering aid and comfort to the enemy of England. Never mind that Louis accepted my betrothal offer instead of his. The point is this: Boulton made an offer that, if accepted, would have substantially aided the French in their war-making powers. He did this before I called a truce. That's treason, and you knew it was when you returned from France. Now, I'm not criticizing you for your failure to mention it; that's my royal preroga-tive, but don't act surprised now that I am mentioning it." Henry em-phasizes the *I am*. "And directing you to write out my formal charges against Boulton. I am thinking about adding his son Jerrard. Give me your advice. Would you add the young earl?"

"Let me think." In truth, the idea that Boulton's betrothal offer was treasonous had not crossed his mental landscape. But there was a cer-tain logic to the charge if you looked at the matter in a particular way. A hefty Boulton dowry to Prince Arnaud would have represented a fi-nancial boon to King Louis, enabling him to more effectively prose-cute his war against England. But why would the earl want to do that? What if he simply wanted his daughter to marry into a royal family? Nothing unusual about that. The chancellor's perplexity is interrupted by the king.

"Argument in favor: Young Jerrard was an integral part of the whole operation. It was he who brought the proposal to the French king. His father gave him a great deal of responsibility in this scheme."

"And what, if any, would be an argument against charging young Boulton with treason?"

"Let's just say he and his father share a secret about something im-portant to me. It would be a good idea to have one of them alive. You see, I don't think that Lord William will put him into the battle. William, of course, will ride at the head of his troops. He's an egomaniac, but you have to respect him on the killing ground. He will fight to the end."

"Well, now," the chancellor reenters the dialogue. "We can still charge Jerrard with treason, even if he isn't with the troops."

"Quite right. However, if he is charged with treason and we cap-ture him, then we really should kill him immediately. That would be expected. On the other hand, if he is merely a prisoner of war, we could torture the information out of him. It's something to think about."

"And what if you torture him, and he won't talk? There are people like that. They will go to their death with their precious secret."

"I suppose. Did you know that the earl has an old-fashioned rack on his property? Last year I encountered a man, a dying man, who had a personal experience on that rack. Likewise his brother, also dead. I wonder how long young Boulton would last on that instrument of anguish. Of course, we could threaten to torture his mother and siblings."

"Your Majesty, torturing women and children? That's what barbarians do. We are civilized."

"Well, being the civilized king of a civilized country, I know that. But sometimes you just have to abandon certain accepted norms when the stakes are high enough. And these stakes are very high."

"So you are saying that if the stakes are so very, very high, any means of obtaining them are okay?"

"I guess that's what I was saying, yes." Henry peers at his chancellor. "Geoffrey, why haven't you asked me what the stakes are?"

"Truly, I do not want to know. If, as you just said, any behavior is warranted when the prize is valuable enough, then I wish to continue being known as the chancellor who does not revel in intimacy with the king. Thomas, if he were still occupying my position, would know everything. That would make him less safe."

"Here's a bit of a secret, a morsel for you to chew on. Thomas does know. And you are quite right. He is not safe. At least his position is not safe." Henry takes only moments to reach a decision. "I think I will not charge young Boulton with treason. Please write up the charges for William, Earl of Boulton. I've marked the page in this book where you will find the official language in Latin." Henry lightly taps the thick tome.

CHAPTER TEN

THE LOGISTICS OF MOVING massive armies of men across the water dominate King Henry's days for much of the spring and summer months. But before he disassembles his continental fighting force, Henry must secure the truce with King Louis. He does this with his promise to augment Emma's dowry to Arnaud. Two months after the wedding, a heavily guarded wagon train crosses Normandy to the French border, where additional guards accompany the carriages, laden with royal treasure, all the way to the French court. The dowry, however, is not presented to Arnaud, who has been dispatched to Fontainebleau with his bride. King Louis steps in and does his sibling duty, thanking the English emissary and armed escorts on behalf of his brother. Henry has made the final payment on the truce, and he is at last free to bring his now-idle continental troops to England.

Almost a century before, Henry's great-grandfather, William of Normandy, had made the same crossing. He, also, had to transport men, horses and armaments to face King Harold of England, the man who had usurped the throne promised to William. Now, and Henry does see the irony, armies are crossing the water, not to make war on the English king, but rather to aid the English king in making war on some of his own subjects. William's brilliance in organizing this massive convoy is part of Norman lore; Henry studies the detailed notes from 1066, still readable in 1163.

Boats are commandeered on both sides of the water. Hundreds are refitted to carry horses, accompanied by their riders, the knights of Normandy, Anjou, Maine, Touraine, and, of course, the Aquitaine, Eleanor's contribution to the couple's vast land holdings. Certain craft, the least comfortable, are designated to carry the heavy armor that these men will don for battle. Small boats, the cogs, are loaded with the armaments of war: swords, lances and maces, both short and long. Special care is taken to prevent the spikes on the heavy round mace heads from penetrating the wooden boat bottoms. These spikes are sharp enough to penetrate armor. In fact, that is their purpose.

Two vessels are designated to carry the latest weaponry in siege warfare. Henry expects to take the battle to the ancient Boulton castle, where he is sure the Aureus is hidden. His arsenal now includes two Mediterranean trebuchets, the last word in modern artillery. Rolling on three wheels, each trebuchet is capable of flinging sizeable boulders over castle parapets. Older fortifications, like that of Boulton, do not have walls high enough to repel these projectiles. The trebuchets will be his advance troops, impervious to the arrows which can fell his infantry and even penetrate the armor of some of his brave knights. In fact, Henry muses, his fallen soldiers may have an opportunity to give their lives twice for king and country. He will stack up the dead and, at the right moment, toss them into the earl's courtyard. The corpses will be bloody. Smelly, too. Very demoralizing. Henry congratulates himself on his plan to utilize this form of psychological warfare, if needed.

Through much of the year, the king travels to the coast, greeting the arriving soldiers. He knows some of these men. They have been with him since his marriage to Eleanor in 1152, when this surprise union produced a concentration of wealth and land holdings that upset the balance of power in westernmost Europe. Henry was forced to fight a number of his neighbors as well as his own brother Geoffrey and, of course, the French king, recently divorced. He had emerged victorious, unifying under his control all the provinces west of the

French border. As an able commander, he always enjoyed the loyalty of his men, and now they are joining him on England's shores.

"Alexandre, hail to you and your excellent warriors. Welcome to England!"

"Your Majesty, this is an honor. We did not expect to see you so soon."

"I am your official greeter. And I'm here to apologize for the English weather. You will soon wish you were back in beautiful Touraine, but I will compensate you for that as soon as we are victorious."

"We have heard about the rain. Is there anything else?"

"Yes. Fog. Hard to see. You have to be nose to nose to know whether you have the enemy or a friend in front of you. Very tough on your archers and crossbowmen."

"I would say that we should fight on a clear day, Your Majesty, if that's acceptable to you."

"Consider it done."

"There's something else."

"Yes?"

"The English ladies. Are they worth making us brave the rough waters of the channel?"

The king rubs his forehead, pondering an answer.

"After giving your question much thought, I believe it is my royal duty, as your brother in arms, to investigate this matter. I will make it my personal quest to learn whether the fair damsels of our foggy land are suitable for you, for all of you."

Amid laughter and comradely cheers, the king rides away.

By autumn, five thousand men, plus arms and battle steeds, have landed in England. The eastern coast is a military encampment.

THE FOREST TRAIL IS WIDE AND BROWN, trodden by centuries of horsemen. Deer hunters, guests of Bertram, the Earl of Sothingham, pursue their quarry from this beaten track. An occasional wild boar is easily felled here, confused by the barking dogs that flush it from the brush. Emissaries from distant estates travel on this same well-worn route. The local peasants use the trail for a thousand errands assigned by the master. They scour the woods for winter kindling and drag it home over this path pounded flat by countless hoofs. In summer, at night, they follow it to their small gardens, guarded by thick brush, a deterrent to damaging short-cuts by impatient riders.

Two men, elegantly clad in hunting gear, ride side by side on the trail. Their horses are held to a leisurely gait.

"Lord William, I am delighted that you are finally visiting me after all these years. It seems that we all have overused your hospitality in recent times. I think too much of our energies are squandered on squabbling with the church or the king, or both. Now that you're here, we can just relax and let our families become better acquainted. Last year I brought down a first-rate stag just over there." Lord Bertram points to the right at a tree split in half, likely by lightning. "I could spend all my time out here in this magnificent woodland, riding my fine horses, just breathing in the summer air, like today. And, you know, my pleasure is not totally self-serving. I am bringing home the bacon, as someone has termed it, when my hunting skills place a fine meal on my table. And you will notice that my house servants are not thin. Hardly." Bertram permits himself a chuckle.

The riders continue, each inhaling the pleasant scents of ash, oak and basswood. Lord Bertram is happy to share his ancestral woodland with a peer who, just last year, had wanted to envelop him in a triumvirate of Sothingham, Westland and Boulton. The link was to be his daughter Gweneth, betrothed to one of the Westlands. The plan had not ever gone anywhere. Boulton had suddenly become distracted by something else. Who knows what? That was fine with him. The Westlands are powerful, but they've always been difficult. To have his daughter marry one of them – which of them, the father or one of the sons, was never really nailed down – would have made the three

AUREUS

barons a very powerful alliance, but hobnobbing with his daughter's in-laws would have been a chore. He much preferred an easy life, galloping in the forest or lunching with his wife, not plotting and strategizing all the time. His own father had called him "a dedicated pleasure seeker," and he was right.

"Thank you for your invitation. I haven't traveled this far west before. The countryside here is very agreeable." The visit is part of William's plan. His sentries have reported the daily flotilla arriving on England's eastern shores. Henry is busy importing his continental army, so he, William, must likewise secure allies with large armies. Always spoiling for a fight. Westland was easy to bring on board. William had conveniently omitted his French match-making misadventure when presenting his case, preferring to emphasize the monarch's commitment to limiting baronial rights while increasing their taxes. He had put quite a spin on this double indignity. The approach to the Earl of Sothingham must be different.

"Ah, Bertram, may I call you that? Whenever I say Lord Bertram, I feel that there is a barrier between us."

"I am flattered, William. Of course."

William, the new best friend, pulls ever so slightly on his horse's reins. The pace becomes slower, and conversation becomes easier.

"Bertram, the lands to the south that abut yours. They belong to the Gramley family, don't they?"

"They do indeed."

"I have been told that the Gramley forests boast the finest game in west England. That can't possibly be true. Your lands are teeming with game, right? I'm sure you even have more rabbits, yes?"

"Well, I can't verify, much as I'd like to. The Gramleys are not very neighborly. No parties such as yours. No hunting outings. It's only a two-day ride from manor to manor. And never so much as a social call. Such lack of etiquette. I have met the earl just once, at the court of King Stephen. That was truly a boring assembly. Now if Henry had been king, I'm sure it would have gone better. Stephen wasn't the astute political monarch that his nephew is. Even I, who avoids court intrigue, can see that. Now, what about the Gramleys?"

"Well, an idea just came to me. It must be the clarity of the air here." William peers into the woods in front of them, seeking the right words.

"And?"

"First, we unite families. That will cement our friendship and united cause. Causes, actually. Then..."

"Wait, you said 'unite families.' How so?"

"I am putting this together just now. My, the primeval forest has an exhilarating effect. Now where was I? Oh, yes, we join Boulton and Sothingham. Say, that sounds good, doesn't it? Boulton and Sothingham. So, we join our families by the marriage of Jerrard and your Gweneth." He sees Bertram pull up his horse and stop. William raises his hand. "Wait. Wait until I spell it out. The ideas are still coming to me." The raised hand goes to his head. "Listen to this. I will assist you in acquiring some new manorial property to the south. The Gramleys'. I'm building up my army as we speak. Together we will become quite a military alliance. A combined army to match that of the king. Of course, we would help each other. So if I were ever under attack, you would come to my aid. That could be Gweneth's dowry."

"This is a lot to absorb."

"I know. It is for me, too. But I see only advantages. And I think that Jerrard is already acquainted with your daughter. That's a real plus. No surprise at the altar." William's voice resounds with accomplishment. "Too bad you have only Gweneth. I have other children to marry off." He glances at Bertram's sober face. "Just kidding."

Bertram, too, stares at the woodland, seeking the clarity that has so energized William. In truth, he doesn't like the unexpected. He prefers to consider proposals alone, or with his wife, before making decisions. Now he is alone in his forest with the earl of many surprises, and it is his turn to speak. The Countess of Sothingham is his confidant and advisor, and he wishes she were here.

"This is such an honor. A betrothal. Your first-rate son and my daughter Gweneth. The Gramley lands to me. A military alliance. Just too much to take in all at once. Let us go back to the manor and open a bottle of the best wine. Oh, and I can fill in the countess as she prepares to join us. And you can discuss it with your wife, as well."

"My wife will agree."

"Oh, my wife is also agreeable with my decisions. It's just that she likes to hear them from me, privately. I will talk to her immediately. Let's go."

A MID-AUTUMN WAR is not ideal, but Henry has transported his forces, and they are ready to fight. As a formality, a courier from the chancellery has delivered the documents charging treason to the Boulton castle. A servant declares that the earl is absent, but promises that the royal writ will be duly delivered upon his return. Two loyal riders are dispatched to bring the earl home. This will take time. The Boulton army must be rounded up. It is a foregone conclusion that Lord William will not turn himself in to King Henry. For hundreds of years, this barony has been on a war footing, and the castle inhabitants know their respective roles. The contents of the armory are assembled in the courtyard. Flower gardens are trampled as lances, swords, axes and spears are spread among the dormant blooms. Cross bows and their missiles, well-crafted arrows, populate the south end of the vast interior open area. Armor, arranged by size, rests on the ground, as if it were a metal sleeping force. Many of the peasants living and working on the estate have their own spears, the weapon of choice of the lowly foot soldiers. This mighty army will meet King Henry head on, although no one in the castle knows why Lord William has been charged with treason. There is much speculation, but, in truth, it does not matter. They must protect this ancient House of Boulton.

Henry anticipates a face-to-face battle, with William at the front of his troops. A clear victory on the field might avoid a protracted siege of the castle. But he must be prepared for that. His troops are moving more slowly than he would like, and the trebuchets, drawn by teams of horses, are resistant to speed and are often bogged down in the mud. All of this is to Lord William's advantage, allowing him more time to gather his forces and possibly garner some allies. Henry has sent riders in all directions to ascertain whether baronial armies are assembling and to spread the word about the charge of treason. He hopes that his forays into the far corners of England for the past ten years have won him some allegiance, but you can never be sure of the nobility. Their loyalties are fickle, and they seem to take special delight at chipping away at a monarch's powers, even when the king has been an Englishman.

The earl's army musters, and the king's army marches. The battle trophy is the Aureus.

CHAPTER ELEVEN

GIANT FIRES light the east England landscape. It is daytime, but the army has halted and is committed to getting warm. Astride his horse, Henry is addressing the battalion of men who have been trained to operate the trebuchets. They are accustomed to rolling heavy stones into this launcher, and they are curious about the resources of the countryside near the Boulton castle. Their leader has inquired if they will find sufficient missiles to fling in the event of a siege.

"If we use these weapons, we are not catapulting stones." Henry has anticipated this question and has wondered why it took so long to be asked. The men simply look at him, awaiting an explanation.

"First, I do plan on a clear battlefield victory, so that the castle occupants see the futility of continuing to resist. However, it's always good to have a back-up plan. So here it is. We will lose men on the battlefield. Brave men. We will put their bodies in wagons. If we must conduct a siege, we will toss the bodies, now stripped of their armor, into the bowels of the castle. They will be bloody and smelly."

There is laughter. The men nod their agreement that King Henry is a clever and amusing monarch.

"Your comfort in this operation, if it does happen, is most important to me, so in that wagon over there," Henry points to a small grey buggy pulled by one horse, "in that wagon you will find the only protection that you will need to carry out your mission, because you will be so much more effective if you are not sick."

The laughter turns to perplexity. There is murmuring. How can the contents of the little buggy prevent sickness? Have the king's healers found a magical root or a concoction of berries to prevent them from becoming ill?

Henry reaches into his vest and extracts a rectangular piece of cloth. He places the center of the cloth over his nose and mouth and ties it at the back of his head.

The murmuring increases, but its tone instantly shifts from confusion to hostility. The battalion leader tries to hush the growing sound of dissent, but the men are clearly agitated.

"What is the problem?" The question conveys annoyance. The king has already commended himself on his contribution to the art of war. Moreover, he is also displaying concern about the well-being of his men. They should be thanking him. He removes the mask and holds it high, in the manner of a battle ensign.

"Your Majesty, sire, these men are from villages where only women wear masks and only because they have committed some kind of small sin. Like gossiping. The mask is a punishment. Perhaps you know of this?"

"No, I don't know of this. I've never heard of it. Look, it's this simple. Dead bodies smell. If we use the trebuchets, you will be handling dead bodies. Stinking dead bodies. You aren't going to be able to load up the trebuchet if you are throwing up."

The grumbling continues.

"Where are these men from?"

"An area in the south of Aquitaine, sire. It is quite remote."

"The queen has never told me about this, and she is from the Aquitaine. Oh, well, I will run it by her and find out where this nonsense is taking place. Then I will ban masking women for engaging in gossip." Henry throws up his hands. "That's what women do. But in the meantime, here's how it is. I am your king. I am your military commander. Clearly I am not a woman. Nor do I gossip. And I am wearing a mask. If I can wear a mask, any of you can. Duncan, distribute the masks. I want to see a mask on every face. That is an order."

The orderly scurries to the buggy and grabs an armful of heavy grey cloths. The battalion stands quietly, their faces sullen. The men are thinking ahead. The nightly campfire camaraderie and ribbing, a mainstay of their treks across the countryside, will become unbearable if their compatriots in the infantry label them as chattering females. The derision that the masked village women routinely face would be nothing compared to the ridicule from their comrades in arms. Hesitant hands receive the pieces of cloth, but nothing happens.

"I command you all to wear the masks. Now." Henry jumps off his horse and now stands just a few paces away from the captain, who is perspiring profusely in the chilly October afternoon. In a slow-moving gesture, the leader winds the cloth around his face and knots it in the back. The men copy him in the same sluggish manner. One by one, their faces are covered; a full contingent of masked men. A full contingent except one.

"You there. Come here." The king points at the unmasked face.

A young man, in his middle teens, steps forward. His face displays no fear. His pace is sure.

"Put it on."

"Your Majesty, I am Laurence, your most loyal subject and devoted to Queen Eleanor of Aquitaine, where I am from. I serve you as an obedient soldier, but surely you, in your mercy, would not order a real man to cover his head like a woman."

"You're wrong, I would." Henry's sword is out of its scabbard before a gasp can be heard. The blow is swift and merciless. Laurence's headless body stands briefly, still defiant; then, in slow motion, it crumbles to the ground. Red drops pelt the king and closest bystanders. The head is airborne for a few moments, then lands with a thud in front of the assembled leather-clad feet. The masked company of men stands frozen, as in a tableau hanging in the royal palace.

"Duncan, dry off my sword with Laurence's mask. He won't be needing it."

❄

"MY DEAREST ELEANOR." Henry's nightly letter to his wife always begins with this endearment. "Today we have rested to let the rear guard catch up. Our battle should commence soon. It will bring much glory to our reign and, also, a surprise that I will share with you. You will like it, and hopefully this gift to my queen will hasten the forgiveness that I have oft begged from you for my occasional misbehaviors. I hold you highest among all the women in the dominion."

Henry stops writing and lays down his quill. He should have told Eleanor about the Aureus. She would have supported his plan. More than just encouragement, she would have provided wise counsel and would likely be at his side right now. Becket, once his closest confident, is now a chief rival for the prize. Ridel, his chancellor, doesn't know about it and doesn't want to. Thomas, Lord William, his son and some unnamed country friar are perhaps the only other ones who really know what the stakes are. To everyone else, including Eleanor, this is a war begat by treason.

Yes, he should have confided in Eleanor. For nearly twelve years, they have been the most powerful team in the civilized world. And yet, he has feared her wrath. Unlike other queens, she has not overlooked his dalliances. To her credit, she has shown kindness to his illegitimate children, bringing them up at court with their own brood. But as she learned of each affair, Eleanor would rave and weep. Then, after a chilly interlude, she would welcome him back into her chambers. They had the babies to attest to her forgiveness. But, as the years passed, there was an added dimension to the passion they had first generated in 1152. A touch of cruelty has crept into her language, into her eyes.

No sense in agonizing over this now. He cannot commit the Aureus to parchment. The courier who bears his letters to the queen could be caught by anyone. Henry employs the most able riders, but the occupation is dangerous. The forest horse paths are populated by thieves, murderers and those who oppose the king.

Henry picks up the feather pen and resumes his letter. "Please kiss the children for me. Tell them their father loves and misses them. I love and miss you, too." A thought crosses his mind. He will add it to the letter. There is still room at the bottom of the parchment. "I met some lads from your Aquitaine today. They told me of an interesting custom in their villages that you may not know about. I'll tell you everything when we are together. Now I am sure that you can't wait to see me. Henry." He draws a heavy line under the word *sure*.

CHAPTER TWELVE

"THOMAS, I AM ABOUT TO go to war with Boulton and any barons dim-witted enough to throw in with him. The charge of treason should keep most of them out of the fray, but I'm not taking any chances. I want you to declare your support for your sovereign and then demonstrate that support in a material way." The king has planted himself in the center of the Archbishop's study.

"The Aureus, Henry."

"Listen, I'm not in a mood to discuss it. Frankly, you owe your position to me, and I'm here to collect that debt."

"The Aureus."

"Furthermore, I have overlooked plenty in the past year, but no longer. I have a list of complaints longer than your nightly prayers, and I intend to get these matters set straight. You have strained my patience."

"The Aureus."

"You sound like an echoing owl in a barn. First, stop trying to take back lands that one of your predecessors lost by royal writ. What's done is done. Second, you have excommunicated John Woodshire, my appointee. That's a direct affront to your monarch. Very bad. But, unfortunately, there's more. I understand that you refuse to contribute to the sheriff's aid fund, a long-standing tradition. The church has always donated to this charitable brotherhood. And you continuously interfere with my courts punishing criminal acts committed by the part-time clergy."

Thomas interjects. "They are clergy. The royal courts have no right to punish clergy."

"As I said, they are part-timers with some minor pastoral responsibility. Twenty per cent of the men in England help with church duties now and then. Your interference undercuts my ability to govern effectively when my courts cannot punish criminal acts committed by such people."

"They are still officially clergy."

"Such a quasi-intellectual stretch does not become you. Please notice that I do not interfere with your ecclesiastical courts when they hand down rulings on priests and bishops, even when their transgressions are criminal and unrelated to their religious duties. I have a keen understanding of where religious power ends and secular power begins. In short, Thomas, I am very disappointed in you. I am going to take young Henry back to the palace. You are likely teaching him to dishonor the king, his father."

"The Aureus, Your Majesty."

"You'll get none of it." Henry walks out.

CHAPTER THIRTEEN

THE LATE SEPTEMBER SUN is powerless to illuminate the great hall of the Sothingham castle. Candles supplement the natural light, already dimming in the middle of the afternoon. Tables, set with fine dishes and fragrant bouquets, line one side of the cavernous hall. The other side is open, awaiting musicians and dancers. Servants dart in and out, completing the set-up for a wedding feast. The guests are in the chapel, attending the nuptials of Jerrard and Gweneth. It is a small affair, hastily organized. The Countess of Sothingham has done her best to make this a lovely event, but she is losing her daughter, her only child, to the House of Boulton, and Boulton is a considerable distance to the east. But her husband has reminded her that they will gain much by this union, specifically the nearby Gramley lands. Lord William has promised he will march on these neighbors, not invited to the wedding, as soon as he can assemble his forces. And the only dowry he is asking is assistance by the House of Sothingham if Boulton is ever attacked. Why would that happen? It certainly is an excellent contract. Gweneth's mother holds back her tears. Jerrard appears to be a fine young man. She hopes he is not like his father, whose reputation for philandering has permeated the far corners of England.

❋

THE SILENT DAWN of the next morning is shattered by hoofbeats on the stony castle entry corridor. Two horsemen jump from their exhausted steeds and throw the reins to the stable boys running out to greet them.

"Where is your master? We must see him. Actually we must see the Earl of Boulton. We have urgent news for him."

A servant is dispatched to the Sothingham living quarters. Soon he reappears, headed to the guest wing of the castle. The two courier horsemen follow until he stops and points to a heavy wooden door. "Through there. The earl and his party are all staying in this section. That's all I know."

The chilly hallway is unlit. The candle lighters, who also participated in the previous night's revelry, are slow to assume their duties this morning. The two couriers searching for Lord William bump into one another. Furniture becomes an obstacle. "Ouch! Look out!"

A door opens. The Countess of Boulton is swathed in a purple robe edged with fur. "What is all this noise?"

"Ma'am, excuse me, we must find the Earl of Boulton." Jason, the senior emissary, taps his cap in a hasty gesture of respect.

"Yes, finding the earl. Ah. Always a challenge. I am Lady Boulton."

"Yes Ma'am."

"Let me see if I can help. Here's an idea. Try the second level hallway. The door with a bird engraved on the door."

"Thank you, Ma'am."

The young courier turns back in the dark stony passageway, colliding with a shadowy figure.

"Ow!"

"Sorry. Is that you, Revnar?"

"It is. Where's the earl?"

"Up the stairs says the countess. It's so dark she didn't recognize me. We need to find the chamber with the bird engraved on the door."

"The old boy is at it again."

"Looks like it." Jason grimaces. "The last time this happened, when we interrupted his little private party, he threw a fit, if you remember. I almost lost my head." He pats his cap, as if to make sure everything is in place.

Revnar remembers. It wasn't pretty watching their master leap out of bed, completely naked, and grab his nearby sword. The two of them had run out into another unfamiliar corridor, yelling their unwanted news as they made their hasty retreat. They were later forgiven. The news, though unwelcome, had saved Lord William considerable trouble with a neighboring noble.

The hallway on the second level is also dark. The flooring is not level. The two men make their way carefully, taking turns to rub a hand over each massive wooden door in search of a bird. Several doors are examined this way. None has an engraving. The hall bends to the left. An alcove leads to an opening, covered with an iron grate, revealing the courtyard below, now bathed in a pale light. They hear faint laughter. It is a woman. A man speaks, indistinctly. The woman laughs again.

"That's him. The sound is coming through the window." Revnar lifts his inspection from the courtyard to another window, also grated, on their same level of the left-curving passageway. "His room is ahead on this side of the hall."

"Why don't we just yell our news through this window? Lord William will hear it." Jason's hand, in a reflex action, returns to his head. "By the time he gets dressed and finds us outside in the courtyard, he will be more reasonable."

"Chicken."

"You're so right, my pal. Tell you what. You knock and go through the door first with our news. I will await you in the hall. Or maybe catch your head as it rolls out."

Revnar breathes in and exhales. "I will knock, deliver the news in record time and get out of the way." He turns to follow the curvature of the wall until his hand feels the outline of a bird in the arched door. The room is now silent. Jason leans against the opposite grey stone.

"Here goes." It is a whisper.

"Good luck."

"Lord William, sire, King Henry's troops are advancing on Boulton castle!" Revnar pounds on the door. His voice is loud and racing at a staccato speed. "We have ridden many days and nights to warn you. The king is attacking!"

The two couriers look at one another. To run or not to run. The door, heavy and creaking, is pulled open by William in a fur-lined robe. He is unarmed. His eyes gleam in the half light. The earl tosses a benign salute at the two young men, who sense that they are not in danger.

"Well, Henry is a bit premature, I must say. My spies report that troops are still coming from the continent. Our impetuous king. He will pay for that, too. Lads," Lord William switches from his short musing to the role of master, "you have done well, and you will be rewarded for your hard ride. One last thing before you get some well-earned sleep. Find Master Jerrard. He was married yesterday, so he will be in the bridal suite in the Sothingham chambers. I've no idea exactly where it is, so you are on your own to find him, but I have confidence in you. Tell him what you've told me. Tell him very quietly. His wife must not hear. He must come to me at once. I will be with the countess downstairs. Her room is—"

"I know where it is." Jason interrupts. He is not worried about protocol.

"Good. Get going." William turns to the bed. "Dear, an unexpected situation. So sorry. It has been a pleasure." As he steps back into the chamber to retrieve his belongings, Jason and Revnar are already dashing along the semi-lit hallway, back to the stairs.

❧

THE COURTYARD of Sothingham Castle is astir with activity. Servants carry off the remnants of last night's festivities. A scattering of guests ambles around the castle grounds, clearing their heads with the brisk morning air. In a few hours, the celebration will begin anew. Weddings are time-consuming, sometimes days long. Probably not this one, though. It was a rushed affair, though the bride's mother, Lady Sothingham, had done her best for her daughter. The Sothinghams were an unusually small family and very close. It was said that the earl preferred his wife to the charms of other women. Gweneth's parents had not only wanted her to marry well, but to marry into a family who would give her the freedom to travel to Sothingham on occasion. This had been a condition in the previous negotiations to betroth her to one of the Westlands. Hopefully the Boulton marriage contract had likewise contained this provision. Such was the morning gossip among the partiers.

The two Boulton messengers race through the merry makers. Jason shouts, "We need to see the Earl of Sothingham. We need to find Lord Jerrard. Can anyone help us?" Revnar is bellowing his own version of these entreaties. "This is important. Please, someone, direct us to the family wing of the castle."

A sleepy-eyed gentleman of high birth points in the direction of the rising sun. "The Sothingham chambers are over there. See, the earl is coming through that archway. I'm sure he has been advised that you're here. You can forget about Jerrard. This is still his wedding night." He winks and walks away.

Lord Bertram strides across the central courtyard toward the two young men. His jaunty pace is that of a mighty baron who has hosted a successful event on his manor. His eyes, however, flicker with uncertainty and a small hangover. What has brought these riders from the House of Boulton, in such a hurry, to find the earl and his son? This is a family matter now; Jerrard is his son-in-law.

"I say, boys, why are you descending on our celebration like there is an invasion of the Scots? Or perhaps it is an invasion of the Scots."

The "boys" have been in the service of Boulton for a while. They know when to be informative and when to profess ignorance.

"Sire," Jason bows, "We were instructed to ride swiftly to find Lord William and his son and bring them home. That's all we know. Our apologies on intruding upon the marriage of your daughter to Master Jerrard. Revnar joins me in apologizing. Right, Revnar?"

"Oh, yes, very sorry sir. Sire." Revnar follows with his own bow.

"Did you find Lord William?"

"Yes, sir, we did. And he has instructed us to bring Master Jerrard to his quarters. Immediately."

"And why they must return home? Right now? Surely they want to know that."

"I was given a dispatch. It was carried here." Jason pats his vest. "It could only be given to the earl. And I did that."

"Have you read it?"

"Sire, I do not read."

"Oh, yes. Alright. I will send someone to get Jerrard. He isn't going to be happy about this. Wait here."

Lord Bertram turns and walks back to the archway. Jason and Revnar watch him recede until it's safe to speak.

Revnar pats Jason's vest. "A dispatch. Carried right there. You're very convincing. Liar."

"Thank you, my friend. I take that as a compliment."

The two riders stand in the stark autumn light. For the first time, they feel the fatigue, the hunger, the dirt that clings to their bodies. They were chosen as couriers when in their early teens. Even then, they had displayed an intuitive intelligence, plus loyalty and superior strength, all part of their job description. And their horsemanship was superb. Now they are close to completing their current assignment. Normally, upon return to the Boulton home base, they would be rewarded. Perhaps a fine coin or a side of deer. They were always provided with the best horses. The countess, who flirted with them from time to time, oversaw the making of their clothes. But in this case, they will not return to reap any reward, even though the earl has just spoken of one. Lord William's sole focus will be the coming war with the king, and the outcome of that conflict will decide their fate as Boulton couriers. The morning sun rises higher, but they feel colder.

AUREUS

JERRARD HURRIEDLY GATHERS his belongings in the bridal bedchamber. Gweneth, wrapped in an oversized robe, watches her husband prepare to depart. At this time on the previous day, she was preparing to become a wife. Now she is preparing to say goodbye to her spouse, who is leaving for an undetermined amount of time. He hasn't told her everything, she knows that. He was summoned an hour ago to meet with his father, the same father who had told her, in the wine-infused partying that had followed their vows in the chapel, that the two of them would be left alone for several days "to get properly acquainted." Now her husband is leaving so soon after introducing her to what a betrothal really means, what people do when they get married. A single tear rolls down her right cheek.

"Gweneth, I am so sorry. Believe me when I say that I would rather stay here with you than do anything else. We've just started to, uh, explore." A grin explodes across Jerrard's face. "Hey, you're blushing. My blushing bride." The grin fades. "It was going to be just us this morning and all day." How do you tell someone goodbye just as the whole marital adventure has just begun? His father had said jokingly, "You might even fall in love with her."

"Gweneth, please say something."

At first, Gweneth just shakes her head.

"Please."

"I fear that you won't come back to me."

Jerrard's arms envelop the tiny robed figure. He kisses the top of her head. "I will come to no harm. I will come back to you."

LORD WILLIAM HAS SENT a Sothingham guard to request an audience with Lord Bertram immediately. The request has been granted. William walks more slowly than his normal pace, rehearsing his approach to his host. Only hours before, William had wrapped Bertram in a bear-like hug while espousing the benefits of close familial ties. He had been sure that Henry's army from the continent would take much more time to assemble and prepare for war in England. During this interval, he had planned to continue his own military buildup which, he would tell the Sothinghams, would assure a quick victory over the House of Gramley. In short, he would be the perfect in-law. Then, when the fight with Henry began in earnest, he could, with some feigned embarrassment, call upon Sothingham to commit his considerable forces as part of the dowry agreement. Now, one day after the wedding, he would have to face the Earl of Sothingham, who likely had a headache, with this dowry matter. It didn't help that he had to drag Jerrard away from the lovely Gweneth.

"Good morning, William."

"Good morning, Bertram."

The study is well appointed with art, tapestries and luxurious rugs. Golden sconces glitter in the mirrors. Lush furnishings complete the décor. It is a room meant for high tea or to seal an honorable agreement. The ambience is one of aristocratic good will and noble sentiments. William of Boulton senses the nuance and wishes this meeting were taking place elsewhere, in an environment more attuned to the realities of difficult choices. He would rather they were meeting in the castle armory, surrounded by weapons of war, reminders of the means by which so much of baronial wealth was obtained, and defended.

"Once again, my dear Bertram, the wedding was splendid. I hope you are not overly tired this morning."

"I am fine. What is going on? Why are your riders here? Why must you yank your son from his marital bed? Is he going to leave here with you and your entourage? This is all very distressing."

"It is distressing for me and my family as well. I am here to tell you the very bad news that I've just received. I just can't believe it. An army is advancing upon my lands. I must return home and prepare to repel the attack."

"Whose army? Who would attack the House of Boulton?"

"Here is the baffling part. The report says that the soldiers are from the continent, all the western provinces. I have no enemies there."

Lord Bertram endeavors to make sense of this revelation. He cannot. "Boulton, if this army is from the continent, from the western provinces, then these are King Henry's soldiers. Are you telling me that our king is about to make war upon you?"

William shakes his head in a convincing show of bewilderment. "I am as incredulous as you. Maybe it's all a mistake, but I must leave now to find out."

"You surely don't need my new son-in-law to do that. My daughter deserves to take pleasure in a bride's delights."

"But I do need him. He is my right hand. And he is a good soldier. There is another thing. Something that we agreed upon. Hopefully I won't need your help, but if indeed I am under attack, by King Henry or anybody else, I will of course require your daughter's dowry, your army, to assist me. Oh, my, this is quite embarrassing. I have been planning to put my forces at your disposal for the Gramley adventure. Yes, I am quite embarrassed."

The Gramley adventure. Lord Bertram takes a quick breath. Yesterday the rich Gramley lands seemed so close to his grasp. He had almost felt like those dense forests and rolling meadows were already under his domain. Right now they seem to be receding, moving to another part of England, out of his reach. There is a flutter of an idea that he has been duped by the earl, but he dismisses it. Such a scheme, so convoluted, seems preposterous. But he has promised his troops to Boulton, and now he is being asked to deliver. His hangover, fading not long ago, returns to a point between both eyes, as if an arrow had been aimed by a Boulton archer.

"Two of my commanders are here for the celebration. I will summon them. They will organize my forces. The peasants should be easy. They are done with the harvest. We will have to round up the others. How close is the advancing army to your lands?"

"Several days, I would guess. It depends on their numbers."

"Do you have any idea of their numbers?"

"Several thousand, I am told."

"William, what have you done? Assuming it is King Henry, what have you done to anger him so much?"

"I simply have no idea."

CHAPTER FOURTEEN

THE BOULTON LANDS are but a day's march away. Henry confers frequently with his commanders; he also studies the copious notes written by his great-grandfather, William of Normandy, now known as William the Conqueror. How ironic that his most illustrious ancestor and his biggest enemy share the same name. How coincidental that the Battle of Hastings took place in mid-October. If Henry can control the timing, he could call his coming victory an anniversary celebration.

The notes, so helpful in transporting his continental army, contain a sequel, a description of the battle tactics at Hastings. It has occurred to Henry that since no one outside his family has ever read this account, these parchment renderings of a successful military campaign could be useful even now. There had been, over the past century, a few changes in the art of war. Unlike the flimsy armor once worn by the Norman cavalry, his knights now wear heavier metal; their horses are better protected, too. The Boulton knights would be similarly suited up. But the lineup for battle is essentially the same: archers and crossbowmen in the front line, foot soldiers carrying spears, pikes and maces in the middle and mounted knights with their lances bringing up the rear.

William of Normandy had been aided by the depletion of King Harold's forces in a previous battle with invading Norsemen. Henry does not have that advantage. Reports of the size of the Boulton forces are coming to him daily. The earls of Sothingham and Westland have thrown in with Lord William. Westland would be a natural Boulton ally. These two families have been cooking up schemes to advance baronial rights since the days of Alfred the Great. Sothingham was a surprise, but the means of securing that ally was predictable. A marriage contract. Lord Bertram has a huge army at his disposal, but his indisposition to engage in warfare is legendary. His army is well fed and well paid, yet they rarely fight. Perhaps they are a bit rusty in battle skills, but he can't count on that.

Scouts have also reported a contingent of Scottish forces. William has certainly been busy. The Scots have no particular interest in the Boulton fortunes; they live to harass the English monarchy no matter what the issue. Treason would appeal to them. They are excellent warriors. A human being had to be tough to simply exist in that unforgiving northern land.

Henry calculates that the opposing forces number around 5,000, roughly the same number of men under his command. The scouts' orders have been to ascertain how many are archers and crossbowmen, infantry and cavalry, but it is difficult to get close enough to get an accurate count of each group. Each army employs sentries who are on the lookout for unfamiliar riders. And each army has experienced the realization that, after days of waiting, certain riders are not going to return.

A few paragraphs in the now-faded 1066 parchments had caught Henry's eye a long time ago. The Norman forces had thrust forward in an aggressive onslaught, then strategically retreated as the counterattack was allowed to gain force. The enemy seized the opportunity to advance quickly, too quickly, and they were caught in a calculated vise. This ploy had worked twice. During the second retreat, an over-eager King Harold had galloped into the middle of the fray and was felled by an arrow which pierced his right eye. William the Conqueror was crowned King of England, and now his great-grandson is privy to a winning battle plan that his opponent has never seen.

�֎

"FATHER, THERE IS A COURIER here from the Archbishop." Jerrard stands at the entry of the earl's study. "He says he was almost killed by our sentries."

"Interesting. The Archbishop is calling upon us, in a manner of speaking. Well, I'm not surprised at the sentries' reaction. Everybody knows that Henry and Thomas are special friends, even though we hear they are not as close as they once were. Send him in."

The courier is ushered in by a servant. He is breathless and rumpled. There is a cut by his right eye, and his lip is swollen. And he is outraged. "I have ridden for Archbishop Theobald and now Archbishop Thomas, and no one has ever treated me this way. Secure right of passage has always been accorded to messengers of the church. Lord William, why do your men not recognize my protected position?"

"I apologize for the fervor of my men, but you must understand that they believe the Archbishop favors the king. What is your message?"

"The Archbishop is staying at the Wilshire Abbey on your manor. He has ridden in disguise in order to meet with you, but he will not come here. He feels that he might be in danger from your army, and I think he's right about that." The courier touches his fat lip. "Archbishop Thomas requests your immediate presence at the Abbey. He has something urgent to discuss with you."

"Do you know what he wishes to discuss?"

"Oh, no, sire. I am not privy to such things. May I return to the Abbey and tell him you are on your way?"

"My son and I will ride with you." He turns to Jerrard. "Get our horses and tell the commander that we will return before nightfall."

✖

"ARCHBISHOP." WILLIAM KISSES the golden ring. Jerrard follows his father's example. William continues. "This is a great honor. In other times, the countess and I would welcome you with a first-class banquet. Perhaps another day. May I present my son Jerrard, who accompanies me as my primary advisor." As Thomas makes a slight bow in the young earl's direction, William looks around at the stark décor of the entry hall. "I haven't been to the abbey for years. Abbott Eldred stops by occasionally to inquire about the condition of my soul. Is he here today?"

"He is not, but he has suggested that we converse in the chapel. It's just this way."

The three men enter a dark chamber illuminated by pale candlelight. Faded paintings of martyrs and angels hang between the sconces. A simple cross hangs behind the altar. The atmosphere is holy and austere. It is a sanctuary unaccustomed to the language of power.

"You wish to know why I have summoned you, of course. And I know you are busy preparing for battle, so I will be brief."

"I appreciate that."

"Good. I am aware that the coming battle is not about treason, which is, as they say, a sort of smoke screen to disguise the real controversy, the Aureus." Thomas stops to assess William's reaction, but other than one flicker of his eyelids, the earl does not register any response. Jerrard, likewise, gazes steadily at the cross. It is what Thomas has expected. Boulton caginess is a centuries-old family trait.

"You have the Aureus, and Henry wants it. So do I. For the Church, to whom it belongs, but we will let that rest for the moment."

William waits.

"I am in the position to do something for you that no one else can do." Thomas allows his words to hang in the stillness of the chapel. "My informants tell me that your and Henry's forces are about equal in strength. So unless one of you has a magic potion or secret weapon, the chance of winning is about fifty-fifty. Have you made provision for what happens to the Aureus if you lose?"

"I don't plan on losing."

"If you're going to cover all eventualities, you should have a plan. I have consulted with a Higher Power and have been given guidance in constructing a mutually beneficial course of action. Here it is. I can hide your treasure in plain sight, that is to say, somewhere in the cathedral. If you win, you know where it is. If you lose, your family can count on the fact that the Aureus is safe with me."

"Whoa. Just a minute. Your offer, attractive as it is on the surface, doesn't pass the smell test. When were you going to spring the papal decree on me? After you have all those coins in your possession? Is that when? And if this ever becomes known, you will be charged with treason. Do you want to be named as my co-conspirator? Treason is punishable by death, you know."

"First, I am immune from secular prosecution. Second, I was coming to the papal decree, but I'm glad you mentioned it. Let's start with a doubtful – doubtful to you anyway – yet possible outcome of these hostilities. If Henry wins and secures the Aureus, he will play winner-take-all. Obviously. As things stand right now, if you win, there will also be no sharing. And I am not invoking the papal decree. But if you lose, you lose it all. Henry will dismantle your castle, stone by stone, to find it. So you need a secure place to hide the Aureus. In this way, your family will still have considerable wealth even if your castle is rubble and your lands confiscated by the crown. I can make that happen, but you need to put the Aureus in my safekeeping before the battle. Our shares would be the same, whether you win or lose."

"Did you have a percentage in mind?"

"Oh, I think that a fair figure would be the same as the odds for your victory. Fifty-fifty. I would also suggest that Jerrard here accompany the prize to the cathedral and be its guardian, dressed as a cathedral monk. I will have a cassock made to order for him. You see, I think of everything."

"Wasn't your pal Henry ever willing to share with you, his closest advisor, if you aided him in getting the Aureus?"

"That is an intrusive question, but I am in an expansive frame of mind and will therefore answer it. Yes, once upon a time. But that time has passed."

Jerrard has listened silently to this unusual negotiation, but the previous exchange bothers him. "Your Grace, oh, and thank you for the cassock offer. But I am truly curious. It is known across the land that you and King Henry were the best of friends. You owe the archbishopric to him. Yet you are offering to aid us, whom you hardly know. Is this God's will or something else?"

"Very insightful."

"Thank you."

"Frankly it is about loss. And anger at that loss. Henry, my truest friend, gave me a priceless gift; he made me the Defender of the Faith in England. And when I carried out that responsibility, he withheld his friendship. That was my loss. My loss." Shaking his head, Thomas turns to William. "You, my dear lord, have never had a place in my heart. You cannot make me angry."

The Earl of Boulton nods. "I promise this: We will never be friends, just allies. Jerrard, prepare to accompany the Archbishop."

❋

"FATHER, I THOUGHT I would be fighting beside you. I left my bride to do that. Now you're sending me off to pray in the Canterbury Cathedral. That is not what the eldest son does in time of war." Jerrard kicks a stone across the hardened earth in the Boulton castle courtyard. "And praying instead of bedding the bride is not what a new husband does either."

"Your task is to protect our family's most valuable asset, and it's not our castle. If I lose, it will be our greatest, and only, asset. You know, of course, that our armies will win. Consequently, I must figure out a way to dissolve my agreement with the Archbishop. Study him carefully. Learn his weaknesses. We already know one."

"Really?"

"Thomas has always been celibate, so I hear. But he does have passion. A different kind. You heard him speak of loss. Well, I think the loss of Henry's affection and comradeship has troubled him greatly. Your dad here has never been bothered by such things. My passions are of the flesh, and so I have been spared the sorrow of loss. Hopefully I've passed that trait onto you."

Jerrard's toe searches for another stone to swat. Finding none, it pounds the ground. The son looks at his father but does not speak.

"Perhaps those are not the right words to deliver to a young man separated from his bride on the day after his wedding."

"That's probably it."

"Well, examine the Archbishop as if you were dissecting a deer for the cookery. We will need every kind of weapon to regain our prize from a man who believes that God is on his side."

A spacious carriage bearing the insignia of the Bishop of Boulton moves slowly to a halt near where father and son are standing. The driver dismounts.

"Sire, the Archbishop of Canterbury has commandeered this buggy from my bishop to convey members of your family to his home. Are they ready to leave? We still must pick up the Archbishop at the abbey. We have to get far from here before dark."

"My son Jerrard here will be your only passenger. We'll load up his belongings." He motions to servants pulling small carts piled high with clothing and other trappings of rank, a clear indication that the earl believes his son will shed his cassock in a short time. One cart lumbers along carrying a large box which is loaded onto the buggy's rear. "Say goodbye to your mother, brother and sisters. The House of Boulton will prevail. Do not worry. Guard our treasure with your life."

CHAPTER FIFTEEN

THE EARTH FEELS the tremors of ten thousand marching feet. The King's troops, his personal royal militia and his massive continental armies tromp toward the combined forces of Boulton, Westland, Sothingham and Scotland. Wagons carry food, weaponry and fodder for the horses, who must be kept happy to ensure their spirited contribution to the battle. Village blacksmiths, impressed into service to repair and maintain the iron weapons of war, ride in wagons carrying fire pots, anvils, hammers and tongs. The dust raised by all the tramping feet and rolling wheels becomes a giant cloud, obscuring the sun by day and moon by night. Long before the two sides meet, the dust cloud becomes one huge curtain over the countryside.

Moving along in the supply train of each army is a miniature horse-drawn buggy piled with cloths to bind wounds and poultices to prevent infection. Certain knives are useful in cutting away damaged flesh, and they, too, are part of these medical supplies. However, the most important instrument to alleviate suffering, the latest improvement in the arsenal of twelfth-century warfare, is not found on these carts. Instead, a long narrow knife, known as a misericorde, is carried by the mounted soldiers, to be used in a mercy strike to end the suffering of a wounded warrior not expected to survive. This slender razor-sharp blade can pass through most mesh-like armor and through gaps, like the underarm, in the heavier iron plate suits. It easily finds its way through the eye visor to reach the brain. The coup de grace is delivered to friend and foe alike. A medieval army prides itself on its humanity in its treatment of the mortally wounded. Those who have fought in the Crusades in North Africa often speak with disdain of the enemy leaving soldiers to moan and die on the plains outside Jerusalem.

With the Boulton castle as a backdrop, Lord William has chosen to defend familiar ground on the rolling plain northeast of his home. His armies form an arc fanning widely toward the advancing royal forces. The Earl of Westland rides beside William, reviewing the placement of the troops. Lord Bertram has sent his fine army, headed by a trusted commander, and they are well stocked and superbly armed. He has spared no expense in outfitting the Sothingham troops, but he has chosen to remain home with his wife and daughter. After all, the marriage contract did not stipulate his personal attendance at this Boulton/Plantagenet confrontation. He simply does not understand the need to fight all the time. There are so many other diversions, and life is just too short. An exception, of course, is William's proposal to aid in absorbing the Gramley lands. Bertram would definitely participate in that conquest, since victory would double his hunting forests. It's the primary reason he fervently prays for a Boulton victory against the king. Personally, Bertram has always liked Henry.

The Scottish army has been assigned a front and center role, riding just ahead of the Boulton army. The Scots accept this task with relish. They covet the opportunity to present the first challenge to the advancing English forces. Sothingham's army is placed on the left flank, Westland's on the right. The combined cavalry of this united force numbers far more horses and riders than those fighting for King Henry. A number of horses had been lost in the channel crossing, and there were not sufficient replacements for the knights who rode them.

The royal troops advance to the southwest. Unlike the Boulton forces, Henry's army is combined on the basis of function; all archers and crossbowmen, regardless of regional identity, are marching together at the front of this mass of men. The infantry, greater in number than its opposition, is made up mainly of the king's own private militias, augmented by continental forces who specialize in the use of spears. The locals marching alongside them are better at wielding the mace and axe. The spearmen speak a different language, but they shout and curse just like the home boys, who are fascinated by these jaunty men from across the water. They all tramp in unison, a cohesive fighting force. This blending of English and continental forces is Henry's idea, a divergence from his great-grandfather's policy of maintaining regional separateness. He wants all his men to fight as an operational unit.

The knights in the royal army are outnumbered, but the continental contingent is far more seasoned at battle. They have been jousting with the French army for years. Their English counterparts blend with them; they are the highest ranking soldiers and their superiority of position imparts a natural camaraderie between these armored, mounted men.

Henry, a student of war, assumes William possesses better military skills than King Harold, who was duped twice by the same ploy. He has decided that there will be an all-or-nothing strategic retreat after the initial charge. The notes on the Battle of Hastings describe in detail how far, in yards, William the Conqueror retreated each time. Henry has marveled at this; his great-grandfather, in the heat of battle, taking the time to calculate the distance of each reverse movement. The second, which produced the ill-fated royal charge, was much deeper than the first. King Henry will follow this course of action. Yes, wily Boulton likely cannot be fooled a second time, but his weakness is his ego. Henry can visualize William, basking in vainglory, charging into a perceived rout. It is a satisfying mental image. He hopes it will work.

The armies face one another, stretched along the rolling Boulton plain. Lord William rides at the head of his troops, just behind the Scottish force. Henry and his militia sit on their horses at the edge of an elevated grove of trees. He cannot resist a bit of historical irony. His favorite minstrel, Darrel, outfitted as a knight, rides to the front of the army, tosses his sword into the air and catches it while singing the

Song of Roland, just as William the Conqueror's minstrel had done ninety-seven years ago. Unlike his predecessor, Darrel lacks fighting skills and is not charged with making the first kill. That honor remains for an archer. The royal forces advance, and the battle begins.

Arrows fly both ways across the vast landscape which separates the two fighting forces. On each side, a half-mile wall of men walk, then run forward. The armies clash. Spears, axes, maces and pikes perform their bloody mission. Bodies pile up on both sides. Still the foot soldiers push on. Knights of both armies, straight and quiet in the saddle, await their turn. The field of battle is red and moaning. King Henry's more powerful infantry is advancing, slowly, stumbling over the fallen. They have opened a swath for a rush at the cavalry, still silently mounted, waiting for William's signal to charge. The Boulton bowmen fire forward at Henry's knights and sideways at the massive infantry charge, which has pierced a deep chasm in the Boulton lines.

William gives the signal. His knights surge forward, following the men on foot who are shouting and screaming. Each infantry carries spears and spiked iron balls that will cripple horses unable to avoid them. The battlefield is crowded with the living and the dead. There is no room to dodge and parry. The knight's lances do their lethal work. The pikes, thrust upward, do the same. The battle momentum still favors Henry's troops, but suddenly the royal infantry stops, turns and begins running back to its lines, past the enemy foot soldiers, past the enemy archers and crossbowmen, back to a widening empty gulf in their own army. The Boulton chargers, hampered by fallen bodies, struggle to catch up with this retreating foe.

The earl, at the head of his mounted forces, delights at his good fortune. Even in the vortex of the battle, he is smug. His army does inspire fear, he knows that. Too bad Henry counted on such a motley crew of foreign fighters. He must remember to congratulate his victorious troops on their courage. He raises his sword and gallops into the frenzy of retreat. What a moment. He is going to trounce the Plantagenet pretender.

His voice resounds above the cries of battle. "Henry, you sprig of broom. You planta genesta or whatever the hell your dad wore in his bonnet." William's sword waves over his head in a victory flourish. "You're history. So is Plantagenet. Long live the House of Boulton! You're a sorry piece of—"

The arrow's shaft is all that can be seen. The tip is somewhere behind William's right eye. He is still sitting on his horse while the Plantagenet foot soldiers, now joined by the armored knights on horseback, surround his army. The Scots are still fighting to the death, but the Sothingham and Westland troops begin to fade away. This battle is lost, and to stay for the aftermath seems a bad idea. One of King Henry's crossbowmen is smiling. The king salutes him.

Leaderless, the Boulton soldiers now fight for their lives on the massive battlefield. Those on the fringes begin a hasty retreat toward the castle. The main gate remains open, ready to receive those who can outrun or outride their enemies. There is little time. Lord William's last order to the castle commander was to close the gate and drop the portcullis if the king's army neared the entry. They must fight without concession to protect the massive fortification of the House of Boulton. Confident of his coming victory, William nonetheless had speculated that Henry would suspect the Aureus was elsewhere if the castle was not defended. He had wondered, in a rare moment of reflection, what would happen if King Henry was triumphant on the battlefield and in a castle siege. Surely he would tear the entire place apart looking for the treasure. What then? William had stopped himself at this point. Why borrow trouble? He, the Earl of Boulton, was going to be the winner, period.

HENRY IS IN HIS TENT, alone. It is dark. Outside, the distant moans of the wounded float across the night air. Thanks to the misericorde, some moans have been muted. His men, exhausted, sleep among the dead.

A single candle flickers over the king's hand as he glides the quill pen over a small parchment. "October 14, 1163, My dearest Eleanor, On this day, 97 years ago, my great-grandfather was victorious at the Battle of Hastings. Today your husband is likewise the victor over the treasonous Earl of Boulton and his forces. I thank God for this. Soon I will behold your beautiful face and you can tell me how proud you are. Kiss the children. Your loving Henry."

CHAPTER SIXTEEN

THE DAWN CASTS AN EERIE GLOW on yesterday's plain of battle. The grass reflects red to the rising sun. Soldiers from the victorious army mingle around, but the dominant morning force is the panorama of the dead. Wounded horses have also been given the coup de grace for their faithful service.

Henry, on horseback, is busy shouting orders to the wagon drivers and the blacksmiths. "Pull between the bodies. Duncan, organize the infantry to load the dead. But make sure they're dead. Remove armor and load it on the smithies' wagons over there. Weapons, too. That's a good lad." He rides to the food wagons, pulling up his horse in front of a blood-spattered man carving up a dead grey steed. "I see you're busy with the horsemeat. Keep those fires going. We'll be here for a while. The men deserve a fine meal."

"Sire, we need more salt. There won't be enough for all these horse thighs."

"We'll get more once we're inside the castle. Surely the earl has plenty of that, along with his fine wines. When we secure our hold on that creaky old fort, we will have a superb banquet, and all my men will eat from William's larder and drink from his wine cellar."

"Thank you, Your Majesty. Long live King Henry." The gnarled wagon chef waves his cap at the king.

❀

THE CORPSE WAGONS rumble slowly toward the Boulton castle and stop out of range of the arrows pointed at them. The two trebuchets are positioned alongside this caravan of the dead. Henry's plan from the beginning has been to demoralize the castle defenders, now without the Earl of Boulton. The castle commander, known to Henry, is capable and has been in the earl's service for many years. His name is Orik, and he is now in charge of the Boulton family and possessions, but not likely in charge of the Aureus. That brings Henry back to the whereabouts of Jerrard; surely he was not on the battlefield. But is he really in the castle? If yes, then the Aureus is there, too. But if not… mmm.

Watching the grisly procession, the king ponders his overall strategy. Riders from his militia are already fanning out over the countryside to proclaim royal victory over the treasonous earl. That should resonate throughout the land and certainly act as a deterrent to future baronial misbehavior. Perhaps he should pardon the earls of Westland and Sothingham. He will think about that. The captured Scots will pay a price; the unlucky ones will be tortured to death, and their more fortunate companions will carry the hideous corpses back to be buried in their beloved frigid northland. It will be a message which, if heeded, will keep the Scots off his back for a while.

His grand design is to avoid a winter siege of the Boulton castle. Sieges in any weather are, in Henry's opinion, a waste of valuable time and manpower. This particular fortification lacks a moat, which is a useful defensive feature, but even a moatless castle is difficult to storm. Trying to build a tunnel under the thick walls is almost always a futile endeavor. Missiles of every description rain down on the hapless men digging furiously to create a hole deep and wide enough to be a tunnel entry.

The Boulton castle, being quite old, has square towers, which are relatively easy to topple, if a sufficient number of men survive the hail storm of rocks and arrows long enough to dig under the foundation. There is also a newer challenge, the construction, in the last century, of machicolations, the stone boxes which visibly project from the top of the castle walls; the holes in the box floors are there for the purpose of dropping boiling oil on the men below. Henry is sure that the areas behind these boxes are well stocked with oil, pots, firewood and heavy leather cloths to protect the hands that will do the lethal pouring.

Having been a guest at Boulton, Henry has seen, on his approach, the upper battlements atop the stone curtain wall that surrounds the entire fortification. The gaps in the tooth-shaped parapet provide a place to fire deadly projectiles at an advancing army; the raised sections between these gaps provide protection. They appeared to be well maintained. When riding through the elaborate gate as a guest, he had not missed the arrow slits on his left and right, at mid-body height; when looking upward, he could see the bottom of the portcullis, ready to drop by a pull of a chain. He had also noticed the murder holes over his head, openings for boiling water or oil, if needed.

No, Henry had been nurtured on the battlefield, not on laying siege to an ancient stronghold. He will offer peace with conditions. If they are not accepted within a specified period of time, he will throw the rotting bodies into the castle courtyard. The stench should be persuasive.

"Your Majesty, I have some information for you." Henry's principal steward is waving and pulling his horse's reins simultaneously. "The Boulton men we captured. Over there." He points to a group of peasants, likely a part of the infantry, seated on the ground near a grove of trees. "One of them told us that young Jerrard left several days ago in a carriage he had never seen before. He helped load it with the young earl's possessions. It looked like he was going to be away for a long time. The man wondered about this because they were preparing for battle. Oh, and he said that they put something heavy into the carriage. He doesn't know what it was. Probably not important, but I wanted to tell you everything he said."

"You're right, it's probably not important, but it's also good that you have reported everything he said. You have done well. Come to my tent tonight, and we will toast your skills in the service of the crown."

The steward's expression beams his appreciation. "As ordered, I will report to your tent tonight." A tug on one rein turns the horse's head toward the assembled captives, and he rides away.

"Well, well. William, you old fox. Where did you send the young one with the 'something heavy' in the carriage?"

A CHILD FROM the nearby settlement has been chosen to lead Lord William's horse to the castle gate. The body of the rider is draped across the saddle. To avoid injuring the animal, the earl's body lies on his back, his legs flung over the horse's left flank and his head, arrow shaft still protruding from his eye, on the right. To prevent the stiffening body from toppling off, his legs and torso have been secured by rope to the saddle. This was the earl's favorite steed, and it is obvious that the horse knows who he is carrying.

A parchment missive, in Henry's distinctive hand, is tucked into William's belt. The king has revised his strategy, but he must not reveal it. There is no prize for him inside those fortified stone walls. Yet, he must act the conqueror. And his men need a celebration. Hopefully the countess has useful information about Jerrard's location, but he can't be sure of that. William probably didn't share much with her. He, Henry, will likely have to threaten her and the Boulton children with residence in the Tower of London. The prospect of being permanently cut off from the world has certainly been persuasive in the past.

CHAPTER SEVENTEEN

THE ARCHBISHOP OF CANTERBURY and a single friar kneel in prayer in the cavernous cathedral, now cold and drafty in the late October afternoon. The tone of their incantations is solemn. They beseech God to grant everlasting life to the fallen warriors in the Battle of Boulton. The Archbishop's voice resounds through the empty nave. The friar's voice is muted; his prayers are uttered with sadness. He asks for God's mercy to be granted to a single warrior. They rise and walk silently to the palatial home adjoining the cathedral.

"Jerrard. Oh, sorry. I must remember to call you by your new name. Brother William, I pray for your family. Henry, if he gets his hands on them, may be merciless in trying to find your whereabouts."

"I told you. Nobody knows. But I fear for them."

"You have reason to. The king is ruthless, among his many personal traits."

"Do you realize that King Louis is also ruthless, in his own self-righteous way? When he accepted Henry's offer of a truce as part of the betrothal arrangement, he must have guessed that Henry, having made a temporary peace with the French, would find other work for his military forces, that perhaps he already had plans to use his continental army in England. My father and I discussed this. Louis took a chance on our king's violent nature. He didn't know about the Aureus, but he did know our king, the same cruel king who is holding my family."

"Your father was an astute observer of men in power. Have you inherited that ability?"

The Archbishop does not expect an answer to his question.

❊

THE SOUND OF approaching horses interrupts their conversation. Thomas is not expecting visitors. These are troubled times. The unexpected is not welcome. He hastens to a small window facing his manicured courtyard.

"I don't recognize the insignia on these men. There are three of them. Jerrard, go to your room. I will meet the riders."

Summoning his most agreeable manner, the Archbishop strides outside the main portico to greet the dismounting visitors. As they tie their horses, he calls out a cheery welcome. "My home is always blessed to have callers. Who gives me this honor?"

The men execute a deep bow. It is their first time in the presence of an archbishop. They are speechless. Finally, one of them steps forward.

"Your Grace, we humbly request an audience on behalf of the Earl of Sothingham. It is with great urgency that we speak to you."

"Sothingham? Wasn't he just at the Battle of Boulton?"

"Oh, no, Your Grace. He was not there. He was at his estate, having lent his army to his son-in-law's father."

Thomas is perplexed, but the sense of danger has passed.

"Please come in and join me for tea. You must be hungry. We will have biscuits and jam."

"Thank you, Your Grace."

The men are seated, awkwardly, in a comfortable parlor. Thomas does his best to reduce the tension. In truth, he is most curious about the purpose of this surprise visit.

"Please, gentlemen, savor the comfort of this room. It is usually the warmest place in my rather large home. The afternoon sun, coming through that window," Thomas points to the vaulted panes, "assists the hard work done by my fireplace. Now, you were saying that Lord Bertram has a message for me?"

The spokesman puts his teacup down and clears his throat. His presentation has clearly been rehearsed.

"Um, the earl wishes to appeal to the king for forgiveness. He believes that you could perhaps act as his intermediary. You see, when his daughter married young Boulton…. No, let me start again. When the betrothal contract was written, the dowry was the Sothingham army, if ever there was a need. Lord Bertram did not know about the charge of treason. If he had known, he would never have entered into the betrothal contract. Now the king is probably after his head. But he must know what I have just told you."

The other two men nod.

"Where is the Lord Bertram now?"

"He is hiding, Your Grace, and most unhappy. He is the king's devoted subject. He wants to go home to his wife and daughter, who is pregnant. He will do penance for King Henry. You know the king. Please tell him this."

"What about Westland? Does he want forgiveness, too?"

"Oh, no. That is to say, we don't know. Lord Bertram specifically says that he was not told of any agreement between Boulton and Westland. He is not a man given to war. Will you speak to King Henry?"

"I will. As soon as he returns from his military venture."

After the men leave, voicing profuse thanks, Thomas makes his way to a small room in the rear of the archbishopric. He knocks.

"Come in."

Thomas opens the door, but remains at the threshold.

"The men came as representatives of Lord Bertram."

"What?"

"Yes, your new father-in-law. He claims to having been tricked by your father into contributing his army to the Boulton cause."

Jerrard says nothing.

"Is that true?"

"I know that the dowry was the earl's army. That's all I know."

"Come now. Did Sothingham know about the charge of treason?"

"My father did not wish to share that with anyone."

"I have my answer. You had best keep praying. You've got a lot of work to do on yourself. Oh, by the way, you are going to be a father."

CHAPTER EIGHTEEN

WITH THE BOULTON CASTLE in the distance, King Henry speaks with the commander of his royal militia. The men, astride their horses, watch the positioning of the trebuchets and the body wagons, now much closer to the castle.

"Sir Mallory, I have given the castle garrison the opportunity to respond to my generous written offer of peace without death or torture. In my opinion, I have been very lenient with them. Of course, the family is a different story. Young Jerrard should be there, but maybe not. That's who we're after. Let's see how hard they resist when we start our assault, which we should begin."

"Your Majesty, you can confiscate the Boulton lands, even the castle if you want to continue with the siege, but you have already accomplished your goal of punishing William of Boulton for a crime against the crown. Pardon me, sire, for my impertinence, but why do we seek his son? He can't hurt you. Do you intend to kill him? And his siblings?"

"I have chosen you as my commander because you ask intelligent questions. So you are not impertinent. Having said that, I will not answer you. There are some things that only the monarch can know. Three days have passed since I sent the Boulton family my letter along with the earl's splendidly dressed corpse. Prepare the trebuchet battalion for action."

"Yes, sire. Thank you, sire."

"After we take the castle, I'll have a better idea about our next step. If young Boulton is hiding there, that's one thing. If not, we will call on Lord Bertram. I have learned that he did not accompany his army here. I want to talk to him before I decide whether to decapitate him or break bread with him. Maybe his new son-in-law is there in the arms of his bride and not here at all. Much to do."

"Yes, sire." Sir Mallory turns his horse toward the objective, the castle. The king is always a mystery to him. Henry is a warrior leader, and he easily commands the respect of his troops. He, Mallory, is honored to lead the knights of the royal militia. The king has often asked his opinion on military matters. But this imported monarch is a complicated man, so unlike his predecessor King Stephen. Mallory remembers the civil wars of the 1140s; Stephen was fighting everybody, even Henry's mother. At one point, he was actually taken prisoner. Mallory cannot imagine King Henry imprisoned for five minutes. He is too clever and way too dangerous. It would be wise to avoid angering the king. Maybe he should refrain from asking impertinent questions in the future, in spite of Henry's tempered praise.

The commander rides to the trebuchet staging area. The battalion from the Aquitaine is camped nearby. Mallory finds their leader. "Begin," he says.

The Boulton skies have never beheld such a sight, bodies flying through the air, soaring like eagles, landing like stricken forest animals in the middle of the castle courtyards, vegetable patches, flower gardens, stable areas and outer entertainment grounds. Some are caught in the upper parapets, legs dangling through the crenels meant for defensive archers. It is a show quite unlike any other put on for an army of spectators, and the audience numbers in the thousands. Each torso-shaped missile is cheered as it sails over the no-man's-land surrounding the fortification. This is a bloodless attack, and the army, quite rightly, is having a good time. In most engagements, a number of them would already be dead or wounded. Instead, King Henry is entertaining them. For the soldiers from across the water, this spectacle is definitely worth the rough channel crossing.

Ignoring the flying show, Henry studies the formidable trebuchets as they are loaded to perform their grisly tasks. The masked men of the Aquitaine work as in a fire brigade. Two men unload a body, passing it along to several pairs, working in tandem, who deliver the corpse to the trebuchet crew. Each body is handled quickly to avoid the unpleasant fluids emanating from them. Even a facial covering cannot completely hide the stench.

"Ho there, Commander," Henry speaks to the battalion chief. "Your shooters have an excellent aim. Please commend them from me."

"Thank you, Your Majesty. I will do that."

The king puts on his mask and rides closer to the operation. The men from south Aquitaine interest him. They are deeply tanned and ruddy, unlike the other lighter skinned people from that region. He has seen people from the south provinces of Europe, darker and stockier than their northern neighbors, and these trebuchet men resemble those southerners. He wonders if Eleanor is aware that her province is home to men of this crimson coloring. She hadn't known about the masks for gossiping women. But why, of course, should she know about the loutish superstitions of common people? Still, he is curious about the shade of the hands, necks and faces of these men and wonders if the rest of their bodies are of the same pigment. He rides back to the commander and lowers his mask.

"Say, commander, your men are a darker color than others I've seen from the Aquitaine. You, too. Why is that?"

"I can only tell you that where the sun does not shine on me, I am pale. It's probably the same for all the men. There is no fog where we live. Like the fog here. And our home is much warmer than the rest of the Aquitaine, I am told. When we plant and harvest, it is usually sunny. That's why we are blessed by God with bountiful food all year round. And I guess that's why we are dark to your eyes. You see us where the sun sees us."

"Ah, excellent explanation. Thank you. Keep firing."

The king resumes his inspection while the nearby audience continues its vocal enthusiasm for the airborne show. The stock of bodies is slowly being depleted. In a few days, all of this lifeless ammunition will be rotting in the court of the castle, and the high walls will block any winds from transporting the fetid air away from its miserable inhabitants. This is most satisfactory to Henry. As he turns his horse to ride to his tent, he spies a man kneeling on the ground, vomiting. Looking closer, he can discern the sun-dyed complexion of a south Aquitaine soldier. He closes the distance between them.

"You there. Tell me what's wrong."

The bowed head does not turn, but a weak voice responds. "I'm sick. Can't you see?"

"Where is your mask? Your king wants to know."

The man wheels around. His face is a picture of fright. There are pale yellow droplets on his chin. He is reaching into his clothing. His hands produce nothing.

"Your Majesty, it was just here. Right here. I took it off because I was sick. I could still smell the bad stuff. The mask didn't work. I wanted it to work. I didn't want to get sick. I swear. Wait, here it is." A trembling hand tugs the mask from inside a goatskin shoe. "Here, sire, I have it with me. Please. Mercy." He rolls until his forehead is touching the dirt, while one beseeching hand thrusts the pristine mask upward. "Please."

Henry steers his horse toward the cowering figure, still pleading for mercy, until he is seated directly above him. His right hand reaches for the silver sword in its scabbard. A long frozen moment follows. Then the king shakes his head. The ignorance of the peasant class confounds him. Wheeling his steed around, he gallops away from the lump of a man.

"Rednecks. I govern rednecks. Sun-baked fools."

❀

"MADAME, YOU AND YOUR COMMANDER are very wise to accept defeat and concede your castle to my forces." Henry stands next to a carriage holding the Countess of Boulton and her children. In the distance, a large white sheet hangs over a stone parapet, fluttering as it brushes against the outer curtain wall. "Here's my suggestion. You and your family should retire to another of your manors for a while. My forces wish to hold a banquet, courtesy of your late husband, but we need some time for your servants to clear out the courtyards so that our appetites are not impaired by the current stench. Your living quarters will be off limits. You need not worry about that. And you may return when it's safe to do so. We will let you know."

"Thank you." The countess dabs her eyes with a handkerchief. Her brood stares off into the distance.

"Now that I have been so generous, it is your turn."

"What?"

"I said it is your turn to be generous to me. Where is Jerrard?"

"Is killing my husband generous? Taking our lands? Is that generous?"

"Madame, I do not answer questions. I ask them. Where is your son?"

"If I knew, I wouldn't tell you. But I do not know. Go ahead. Put me in the Tower. I still won't know. If you had any insight into my husband, you wouldn't even bother to ask me. You would be aware that he would not tell me such a thing."

"Because he would want to protect you."

"Oh, please. Because he did not confide in me on anything."

Henry nods.

"I see. Your husband and I had much in common. Including a disinclination to share. Well, have a nice day."

HENRY AND HIS COMMANDERS are seated in his tent. A bottle of Anjou claret sits on a small table. Another bottle, empty, lays on the ground beneath.

"These are my orders. They are pretty simple. Gratify yourselves in the castle larder and wine cellar. Leave the family quarters alone. Send out small garrisons to make sure that the Boulton soldiers have resumed their peasant way of life. When all is secure, send one of the locals to find the countess and tell her she may come home, courtesy of me."

The commanders chuckle. Having a nightcap with Henry is always a merry event.

"The Boulton lands are quite an addition to the royal treasury. The chancellor is preparing payment to you and your armies, so that is your next stop after you depart this place. I'm taking a garrison and going to Sothingham."

"Your Majesty, his army is intact. That may be ill advised. We can send a large force with you." The continental commander wears a worried look.

"I agree. Please wait until we can organize additional forces to accompany us." Sir Mallory is nodding.

"I appreciate your concern," Henry raises his cup to his companions, "But a message has come from the Archbishop. Oh, and you'll get a kick out of it. Let me read it to you." Henry reaches into his vest and removes a folded parchment. "Mmm." He clears his throat as if to begin a speech. "The Archbishop sermonizes to me, his faithful parishioner." More throat clearing follows. "'Dear King Henry, I thought you would return to your royal duties before this, but I understand that you are having too much fun tossing smelly bodies over the Boulton parapets. What a grown-up diversion!'" Henry glances at his audience and sees that they share his amusement. "'So I must inform you in writing that the Earl of Sothingham has sent messengers to me to beseech you to forgive him. He didn't know of the charge of treason. He is in hiding. No more room. Must close. Thomas.'"

Henry returns the letter to his vest pocket. "I have sent a courier to Sothingham telling him he is safe if I am safe. That should do it. We will see when I pay him a visit, which is very soon. He dislikes war. Maybe he will lend me his army in the future."

"Why go at all, sire? You apparently have already forgiven him."

"The Boulton heir may very well be there, that's why. I want him in my custody."

The men nod their understanding and finish their fine drink. It is late. They bid their monarch good night.

Henry finishes his wine, tapping the table with his free hand. "Jerrard is there only if he is crazy. But someone *is* there who perhaps can help me. We'll see."

CHAPTER NINETEEN

LIKE THE CHURCH ABOVE IT, the crypt of the Canterbury cathedral is spacious and ornate. The rebuilding of the main chapel nearly forty years ago allowed the priors to enlarge and redecorate the cavernous chambers beneath it. This is where the polished coffins and stone sarcophagi would find an eternal home. The process of burying saints and other high churchmen on the main level had, for too many centuries, been an unwelcome interruption of the solemn rituals of the cathedral's interior. Now the dead rest undisturbed by the daily practice of the faith that has honored them with this extravagant tomb.

Thomas and Jerrard stand next to a fine mahogany coffin dedicated to one of the church's early fathers. A likeness of the deceased has been carved into the raised top. His arms are folded on his chest, much like Jerrard's arms, crossed defensively on the front of his brown cassock.

"I know that the king expects me to go to Gweneth. At least he would like me to go to her, but I'm not that crazy. But you could bring her here, saying she should be protected in a convent from Henry's retaliation against her father."

"I already told you. Henry knows that Sothingham wants forgiveness. He may grant it. You never know what the king has up his sleeve. Point is: Gweneth is probably in no danger."

"But, you can't be sure. Think about that."

"And what, my young man, makes you think she would leave her parents?"

"You have to let her know that I am here. She would leave her parents to see her husband."

"Oh, you are truly a Boulton. The wife of one day will abandon her parents, who have doted on her, so I hear, from the day of her birth, and join her landless spouse. And in the process, I might add, bring attention to this place, because you have nowhere else to safely go."

"She is pregnant." Jerrard, miserable and losing the argument, begins pacing the length of the coffin.

"All the more reason that she should stay with her mother. The ladies of Sothingham likely know how to introduce a baby into the world. Unless you can do better."

The Archbishop regrets his tone. But he cannot allow Henry to come sniffing around the cathedral, possibly asking about Thomas's newest friar associate. He wonders: Would the monarch violate the sanctity of this place if he suspected the Aureus was here? He hopes Jerrard is asking himself the same question. The crypt can hold its secrets. It is the weakness of mortals that worries him.

"Your wife needs her parents now. And, they can provide for her and your child."

"I may be landless, but I have this." Jerrard taps the carved boot of the coffin's occupant.

❈

KING HENRY AND HIS SMALL GARRISON ride through the Sothingham gates as if to pay a social call. Having been told of the king's approach, the earl and countess are in the courtyard. Their elaborate dress bespeaks an important visitor.

"Your Majesty, welcome." The earl delivers a sweeping bow. The countess curtsies. Their staff is not in attendance.

Henry dismounts. "Lord Bertram. Lady Sothingham. A pleasure."

It is close to December, but the earl's forehead is visibly wet. Pallor is the color of his wife's cheeks.

"Your Majesty, the men riding with you must be starved. Our boys will attend to their horses." Bertram motions to the children standing off to one side. "And through that door," his hand sweeps to the left, "is a fine feast prepared just for them. We three will eat through there." He points to a larger door, slightly ajar. "My forest boasts the best meat and fowl. You will see."

"I look forward to the meal. Won't your daughter be joining us?"

The host and hostess exchange quick looks. They had hoped that this question would not be asked. Nevertheless, they are ready with an answer.

"Gweneth, our sweet baby, is indisposed today. I think it's her condition." The countess throws a wan smile at the king.

"Oh, my," Henry projects deep concern. "She is not ill, I hope."

"Our daughter is expecting a baby." Lady Sothingham hopes this will end the conversation. Her husband stands silently.

"That is wonderful." Henry radiates rapport and congeniality. "Always good news about new ones coming into the world. My youngest, named for her mother, will be two this coming year. She is such a delight." The king chats as if he were passing the time with his children's governesses and tutors. "You are absolutely right. Your daughter should rest. I will pay my respects later in my visit."

The protective parents were warming to the king's sociable manner until the last sentence. But they lack a plan to prevent the paying of respects, especially when it is suggested by the king. Hopefully the food and wine will dull his enthusiasm for exchanging pleasantries with Gweneth. Best to hasten the king to a fine meal.

❁

THE CRYPT GLOWS A DULL GOLDEN HUE. The still air is cold, but without wind, or even a draft, the atmosphere is that of a late afternoon on an autumn day. Two men stand next to the mahogany coffin, polished to a luster on its sides. The carved likeness on the top has aged naturally, a faded prince of the church lying in an eternal glossy cocoon. Thomas's hand rests atop the prince's wooden boot.

"Jerrard, you know it's going to be a while until we can divide this. Or move it anywhere. I know where my half is going, eventually. But your situation is more awkward, all the more to take our time. Here's what I propose."

Thomas raises his hand from the boot in a gesture that generally precedes the pronouncement of a papal decree, but he is interrupted.

"Listen Archbishop, I need to first find out if Henry is going to pardon my father-in-law. That will make a big difference in my plans."

"You already have a Plan A, Plan B and so on?"

"No."

"I thought not."

"As I said, I need to first find out what the king is going to do to Gweneth's father."

"Alright. Once again, here's what I propose. At the present time, you have disappeared. The House of Boulton is defeated on battlefield; your father, the earl, is dead; Henry has won…what? A castle he doesn't want or need. More land, yes. Though I expect he will make some provision for your large family so that he is not responsible for their well-being. He made war for the Aureus; however, what he won was an opportunity to perform an air show over your castle. I suspect he is in a truly foul mood. You need to project a very low profile."

"I've been doing that."

Distant footsteps intrude on the conversation. Thomas motions to walk quickly to a nearby massive sarcophagus. He drops to his knees and Jerrard follows. Their audible prayers cause the footsteps to slow down, stopping as the elderly friar comes upon the Archbishop and his aide.

"Pardon the intrusion on your prayers, Your Grace. I was just making my afternoon rounds. Tending souls, you might say."

Turning around just enough for his face to be visible, the Archbishop produces a genial countenance. His right hand offers a blessing. "Our conclave of souls thanks you, I am sure, as does Brother William here. Certainly I thank you for your daily journey through this consecrated place."

The friar nods, folds his hands in a prayerful clasp and continues into the golden necropolis. Thomas and Jerrard spend several quiet minutes on their knees.

"My, this stone is hard on the bones." Thomas rises. "You likely don't feel it at all."

"I'm beginning to feel it, Your Grace. This cassock is unkind to my knees."

"Say, I had it especially made for you. You should see the thin material that the other friars wear. I told my housekeeper that I was trying out new fabrics for our garments. Now first, I say that, in the future, we should avoid standing around one special coffin. Second, here's the idea that I have been trying to get across." There is a pause as the Archbishop regroups his presentation. "I've noticed that you are especially gifted in the catechism, liturgy and prayers. Really, your religious training is superb. I wouldn't have guessed that your father would have emphasized that in your education."

Jerrard leans forward, remembering his studies in preparation for impressing the French king. It seems like a very long time ago. Perhaps the time was not wasted, after all.

"Yes, my father thought it was important."

"Well, it's a very nice surprise. Perhaps this will aid him in attaining everlasting life."

"One hopes."

"What I am thinking is that you fit in well in a religious surrounding. Until we have our own Plan A, B or C, you should consider a period of contemplation in an abbey far from royal eyes. You would fit right in."

"You're suggesting that I leave here so that you're the only guardian of the Aureus?"

"Shh, don't raise your voice."

Jerrard lowers his volume, but his tone shouts hostility and sarcasm. "I like the Canterbury Cathedral. The splendor. The Glory of God proclaimed from its spires. The seat of the Holy Church for all of England. Yes, I like it a lot. I'll stay here."

"Suit yourself."

The air is crisp with mutual suspicion, reminding Jerrard of his father's description of the confrontation between himself and the king in the Boulton wine cellar over a year ago.

"AN EXCELLENT REPAST. I congratulate you." Henry leans back from the gleaming table, burdened with empty platters.

The earl and countess are also comfortably stuffed with the produce from their land. Mostly they are exhausted from the rigors of hosting a king who has the power to decapitate them after dessert. Henry has said he understands Lord William's trickery; he's certainly seen enough of it. He has promised to leave their vast properties untouched. And he has specifically used the word *forgiveness*. Surely he means it. One other thing the king has mentioned is the excellent Sothingham army, previously never impressed into the king's service as a result of some long-ago agreement. Now Henry is complimenting Bertram on their fighting ability. Imagine, the current earl reflects, the head of an opposing force paying tribute to his men. Henry had said something like...what was it? "I could surely use those fellows on some of my campaigns. Of course, you would naturally be compensated with more lands and, you know, the usual." Bertram can't help but feel immense pride at the reputation of his troops. But no wonder. He has spent more than any other baron on their upkeep and training. As a result, his vast estate has never been threatened.

"If I may bid you goodnight, it's been a long trip to get here. But well worth it. We've accomplished a great deal. I will bunk with my men tonight." The king rises. The Sothinghams rise. They are too tired to insist that the king retire to their fine guest accommodations. If he wants to party with his men, fine. They are just grateful that there has been no further discussion of Gweneth.

Henry moves quickly through the side yard to reach the door which had swallowed his men several hours before. He does not think the earl is capable of perfidy and harm to a guest, but he is technically in enemy territory and, right now, he is alone. Sleeping in the guest wing would have its own comforts, but there is a different kind of comfort to be derived from a safe slumber surrounded by the best swordsmen in the royal militia.

"I BELIEVE I WOULD like to pay my respects to Lady Gweneth now. My, that was a fine breakfast."

It certainly had been an excellent meal, prepared for the king by the castle kitchen's full complement of morning workers. The Sothinghams had hoped that Henry, well fed and satisfied with the earl's contrition, would take his leave and visit other parts of his domain.

"Oh, Your Majesty, our daughter continues to be indisposed. You understand." The countess leans across the enormous table, allowing Henry a closer look at her imploring gaze.

"I do not understand. Please announce me and have a servant escort me to her quarters."

"MADAME, KING HENRY of England is here to pay his respects."

"Of course, please have him come in." Gweneth's voice has graduated from early teen lightness to the modulated tone of marriage and impending motherhood. Eleanor had made this transition long before he met her, but Henry has observed such female changes in his other relationships, the ones that produced the extra youngsters at court. He enters the room prepared to speak with a young woman, not an adolescent.

"Good morning, Lady Gweneth." Henry executes a slight bow to the reclining figure on an elaborate chaise.

"Good morning, Your Majesty. I trust you have been well fed. Is your business here complete?"

"No, it is not. That is why I wished to speak to you. Your father-in-law is dead. The Boulton lands are confiscated. Your husband is missing. Do you know where he is hiding?"

"I don't know where he is. He is not here, if that is the purpose of your visit, though why you would think he would be so foolish is quite beyond me."

Henry had assumed that their morning conversation would proceed in this manner, but the purpose of this visit was not just to settle matters with the earl and obtain an agreement for the future use of the Sothingham army. He has come a long way to acquire the means to lure Jerrard out of hiding. It's worth a try. Right now, he has no other inducement.

"Have you been to London?"

A slight hesitation precedes the answer. "Yes, many years ago. I was a little girl, and I don't remember much except that it was such a large city."

"Did you visit the Tower? Many people do. Some stay there for a long time." The king's lips stretch into a small smile. His eyes twinkle, then go cold.

The hesitation is longer. "Have you discussed this with my parents?" Gweneth's tone is even, but something else has crept into her voice.

"No, I haven't. I was hoping that it would not be necessary. I was hoping that you would tell me the contents of any message sent to you by your husband."

"Your Majesty, there has been no message. I cannot help you."

"You may be surprised, but I do believe you. That is, I believe that there has been no message. You may soon wish there had been, giving you the option of helping me while remaining here in your ancestral home with your parents. However, now you must help me in another way. You must come with me when I leave today."

"No." The voice is still strong, but it has acquired another dimension: fear. "I am expecting my first child in early summer. Such an arduous trip could endanger the baby. You are a parent. You must be aware of my condition. What can my husband possibly give to you except his head? Is one more dead body that important?"

"You ask sensible questions. Nonetheless, I am not answering them. You should have been eavesdropping on a conversation that I had with my chancellor some time ago. Then you would know my philosophy regarding means to an end. You are the means. If you lose a baby, then have another. The queen and I lost our first-born son when he was just a toddler; so we had more sons. Prepare to accompany me to London. When we arrive, we shall go sightseeing. First stop: The Tower of London."

AN ELEGANT CARRIAGE carrying two passengers and several trunks slowly makes its way toward the castle gate. Behind it ride King Henry II and his garrison. The Earl and Countess of Sothingham, looking diminished in size, watch their daughter wave a brave goodbye. A closer look reveals the earl holding his wife, her knees buckled, in a semblance of a standing position. She cannot believe this is happening. They had fed the king and his men the best from their larder. Lord Bertram had thrown himself at the mercy of the king, and Henry had pardoned him. There had been an agreement on the baronial army being placed under the king's command from time to time. And now Gweneth, a mother-to-be, must go to London with the king. All because of that Boulton family, now headed by the fugitive son who is married to her daughter.

"My dear, my dear, I share your sorrow, but you must not worry. King Henry promises that he will take care of our sweet one. He says the Tower has the finest apartments in all London. And the Queen will provide her own midwives for Gweneth when her time comes. Oh, please do not worry."

"What proper woman travels with only one lady-in-waiting? Our little girl requires many ladies to ensure her well-being. My sweet daughter in London. Practically alone. I shall not be comforted until she comes home to us." The countess is engulfed in sobs.

"She will be attended by many servants. The king assured me." Her husband repeats Henry's promises. He hopes he can believe them.

"Oh, Bertram, you know as well as I do. She is a hostage. The target is Jerrard. How could we have done this to our daughter?"

The earl has no answer. All he can do is embrace his wife and prevent her from falling onto the cobblestoned courtyard.

CHAPTER TWENTY

NEVILLE, BEARING THE ROYAL BANNER, rides just ahead of the king, who is followed by half of the garrison. The carriage lumbers several yards behind them. The rest of the garrison rides as a rear guard. Henry does not expect to encounter any portion of the earl's army. They have had an opportunity to reorganize, but the king's instincts tell him that Lord Bertram would not contradict his own avowals of repentance and fealty. Still, he urges haste in putting the vast Sothingham estate behind them. They had come by the shortest route from the Boulton encampment. The return will be different, and longer. London is their destination. Henry has chosen the roads known to be well traveled. Abbeys and inns lie on their homeward path. Mindful of the two passengers in the carriage, the king has chosen a route which offers occasional comforts.

"Stop here!" Henry shouts loud enough for Neville and other nearby riders to hear. "George, look at your maps. There's a settlement just a half day's travel from the perimeter of the Sothingham lands. The earl was telling me that it's populated by freemen and quite prosperous. He didn't know if it had an inn, but I think we should check it out."

"Sire," George lays his reins across the top of his saddle and reaches into the leather bag that hangs from his belt. He pulls out several parchments. They are in a numbered sequence that only he and a few others in the garrison understand. These men carry identical parchment maps in their pouches. It is a concession to reality. A map man can be killed just like any other fighter in the force. And it is folly to try to rescue a leather bag in the midst of a skirmish. Thus far, for many years, George has avoided this unfortunate end to his career. He remains the number one map man in the company.

"Yes, I checked out our route yesterday. You see, I'm a fellow who likes to keep his head about him." George completes his statement by slowly dragging an index finger across his throat, then dropping his head to one side, tongue hanging out, eyes rolling back, to complete the mock execution. Henry bellows with laughter. The men follow. It is a real plus to ride with a monarch having a sense of humor.

"Anyhow," George is sorting through the numbered sheets, looking for just one. "Anyhow, we are close to Bridge Town. Funny name. Must be a river there." His hand pulls out the desired parchment and he studies its markings. "Oh, yes, I see it. The main settlement is on the other side of the river. This town is marked by a square, not a round dot. That means it has commerce, and some kind of fair is held there. Maybe we will arrive for music and dancing."

"Maybe there will be buxom maidens offering you kisses and gar-lands of flowers for your neck. Maybe they will greet you wearing only fronds from the forest. Maybe, ah, maybe." Henry is in an excellent mood today. His hostage enterprise is proceeding as planned.

George executes an elaborate bow from the seat of his saddle. "Sire, would that your words forebode such an excellent surprise."

"Only the best for my men. Where do we turn?"

"Not far ahead. The way is marked."

❀

HENRY ADDRESSES THE REAR GARRISON. "Remain here with the carriage. Allow the ladies to get out and take care of their needs. We shouldn't be long. If it's a decent place, we'll come back for you. If not, we'll return and push on. I hope not. George tells me that the next abbey is hours away. Keep a watchful eye. Take turns having a rest. You know what to do."

The king knocks on the carriage door, which is opened by the lady-in-waiting. Gweneth begins to speak, but is interrupted by Henry.

"Ladies, we are going to a nearby settlement, called Bridge Town, to determine if it has proper accommodations for you. Wish us luck." Before the two young women can speak, the door is closed. There is the receding sound of hoofbeats. Then silence.

TWO HOURS HAVE PASSED. The winter sun is quickly moving west. The ladies are resting in the carriage. Four sentries on horseback guard this tiny gathering. Most of the men are seated or dozing on the trailside vegetation. The surrounding forest gives up its own sounds. It is an agreeable picture of travelers stopping for a rest.

The horses know first. They whinny and jump around. As quickly as possible, their riders are in the saddle. Swords are unsheathed seconds before they hear the approaching clatter of horses carrying a band of highwaymen.

The commander shouts, "You three, to the carriage. Defend the ladies. Semicircle! Semicircle! Men, for King Henry!"

The shouts echo back. "For King Henry! For King Henry!" Then they are drowned out by the onslaught of horses, men, swords, lances and knives. It is a hand-to-hand brawl. The lightly armored royal garrison is outnumbered and caught by surprise. Their attackers are dressed for a major battle. This trail juncture must be one of their favorite places to ambush unwary travelers. No wonder Bridge Town is prosperous. But there is no time to wonder about anything else. It is a close-up melee of clashing metal. Inside the carriage, two women are screaming.

❀

"MALLORY, STOP. Do you hear something?" Henry has already pulled up the reins on his handsome steed. He and his small contingent are returning from Bridge Town, something of a disappointment as a traveler's stopping place.

Mallory halts. Henry raises his right hand, meaning he wants silence. The men and horses obey.

In the distance, there is a faint sound of something. Something that is out of place in this pristine woodland. As one, Henry and his band understand the source of that sound. Within seconds, they are at a full gallop on the trail. Even with their horse hooves pounding on the hard dirt, the battle noise reaches their ears, the sound of metal on metal echoing through the quiet forest. Animals scurry. Small rodents dive into their burrows. Birds flee from the trees. Something unnatural is happening on a trail normally used for commerce and hunting.

"Henry! Help!" A voice shouts its last words, imploring the monarch to bring aid. The man slides off of his horse onto the ground. The leader of the attack, in full armor, is at the left door of the carriage, but he cannot pull it open while seated on his horse. Jumping off, he grabs the door handle with both hands, while the two occupants use all their strength to pull on the inside door handle. Their screaming has evolved into a chant which recharges their untested strength in keeping the door closed. "No. No. No. No."

Neville is first, rounding the ninety-degree turn with the royal banner pointing laterally at the battle taking place on the trail and nearby grassy areas. He takes the nearest of the enemy right off of his saddle with his pole, while the Plantagenet emblem flutters innocently in the light afternoon breeze.

King Henry is a millisecond behind Neville. He sees the carriage attacker, pulls up his horse and jumps off, sword in hand. The clamor of the new arrivals causes the attacker to turn, just as Henry is upon him. Two swords meet mid-air. A battle between king and enemy leader begins. The women in the carriage press their faces to the windows to watch a contest that will decide their fate.

The swords flay and parry, as the men take measure of one another. A heavy blow to the enemy's armor will not do much damage unless it is placed at an unprotected opening. A similar blow to the king's vest will knock him down. His men cannot help him; they are busy aiding their comrades, and they know the king is an excellent jouster, on the ground as well as in the saddle. Henry is on his own, at least until some of the attackers are defeated and routed.

The king, however, has the advantage. Armor is useful on horseback, but on the ground it is a heavy weight to be borne while dueling with a dancing opponent. Henry sidesteps, then leaps, hops, skips, and jumps while feigning a slice here and a cut there. His legs are weapons; his sword their accomplice. The attacker is soon on the ground, now crimson with his ebbing life.

Holding the metal tip to the exposed throat of the armored highwayman, Henry speaks. "You have used poor judgment in trying to kidnap these two ladies, but you also made a mistake in attacking your king. I am Henry the Second."

Fear in the man's eyes is momentarily obscured by surprise. There is almost a glint of joy. Oh, to be felled by a great king. The fear returns, with good reason. With a thrust, the saber does its work, and the man is dead.

The king's garrison is likewise at an advantage against their heavily armored opponents. Swords are thrust, not to inflict injury or death to the forest outlaws, but rather to their horses. Once the horse is down, the duel is done. Suddenly the survivors turn and gallop away. Their leader is slain, and they sense defeat before it is handed to them at the end of a blade.

Henry stands over the wounded highwayman about to be dispatched by Neville. "Just a minute. I need to get some information. Get this man some water."

Neville looks confused, but he complies. The king rarely questions the fallen enemy.

"Look here, bandit, you have attacked the king of England, his royal militia and two fine ladies. Big mistake. Why are you wearing full armor?"

"I hurt."

"Answer me."

"An accident. An accident."

"What do you mean *accident*?"

"A man known to our town, a man from the nearest Sothingham settlement," the wounded man stops to breathe, "he came to us saying the earl's soldiers were headed this way. He," another pause, "he wanted to warn us. They've come before." He coughs. "We prepared to fight. To protect our land. Finding your carriage and men was an accident. We just wanted the carriage." A rasping noise follows. "We didn't know." The man closes his eyes.

"Listen, listen here. You're forgiven. You hear? You're forgiven." Henry looks at Neville who shakes his head, then turns back to the mortally wounded man. "How far away is this Sothingham force?"

"Sundown, maybe sooner," the voice struggles. "Thank you, Your Majesty." The man slips away.

"It must be my lot to hear last words," Henry says to no one. Then he stands and shouts for his men to come close. "Sothingham has an army after us. The bastard." He thinks but does not say that he misjudged Lord Bertram. But the self-admonishments must wait. Henry continues. "This dead man here said they thought the army was coming to attack their village, like they've done before. In any case, they are close to us. We must get off the trail. Strap the wounded across their horses. Any wounded who can't ride go in the carriage. The ladies will tend to them. Neville, any too far gone?"

"Not that I can see, sire."

"Check. If so, you know what to do."

Neville nods and pats the handle of the misericorde in his belt.

While the ladies protest the transformation of their elegant carriage into a hospital wagon, Henry addresses the driver. "Take the carriage to the outskirts of the town, this side of the river. Remain out of sight. You'll hear us coming."

The driver salutes and urges his horses to the side trail.

"Damn that Sothingham bastard. Just like all the other barons. Can't trust any of them. Wait until he sets up housekeeping in the Tower, next to his daughter. Good thing I didn't sleep in his guest chambers. I'd be dead. Dead!" Still irate at Bertram's perfidy and his own failure to detect it, Henry turns to face his commander who is holding the reins of the royal mount.

"Sire, your horse wishes to be ridden."

"Thank you. Here's what we are going to do. Send a few men to the town, announcing the king knows the attack was an accident and he forgives everybody."

"What? They wanted the contents of the carriage. They would have taken the ladies, too. They are common thieves."

"I know that, but we need the town's cooperation. Tell the people that we are bringing their wounded as a token of my forgiveness. And we're going to help them defend against the Sothingham force. We will put their wounded in front, ours next and then the rest of us."

Within minutes the garrison is riding the trail toward Bridge Town. The moans of the injured riders float back along the trail. It is a somber procession. Galloping is out of the question, but Henry insists on a steady gait. This is a race, though not a fast one, against time. He hopes that the Sothingham soldiers have been riding at a leisurely pace, knowing that their objective is a carriage unaccustomed to speedy travel. As he rides, Henry works through his plan. They will arrive at Bridge Town in late afternoon. While he has seen that the settlement lacks traveler accommodations, its homes reflect the prosperity of its freemen occupants. He will get his men and the carriage across the bridge and into the town where the wounded will receive care. At this point, the Sothingham forces will be on the new trail, seeking a dual prize: the king's hostage and Bridge Town's freehold lands. Henry will announce that he and his men have come to aid the townspeople in their defense. If anyone thinks to ask how the king knew about the impending attack, he will invoke the Almighty, who has summoned Henry to be the savior of this settlement. This pious explanation would be mocked by sophisticated Londoners and Boulton-like barons, but piety always plays well in the countryside. He will become their beloved benevolent monarch.

"George, come up here." Henry waves to his map man, who breaks rank and joins Henry and Neville in the front of the garrison.

"Yes sire?"

"What lies beyond Bridge Town on the other side of the river?"

The parchment packet is removed from the leather bag. George goes through several sheets, with an apology. "Beg your pardon. I had arranged these according to the route along the other trail."

"Yes, fine, no problem." Henry is talking and listening simultaneously. His ears are attuned to distant sounds. He hears none.

"Wait, I see. Here is Bridge Town. The river. The trail. Oh, I must go to the next sheet." George carefully replaces the top parchment with the one underneath it. His index finger traces a route across the ecru coloring. "About a day's ride from the town you come to the Penfield lands. The trail widens, goes actually to a settlement first, then the manor. There's an abbey, too."

"Penfield, good." Henry turns and motions to his commander to join them. "George here says that this trail goes to the Penfield manor. When we arrive at the town, send a rider to Lord Penfield. Announce a visit from the king. Tell him about the highwaymen attack and that we have wounded. Mention the ladies, but not specifically Sothingham. Say we would appreciate a welcoming squad of his finest soldiers. Do you understand?"

"I do, sire. It shall be done."

AUREUS

THE DAY CLOSES SILENTLY. There has been no attack, no sound of approaching hoofbeats. The villagers report no activity on the approaching trail. Henry hears the backstory from his new friends, now basking in forgiveness for their unseemly attack on a ladies' carriage. Over the years, the Sothingham forces have harassed the village in the earl's efforts to acquire their freeholdings. The river and nearby forest have provided a natural defense supplemented by the armaments wielded by the local men, though to keep their fighting skills honed, they have occasionally attacked unsuspecting travelers along the main trail, which has provided a secondary income for the small settlement. As one, the inhabitants agree that this kind of activity is an affront to the king's peace. It will not happen again. An Act of God has brought help in the person of King Henry, who sits on a stool radiating goodwill in every look and gesture.

All know that an assaulting force, if it is to come, must cross the bridge. The town folk, however, believe that the king's magical presence will deter an attack. Henry knows better and posts sentries, then visits the wounded, bids the ladies goodnight in their carriage and prepares to retire until he is awakened before dawn.

EVEN BEFORE THERE IS A SUGGESTION of light in the eastern sky, archers are posted, just out of sight, by the structures nearest the bridge. At this close range, the expert royal bowmen can shoot their missiles through the eyeholes of head armor, should it be worn, without the arrow even touching metal. But to many in the king's force, this is an unusual formation, because they cannot be seen. Some of them, accustomed to the standard battle charge, grumble that this is not a manly way to challenge the enemy.

"See here," counters the commander-in-chief, "we want to fill the bridge with dead bodies and horses. So we hide until the bridge is filled with riders. Then attack. And you, son," he points to a young doubter, "you will live to see another day. You should be happy."

"Sire, it's just that we have never done that before – you know, hide and shoot arrows."

"You're new, aren't you? What's your name?"

"Lothar, sire, I am Lothar, and I am honored to ride with your royal militia."

"You aren't from the south Aquitaine by any chance?"

"Oh, no, I'm from Anjou. It's a privilege to cross the water and ride with you."

"Ah, good, from Anjou, my home. Have you ever worn a mask?" The question produces the desired confusion. Lothar's brow becomes furrowed, while the king's commander, Mallory, standing nearby, simply grins. The monarch's pre-battle, off-beat banter is a familiar staple of their campaigns.

"A mask? Uh, oh. You mean the cloth across the face. Here." Lothar gestures across his cheeks and nose. "No, I've never worn one, but I saw some men wearing masks at the trebuchet."

"Would you wear a mask?"

"Yes, sire, if you ordered it."

"So, you would wear a mask if I ordered it, even if you didn't like masks. Correct?"

"Of course, you are my king and your word is the law. Who would do otherwise?"

"Commander," Henry, wearing a satisfied smirk, turns to his lead soldier, "we need to recruit more Lothars and fewer red necked Laurences. Right?"

"Right."

❖

AUREUS

A DRUMBEAT OF APPROACHING HOOVES shatters the morning stillness. The villagers have melted into the forest. Bridge Town appears deserted. Soon riders enter the clearing which leads to the stone bridge, a relic from Roman times, which means it is very well constructed.

The Sothingham commander waits for his company to completely assemble before he begins the bridge crossing. He can see nothing unusual in the settlement across the river. This whole situation is perplexing. Dead men at the trail juncture. Yet the king, his men and the carriage have left the main trail and traveled to Bridge Town. So they have likely come here unchallenged. But the village men have always defended on the trail or on this side of the river. Why change their strategy? Oh, well, he will subdue the village, an unexpected bonus, and then catch Henry on the new trail within a few hours. The king likely has wounded soldiers as well as the carriage to slow him down. And no point in trying to figure out this quirky village mentality. He gives the order to cross the bridge.

Four abreast, the Sothingham force, attired in fine uniforms and carrying the latest sabers in their scabbards, begins the crossing. Their formation is smartly regimental. Lord Bertram would be proud of this garrison carrying his banner. In less than a minute, just a few feet separate the lead horses from solid ground on the other side.

The arrows sing their way into the mass of horseflesh and well-groomed riders. Men fall. Horses fall. They pile up at land's edge. The bowmen have concentrated on the lead horsemen and those in the rear. As each end of the bridge fills with a pile of soldiers and their steeds, the riders in the middle cannot find a way out. Many dismount, stumbling over the fallen in an effort to exit the bridge the same way they entered it. Some jump into the river. It is a rout, and not one of the royal force has had to unsheathe a blade.

❀

JOAN CATHCART

HENRY CONFERS WITH THE VILLAGE ELDERS, instructing them to leave the bloody mess alone for a few days.

"It is God's will that they remain there," the king intones. "Until they start to smell. Then shove them into the river. They will float by the Sothingham castle sometime next week."

The village men fall on their knees, blessing Henry the Second and the House of Plantagenet.

"Thank you. Please rise. We appreciate your tending to our wounded and lending us your wagons. They will be returned to you once we reach the Penfield lands. You are a credit to England. Good bye."

CHAPTER TWENTY-ONE

"WELL, THOMAS, here we are toasting another new year. 1163 was a busy time, wouldn't you say?"

"You were certainly busy, beating up the Boulton family, throwing dead bodies into their castle courtyard. By the way, I hear that was quite spectacular. Maybe such air shows will be the events of the future. And you will go down in history as the first English monarch to develop a flying circus, so to speak."

"Ha ha. Thomas, you've always had a way with words." However, Henry makes a mental note to mention this to the royal chronicler. If reported without Thomas-like sarcasm, this achievement with the trebuchet could be seen as a valuable, and *yes* unusual, contribution to siege warfare. "So, go on, dear Archbishop, recapping last year in your own inimitable way."

"Thank you. Let's see, where was I? Oh, the flying circus. Then, without stopping in at the palace to check on your growing family, you dash off to kidnap the Sothingham girl, daughter of a well-respected baron and presently married to the Boulton heir. By the way, how did you explain her presence to Lord Penfield?"

"I didn't. She and her lady-in-waiting stayed in the nearby abbey, well-guarded by my men. Penfield didn't even know that one of the ladies was a Sothingham. Maybe he does now."

"Kidnapping a bride. Henry, have you no honor."

"Not when it comes to a pot of gold coins, but let's go back to Penfield. His chef works such magic on pheasants and partridges...the food was magnificent. I should have abducted his kitchen staff, too. I don't eat that well at my own palace."

"And the bride you kidnapped is pregnant."

"That happens to brides, so I hear."

"Do you mean pregnancy or kidnapping?"

"Apparently both."

"And now you think you will flush young Boulton into the open by putting his wife in the Tower of London. Do you expect him to come begging at your gates, or perhaps do you think he will try scaling the Tower to liberate her?"

"I would rather that he do the second. It would be fun to watch." Henry takes a long sip of wine. Last January's new year toast with Thomas had been revealing and argumentative, but it had also been amusing, a sort of camaraderie with a twist. Now Thomas's wine glass remains untouched. There are new lines at each end of his mouth and his eyes. He exudes the dignified aura of an archbishop, which displeases the king but which also reminds Henry of another matter.

"By the way, Your Grace," Henry stops to allow the hollow honorific to drop into the conversation, "I am calling a council of barons and bishops to meet at my palace at Clarendon later this month. The purpose is to realign the relationship of church and state back to where it was during my grandfather's reign. You will attend, of course."

There is a hesitation. Thomas had expected a reprieve in this contentious issue. Henry, he was sure, would now concentrate all his efforts into luring Jerrard from his hiding place to see his wife. He had imagined restoration of the Boulton lands to be thrown into the mix of inducements. Perhaps other endowments to the family. And, there was a new baby coming. Some part of him wants to taunt Henry, revealing that his quarry is at Canterbury, right under the king's nose. Well, that won't happen. But what a moment it would be, telling this violent, head-strong, narcissistic, amoral head of state that he had been fooled. How could Thomas have invested so much of himself in a friendship with such a man? Truly his ability to judge character had been taking a long nap. Had he been seduced by superficial comradeship, or the perks of high office or maybe just being known as the king's closest confidant? Now he can only pray that God will grant him absolution for such earthly missteps.

"Yes, I will attend. It is my duty to defend the Mother Church from the depredations that you increasingly inflict on Her."

"Fine. Well, it has been a pleasure sharing a toast to the new year. Now I must get over to the Tower to rig up a scaling device to assist young Boulton. If you know where he is," Henry smirks at his little joke, "tell him his wife begs to see him. Simply begs."

"YOU MUST LEAVE HERE. Immediately. I will get you to the continent, where you will be safe."

"And my wife and unborn child?"

Thomas and Jerrard are in the Canterbury crypt, standing next to an ancient casket at the far end of a golden corridor. They now avoid the single coffin most important to them, as if being near it would somehow suggest their singular interest in it.

"They are bait, and I will not let you bite. We have, as you may remember, an agreement. A fifty-fifty split."

"I will take my half and ransom my wife."

"And you will possibly end up with nothing. More important, so will I."

"The church will manage without this fortune. It has done well for centuries without it."

"Tell me this. Your father never intended to share with me, right? I'll bet he told you to watch me carefully, get to know my weaknesses, find a way to wrest my share away without having to kill me for it, since killing an Archbishop of Canterbury is something no one would want to do."

Jerrard leans against the cold wooden coffin, arms folded. He looks straight ahead, then nods. "Yes, that's what he told me to do."

"And have you been studying me, looking for the cracks in my armor, so to speak?"

"No."

"Because?"

"I've been thinking about this. If we had prevailed in the battle with King Henry and if my father had lived, I would still not have been a party to breaking a solemn agreement, whether with an archbishop or anybody else. I would have defied him on that. But now, my choices are different. I have, with your guidance I might add, tried to find some answers through prayer. As you suggested, I am working on myself."

"I would truly like to believe you. But, in any case, you must leave immediately. You'll have much opportunity for prayer in an abbey I favor. It's across the water, in Pontigny, part of the Cistercian Order. You cannot help your wife here. She is much safer as long as you are not found. The king is back in London, not that far away, making the situation even more dangerous."

"I must think about it, about leaving here. Gweneth is in London. So close."

"That's the problem. So is Henry. He could pop in here anytime. That's why you must leave now. Pontigny is known to attract the most pious and literate monks. With your religious training, you will fit right in. After I attend this bothersome meeting at Clarendon, I will try to join you for a visit."

"Alright. I'll go across the water. Probably it is safer. And the Aureus?"

"It will remain with the dead until you and I are both free to do what we want with our respective booty. That may be a long time."

AUREUS

❊

LATE SPRING RAINS and longer daylight have both dampened and brightened south England. The country is enjoying its continued respite from war with France and the absence of civil unrest within. The king has prevailed in his standoff with Thomas, but only after both of them have managed to involve all the royal houses of Europe in their conflict, as well as the pope, who surprisingly refused to take sides. After Thomas and the English bishops sign the Constitutions of Clarendon, aligning the church/state relationship to where it had been at the beginning of the century, the furor subsides. All who know the king expect Henry to be elated and cannot understand his continued peevishness in light of his triumph. Except Thomas. Henry still does not have the prize. More important, he no longer has the bait. Gweneth has died in childbirth.

Thomas feels obligated to go to France with the news, but the Constitutions require him to seek royal permission to travel. Lacking a justification which would satisfy Henry, Thomas embarks on a tour of English abbeys. When he arrives at the small monastery in Hastings, he quickly charters a cog to transport him and two attending friars to mainland Europe, where they travel to the Pontigny Abbey, in the heart of King Henry's continental domain.

CHAPTER TWENTY-TWO

"ARCHBISHOP, THIS IS AN HONOR." Jerrard falls to his knees and kisses the grand ring. Others at the abbey follow his greeting. There has been no warning. All are overjoyed at the sudden appearance of England's highest prelate. Monks are sent scurrying for wine. The abbot shouts for someone, anyone, to check the storage building for its stock of food. A friar is dispatched to the nearest estate to beg for any available delicacies that would delight a high churchman. And, of course, an invitation is extended to its noble occupants. *Oh, please, the abbot insists that you dine with us.* Only Jerrard is troubled. Thomas has not sent word of an impending visit.

"Brother William, how nice to see you here. Do come walk with me. I bring news from London."

They step quickly outside the low stone wall surrounding the abbey, now celebrating its fiftieth year. Fields tended by the friars surround this monastic settlement. Thomas walks down a wide furrow followed by the young monk.

"I'm sorry. Your wife is dead. In childbirth. The news was suppressed. I didn't find out right away. I…"

"Dead?"

"Yes, she was assisted, I understand, by Queen Eleanor's ladies. I don't know exactly what happened, but it happens so often. It is God's way. You have a daughter."

"Daughter?"

"Yes, she is at court. The king has included her in his rather large brood, but she will receive excellent care."

"Henry has my daughter?"

"Yes. I'm sure he still entertains thoughts of using her as bait sometime in the future. I don't know her name."

"Gweneth."

"Your daughter?" Thomas is confused. How could Jerrard know his daughter's name?

"No, my wife."

"Oh, yes, I see. Foolish of me. I am so very sorry."

"We had very little time together. I told you I should have paid a ransom for her." Jerrard's voice rises.

"Shh. I came here without Henry's permission to tell you. He is keeping this death a secret. You must not feel that the outcome would have been different if she had been released from the Tower. She had the best midwives, the queen's midwives. Women die all the time in childbirth. It's the way of the world. It is the way of God. I have prayed for her everlasting soul. She is resting in peace. I will go on to visit with King Louis, so that this place does not attract Henry's attention. He will be furious that I have come to France. It's likely that he will punish me for my disobedience to the crown." Thomas's voice drops to a whisper. "It's all because of the Aureus. Henry doesn't have it, doesn't know where it is, doesn't know where you are. In short, he is the mightiest king to sit on the throne of England, and he can't have what he wants. He is, to put it mildly, in a very bad temper."

"Thank you, Thomas. Perhaps, if Henry is angry enough, you will come back to Pontigny for a while." Jerrard wipes his eyes. His simple light brown cassock sleeve is dark with moisture. "Excuse me, I will not attend dinner. I'm sure the abbot will have the best for you. I will be spending my evening in the chapel."

❊

NORTHAMPTON, IN ENGLAND'S MIDLANDS, is a new city, founded earlier in the century. It already boasts a castle that was popular with the king's grandfather, Henry I, and a new monastery. Henry II likewise delights in spending time in this growing town. This part of the country reminds him of Anjou. The local people are simple, but they are also loyal, always an appealing attribute to a monarch.

Henry has chosen the castle as the site for the trial of Thomas Becket, miscreant who has failed to respond to a lawsuit regarding land confiscated by the church. He has decided to drop the initial charges: failure to obtain royal permission to leave the country. Egged on by his own frustration and petulance, Henry has much bigger plans for his former friend.

"Good morning, King Henry."

"Good morning, Thomas. You are early. The proceedings begin tomorrow."

The two men stand in the empty castle courtroom. The king had not expected this early arrival, but his servant interrupted his morning prayers to say that the Archbishop was in the courtyard with his retinue of monks, clerks and a military escort. Obviously Thomas was upset about something.

"What brings you and your splendid traveling companions to my home away from home?" Henry's outstretched arms announce hospitality, but his eyes are unwelcoming.

"Your squires and other men of the court have occupied my assigned lodgings. You can see that I am traveling with a large number of people, as is befitting my station, and we all expect to experience the comforts of the inn assigned to us."

"I'll attend to that right away. Anything else?" Henry has no intention of moving anybody to make way for the archbishop and his crowd. But he will let Thomas find that out the hard way, possibly having to camp out in the sparsely furnished monastery dedicated to Saint Andrew. He envisions the archbishop sleeping on a stone bed, wrapped in his hair shirt for warmth.

"Yes, there is something else. I would like to go to France to meet with the Pope, who is there for an extended visit. You see, I am asking permission."

"And you see that I am not granting it. No, you may not go. You will deal with me first. And, who knows, you may be in prison after that."

❊

THE GRAND COURTROOM at Northampton castle has come to life. It is the first notable trial to be held there, and the lead participants are the two most powerful men in England, the Archbishop of Canterbury and King Henry II, founder of the House of Plantagenet. Barons and church prelates vie for positions to more easily view the proceedings. They have been told that Thomas will be prosecuted on many charges. The chatter assumes guilty verdicts. But can a secular court imprison a sitting archbishop? A few quietly wonder if a death penalty is possible. One baron suggests castration, but he is laughed down by the comment that Thomas's commitment to chastity would render such a punishment unbefitting, even comical.

The first charge, failure to respond to the land lawsuit, brings a quick verdict. Guilty.

The second charge, illegal confiscation of the above-mentioned land, is likewise adjudicated in a speedy manner. The verdict is a surprise. Not Guilty.

What? Not guilty? Henry is irate. After a brief adjournment, further charges are announced.

The court chronicler reads from a lengthy parchment. "As chancellor, Thomas Becket did engage in embezzlement of crown funds. He has never accounted for all the revenues passing through his hands while occupying that position of trust. The missing money exceeds, in amount, more than the crown's annual income from all lands on the continent. Thomas Becket has failed to repay money borrowed from the royal treasury. Also, he has failed to repay personal loans from the king. He is a traitor and, as such, has no claim on the king's mercy."

Thomas speaks. "No man has labored harder than I to maintain the integrity of the office of chancellor. If mistakes were made, they were absolved by the king when I left the chancellorship to become archbishop. King Henry also canceled repayment of my loans at that time. I will happily repay what I can now, if that pleases the king. In any case, I am not subject to the judgment of this court. Laymen have no power over me. My bishops cannot take part in this trial. This is a travesty!"

Silence envelops the vast hall. Thomas walks toward the massive double doors leading outside.

"I am going to pray now. Please continue your wrongful prosecution. Tomorrow I will come to hear my sentence."

The doors open to a crowd of onlookers. Some cry "Traitor!" Others, many others, cheer as Thomas makes his way to the stable. "Praise you, Archbishop! May God deliver you from harm."

ST. ANDREW MONASTERY sags under the collective weight of the archbishop's entourage and escort. There is insufficient space for the humans and no stables for the horses. To Thomas, Henry's pettiness in co-opting his expected lodgings is just another offshoot of his royal rage. The king is bandying around the word *traitor* as if he were accusing his former friend of cheating at darts. Thomas allows himself a moment of gallows humor; if only Henry knew that his treacherous, thieving, embezzling, deadbeat archbishop also co-owned the Aureus. Indeed, if he knew that, Thomas's head would already have been separated from his torso in front of the multitudes in the courtroom gallery. Well, almost. That would be a stretch. The king would never, even in a fit of extreme anger, never do that. But would he imprison a sitting archbishop? A dicey question.

A nighttime October storm drums down on the monastery roof. Four men in monks' cassocks climb upon horses belonging to the archbishop's military escort. The pre-dawn downpour drowns out the sound of hoofbeats as the steeds thunder through the gate. For the next week, Thomas and three friars make their way to the coast, where they board a boat for the continent.

When he is told of Thomas's escape, Henry's response is a surprise to those present. The king's increasing testiness would have suggested an intemperate outburst. Instead he leans against a marble pillar, arms folded across his chest. His face wears a look of wry amusement.

"How things change. A year ago today, I was celebrating my victory over the treasonous Boulton. Afterward, I wrote to Queen Eleanor, sharing my exhilaration. I remember that. Remember it very well. I shall not write to the queen today."

On the following morning, the king's rage returns. "Write this down! Write this down!" he bellows at couriers in the courtroom. "Thomas Becket is guilty. Guilty of all charges. He knew he was guilty. That's why he ran away. Strip him of his income. And his family. And his servants. Send them all away to France, where they belong."

CHAPTER TWENTY-THREE

AS WINTER ONCE AGAIN DISAPPEARS into spring, the French royal family likewise departs from its Paris palace to the delights of Fontainebleau. The monarch's growing family ranges from a twenty-year-old daughter to a baby son. The children look forward to the freedom of the countryside, where they can play outside of restrictive court protocols. King Louis's extended family is joining him for another long holiday where feasting is a primary entertainment. Watching the children romp around is another pastime. Servants stand by, prepared to step in and minister to minor scrapes and unhappy outcomes. The elegant mothers merely watch, knowing their little ones are cared for by loving nannies, nurses and tutors. There is a flutter of attention around baby Philip, who must someday bear the weight of all France. Right now he is crying because he is wet and hungry.

"My dear Emma," King Louis leans toward his sister-in-law. "No holiday is complete without you and Arnaud. Queen Adele wanted to redecorate your suites, but I told her to await your visit. Perhaps you would have some ideas to contribute. You know, color, art work, perhaps some tapestries from the south."

"Louis, very kind of you. I will discuss it with her." Emma, now almost sixteen, sits in a comfortable lawn lounge. Her chestnut curls have been cajoled into an elegant swirl topped by a tiara that glitters in springtime pastels. She holds a fan which she does not need today.

"Have you held my little heir? I must say, it took a while to get a boy. Thanks to God he is healthy. Do you hear those lungs?"

"I do. How have his sisters adjusted to being supplanted in your affections? And the affections of the queen?" For as long as she has been part of the royal household, Emma has asked unexpected questions. Many consider her to be bold, an unfortunate byproduct of her English heritage. The king is usually charmed by her unconventionality. Her husband Arnaud simply does not understand her.

"Oh, they understand the order of things. Even Alys, who is only five. She calls him 'Your Petite Majesty.' Isn't that charming? But, my dear, it's a good thing that my beloved queen brought us this baby boy. If we had continued having girls, it would have been your job to produce the next king of France, and thus far you and Arnaud have not made any contribution in that department. In the court, there is much chatter, and I don't like that."

"Then Louis, you must tell the chatterers to be quiet. Or else. But because you are king, I will tell you this: I have done my part. Maybe you should have a talk with your brother."

"Maybe you should take care and not ride so often, if you understand my point."

"I do understand your point, but unless there is a royal edict prohibiting me from riding, I shall continue to do so. Now, I think I will pick up 'Your Petite Majesty' if the nannies will allow it. It's a wonderful party, dear Louis."

THOUGH YOUNG IN YEARS, Pontigny Abbey has already acquired the status of a venerable monastery. It is surrounded by vineyards, producing grapes that the monks carefully coax into fine wines exported to France and the Holy Roman Empire to the east and England to the west. King Henry II has visited it on occasion when traveling to his continental possessions. Now it is home to an exiled archbishop. The residents have become accustomed to their famous guest and his cassocked attendants, who, like all the others, work the vineyards and pray in the chapel; with modesty, they have adapted to the monastic routine. Of course, there was much ado when Pope Alexander dropped in, on his way home from a visit to the French king, to meet with the famous English churchman. Other than this event, life at Pontigny proceeds at its own cloistered tempo.

Springtime breezes flutter around the stone-built abbey, beckoning its inhabitants to prayerful contemplation in the out-of-doors after months of worship in the chapel. But even in blustery winter, Thomas and Jerrard preferred to walk the dormant vineyards rather than converse within the chilly monastic walls. Now these outings have become more of a pleasure, even if the sun is still sometimes an elusive visitor.

"You have won the respect of the abbot, Brother William. He admires your facility with Latin and the Book of Prayers. I, too, believe you have an unexpected calling. I remember when you first came to Canterbury, in hiding. I was really quite surprised with your religious training."

"I recall your saying that. My opportunity for reflection compels me to tell you exactly how I came to be so well versed in the scriptures. You may find this to be amusing. Or not."

"Go on. I'm listening."

Jerrard stops to kick a brown stick from the path. The day is grey, accented by brown, the shade of the path, the withered grape vines, the earth-toned cassocks and capes. It is a day needing some color, if only in the dialogue of these two men.

"My religious education had been sketchy until my father arranged my trip to France to handle the betrothal of my sister Aldreda to Prince Arnaud. You know all about that. But what you didn't know is that he put me through a crash course in religion in order to impress King Louis of France. Daily I was instructed by a monk from the local abbey. His name was Merlin. He was a dedicated teacher. After each lesson, he would stay to give a report to my father. I think he also savored my father's wine."

"I know Merlin. Our merry England is indeed a small world."

"How do you know him? Wilshire Abbey, at Boulton, is not exactly a national shrine. No one visits there."

"It happens that Merlin overheard a conversation between your father and a servant. That's when your father found out about the Aureus. Merlin came to me with this information, hoping to gain something, in this case a life-time supply of fine wine."

"That's the fellow, all right. Did you give him the wine?"

"I did. Otherwise, you would be sole owner of *our* treasure, though I don't know where you would be keeping it now."

The men stop at an ancient stone bench, a fixture of this land long before the abbey was constructed. Thomas sits. Jerrard stands facing him. He has been preparing for this moment.

"As I mentioned, my unexpected opportunity for reflection has caused me to rethink much about my life." Silence. The change in subject requires a few quiet moments of emphasis. He resumes. "I was destined to be the Earl of Boulton and master of a fine estate. I expected it. The Aureus changed all that. Perhaps forever. Perhaps not. It changed your life, too, but I think that you and the king would still have become estranged. It is not just the crown versus the papacy. It is something about the honor of God and your role in defending that honor. And possibly it is also something about loss, as you once said."

A sudden gust of wind sends a collection of leaves and twigs down the path. A few clutter around their feet. Thomas stares at his hands. At this moment, the feeling of loss is a terrible weight, more than Jerrard can know.

"Go on."

"For now, I must pray to find answers for my future. You see, the monastic life has been a substantial, and unimagined, comfort for my considerable losses. My father. My earldom. My wife. My baby daughter being coopted into the Plantagenet family. I have no news of my mother and sisters. So I am waiting for guidance. From above."

"That's quite a mouthful." Thomas brushes his hood back off of the head. "Perhaps you are our next archbishop. I'm sure Henry would not be disappointed to learn that I've expired from some nasty disease far away from home. Well, at least we now see eye to eye on the disposition of our treasure."

"I don't think so."

"Did I misunderstand? Have you not come to see Aureus ownership through the eyes of the Mother Church?"

Jerrard leans forward. "You recall, if I may be specific, that my father instructed me to study your weaknesses in order to figure out a way to take the Aureus back from you after he defeated Henry?"

"Yes, you told me that. It was very forthcoming of you."

"You, too, have also been peering at my inner self, seeking the places where my armor can be pierced. My weaknesses, in other words."

"It is a natural progression of thought. In pursuing my duty to the church."

"Of course, Archbishop. Riches to Rome. Honor to the Almighty. Right?"

"Sounds right to me."

"Well, think about this. The church supports the traditional social order of our realm and that of other continental powers. The House of Boulton has been part of this fabric for centuries. The Plantagenets are royal upstarts, and the head of this house has upset our well-ordered universe. That's the first thing. Secondly, the charge of treason against my father was, to me, always questionable. Too much of it was based on an assumption, an assumption mind you, of what the French king would do with a financial windfall. Would a court have accepted this as evidence to convict if the king had chosen to hold a trial? My father did not give money, troops or secrets to the French. He did not commit treason. My task, I believe, is to clear up this stain on our family. Then proceed to regain our lands and position. And, lastly, take custody of my daughter. All this may be expensive. But I would expect you to aid me in restoring my position. So I hope you and Henry patch up your argument soon."

Jerrard turns and walks back toward the abbey.

"So much for discerning his weaknesses." Thomas bows his head.

CHAPTER TWENTY-FOUR

"CHANCELLOR, MY PATIENCE is wearing very thin." King Henry is pacing the royal receiving hall. The only other person in this vast space is Chancellor Ridel, who has grown accustomed to monarchical outbursts. He does not speak, knowing that this will be a one-way conversation.

"Look back. I appointed my good friend Thomas as archbishop in 1162. Almost immediately he began to change his loyalty. Then, in late '64, he exiled himself. Since then, for nearly two years now, I have put up with his letters, excommunications and, if you can believe, a constant barrage of papal inquiries. I convene a council, and what happens? Nothing! Nothing! I am the king, and this man in a friar's cassock is making a mockery of my power."

The Chancellor picks at his sleeve.

"Well, have you no ideas on this matter?"

"Bishop Foliot is doing a creditable job of running Canterbury. Why don't you name him the new archbishop?" Geoffrey Ridel opens his hands as if this should have been done long ago.

"Can't do that. Thomas is a sitting archbishop with too many friends in high places. Including the papacy."

"Still, it is a tempting choice. However, Your Majesty, I do have another idea."

"Well, let's hear it."

"I am thinking my way through this as I speak." The chancellor rubs his forehead to formulate his plan. "It would be a good idea, in my opinion, to get Thomas off English-held soil, where he can communicate easily with his allies in our realm. France would be a better home for him and his little band of monks. He and King Louis would get on quite well; they can discuss prayer and piety long after others have retired to their beds. He will be less meddlesome for you."

"I like that, but how do we persuade Thomas that France is better than Pontigny?"

"I'm coming to that." The Chancellor feels emboldened enough to raise his hand for silence. "Pontigny is part of the Cistercian Order, founded by Benedictine monks in the last century."

"Chancellor, I don't need a history lesson." Henry's exasperation returns.

"Listen, please sire. The Order is holding a general meeting in a few months. I would happily attend on Your Majesty's behalf, protesting the aid given to a royal fugitive at one of their monasteries. And I could say that you are contemplating the expulsion of the entire order from your lands. It's just an idea."

"A good idea. Thank you, chancellor. I do need more advisors like you."

❈

AFTER THE GENERAL CISTERCIAN CONCLAVE, a delegation stopped off at Pontigny, citing a need for rest, food and spiritual fellowship on their way home from a most pleasant meeting dedicated to Benedictine business. They were delighted to encounter the exiled Archbishop of Canterbury during their visit. In fact, they took the opportunity to discuss one of the meeting's great concerns. There had been a rumor circulating among the attendees, none knew its source, but nevertheless a rumor that King Henry was considering the expulsion of all Cistercian monasteries in his lands. Had Thomas heard this same rumor? No, he hadn't. The men of cloth thought not; Thomas's exile might have cut him off from court chatter. But the Archbishop need not worry; his presence was an honor to Pontigny and the Cistercian Order. No one would ever contemplate asking him to leave. Such an act was unthinkable. There was much nodding as this was stated. Of course, as one devout elderly monk suggested, Thomas surely would not want anything harmful to befall this abbey which had welcomed him in his time of need.

The following day, a monk in Thomas's retinue left the Pontigny Abbey, riding east. He was atop the monastery's sturdiest horse. Within one week, the brothers working the vineyards were startled by the return of the monk accompanied by three smartly attired couriers from the court of King Louis VII of France. Their mission was to formally deliver an elegant parchment handwritten by Louis himself.

"Thomas, this summons, if you will permit a bit of humor, is long overdue. You must come for an extended visit. There is a fine monastery just south of Fontainebleau. And, of course, you must be my guest at the chateau often. I will be honored by the visit of a religious scholar. We have much to discuss. The men delivering this invitation will accompany you and your friars to France. I look forward to your arrival. Louis. Monarcha apud Deum"

"CHANCELLOR, THANK YOU for coming to see me on such short notice." Henry is expansive, waving Geoffrey Ridel to a richly embroidered chair in a small formal receiving room.

Ridel sits down, thinking that this sumptuous seat is surely mere ornamentation. Most visitors to this chamber remain standing. Perhaps he is the first to actually sit on this bit of artwork disguised as furniture. No matter. The king is in good spirits.

"I am always on call for the king."

"Well, I want to tell you that the Archbishop and his band of brothers are now in France, by invitation of the French king. They are situated in a monastery near Fontainebleau. I'm sure Louis is simply transported to be able to endlessly converse on churchy matters with his pal Thomas. And I am indebted to you for suggesting the means by which this invitation surely came about."

"It is my honor to serve you. Thank you."

"Geoffrey, I like your attitude. I should have made you Archbishop. We would make a great team."

"My lack of religious training would have been no impediment?" The usually grave chancellor permits himself a tiny bit of humor.

"Not at all. You could have studied on the side, as they say. Anyhow, another matter, the one I allude to from time to time. Still no trail, no clues?"

Chancellor Ridel shakes his head. "From the day of the Boulton battle until now, he's never been seen, and no one has heard one word about him. As I always say, he has disappeared from the face of the earth."

"I should have threatened decapitation of the entire family. That always works when you have many potential victims. Now I've lost momentum. Who knows if our fugitive would hear of it, or if he is even still alive."

"Yes." Every time Henry brings up Jerrard, the Chancellor asks the same question, but only in his mind. Why chase down the son of a disgraced dead nobleman? The family has lost land and power. The widow and children live in a small part of the castle, subsisting on the harvest of nearby fields and the small herds tended by castle servants. There is still something that Henry isn't telling him, and it is still something he doesn't want to know.

CHAPTER TWENTY-FIVE

ARCHBISHOP THOMAS BECKET and his four monks are welcomed into the fold of the Fontainebleau Abbey on the edge of the king's large estate. It is a new monastery, built as an after-thought to complete the needs of a pious monarch at his royal getaway. Grain fields surround its stone-constructed buildings. Nearby vegetable gardens are thriving. Just beyond, vineyards produce grapes to be stomped by feet in service to the crown. The forests here teem with wildlife; the lakes and ponds provide a variety of delicacies for the king's table; his archers bring more meals from the skies. The monastery monks, however, do not have agricultural duties. They serve King Louis VII in another way. They copy bibles. Thomas and his retinue must now learn how to participate in this sacred process. In his invitation, Louis had not mentioned the abbey's function. Perhaps the details of everyday life, whether royal or monastic, simply never occur to him. They have never occurred to Thomas either, nor to Jerrard, for that matter. These two men are in a new world.

"We have a stillborn! A stillborn. Praise to the Lord!" Abbot Germaine runs by the miniature cubicles where the monks sleep. Thomas's room is only a few square feet larger than the others. He hears the abbot continue his midnight wakeup call, prodding the friars from their slumber. "It's a fine one. Bloody, but good size. Hurry! We must start the skinning."

The English contingent has been in the abbey for only two days, just getting acquainted with its inhabitants, schedule and physical layout, scarcely long enough to learn its inner workings. But they are game for the night's challenge and shuffle behind the more seasoned monks to one of the outer buildings, now illuminated by many candles. A small wagon stands by the wide door, its hay stained red.

Inside, on a rough table, a newly born goat lies amid mucus, blood and flecks of hay. The animal is fully formed, healthy looking. It should now be learning how to stand up or figuring out how to draw milk from his mother. Instead, its eyes are open and glassy, and the abbot is fairly ecstatic.

"He will give us some beautiful parchment. Young skin is a joy to work with. Archbishop, you will see." Abbot Germaine turns to the scurrying monks. "Hurry, get the blood buckets so that the butcher can perform his magic."

Thomas and company stand aside. They don't have an assignment, so they will simply watch and learn.

A butcher from the Fontainebleau kitchen performs his work with precision. Notches and grooves in the table direct the red flow to the buckets below. Soon there is a pile of meat, a severed head and a stack of skins. The butcher's helper throws the dripping meat and head in the wagon, and quickly they are gone.

The friars throw the shards of skin, carefully cut into large sections, into vats now being filled with water from the abbey wells. As the clear liquid turns pink, then red, the men wash down the table and nearby floor. Soon the dissection room offers no evidence of the night's work. There remain a few hours for rest until dawn announces the day. The Englishmen follow their compatriots back to the sleeping compartments. Thomas and Jerrard lag a few paces behind.

"When the abbot told us we would be copying bibles, I didn't realize that we would be starting with parchment making." Jerrard is shaking his head with disbelief.

"Well, look at it this way. We will be learning new skills, in case I am replaced and you can't reclaim your earldom."

"Thomas, that's the first humorous thing you've said in a long time."

"Who says I'm joking?"

❈

THE KING'S SECOND INVITATION arrives as autumn surrenders to winter. The tone is identical to the letter which produced Thomas's departure from Pontigny.

"My dear Thomas, You have been in my fair land too long without a visit, and that is the king's fault. So many affairs of state to attend to, even here in the country. I would be delighted if you would be my guest at Fontainebleau. We will be in residence early in the new year. You may stay at length. My family visits frequently, and all would welcome your illustrious company. Please bring your attendants for your own comfort. Louis"

Thomas wrinkles his nose as he enters the vat room, where a pungent odor permeates every crevice and corner. Jerrard is throwing piles of calf, sheep and goat skins into large containers filled with water and minerals, primarily lime.

"Whew! Are you sure you want to be assigned to soaking? You're going to smell like a billy goat."

"I'm learning the whole process. After these have soaked for a while, we scrape the hair off one side of the skin and fat on the other. The lime water makes that step easier. Do you want to see the scraping done? Really interesting."

"Uh, no, I have letters to write. There are several excommunications that must take place in England, and I must complete them before I do anything else. The abbot has excused me, at least for the time being, from the parchment process."

"Remember what you said about new skills. I'm looking forward to cutting the dried parchment off the stretching looms. Then it's a finished product. Plus, it's a less smelly procedure." Jerrard's voice picks up an enthusiastic pace. "Then I graduate outdoors to finding tree galls, you know, the ones made by gull wasps, about this big." He points to the thumb end of his left hand. "And I cut them off the oaks, which are everywhere, and then I drain them and combine their liquid with tree resin and water, and then…"

"Enough! You sound like you are taking to the monastic life. That seems uncharacteristic, considering your upbringing."

"I've been living this life for three years, and I've learned to embrace its rhythm, in a manner of speaking. As I was saying, I will learn how to make gall ink, black ink. Later I will learn how to make colored ink."

"You exhaust me. To think that my task will be merely quill making, fashioning a receptacle for your many colored inks."

"Just make sure you don't kill any wasps. They are essential to our work."

"Listen, another matter. I have an announcement, but let's go outside and get some fresh air."

In truth, Thomas is less than enthusiastic about turning out quill pens. He is a scholar, not a tradesman who works with his hands. Jerrard appears to be more versatile, but then again, he is much younger. The two men walk silently down a tree lined path.

"Jerrard. Oops. I mean Brother William. The king has sent me an invitation to Fontainebleau. An extended visit after the new year, mind you. You must come along with the other English friars. The abbot will release you from your duties for a while."

"Haven't we been over this? King Louis knows what I look like."

"First of all, he hasn't seen you in a few years, *and* you have changed. Even if he looks straight at you, you are totally out of character. He remembers the young Earl of Boulton as an elegantly attired adolescent noble, not a monk in a brown cassock. Don't worry about it. I wouldn't take you into a dangerous situation. Besides, it will get you out of that putrid soaking room. I'll bet that lime water is bad for your skin."

"I use comfrey root. The brothers say it helps with the itching. Anyhow, I've always wondered if King Louis understood the oath I took before him. I doubt it. It's just another reason to avoid him."

"What oath?"

"It's difficult to explain. I mean, I don't want to explain. But I took an oath that I was telling the truth. And I was. But King Louis might not believe that. It all depends on how he remembers it. Oh, never mind."

"I will never mind. You're not making sense. Come with me to Fontainebleau. The other Canterbury monks are making the journey. Look, I will converse with the king. We have much in common. Truly he won't be interested in a lowly friar. You can pray with your peers or hobnob with Louis's relatives. I hear that Prince Arnaud's wife Emma, the one who beat out your sister Aldreda, is quite a lovely lady. You can talk to her."

"Sure."

CHAPTER TWENTY-SIX

"CHANCELLOR, READ THIS. A letter from Pope Alexander. What a way to start a new year. I had hoped that 1167 would see an end of this Canterbury mischief coming constantly from France. Instead, the Pope merely says that he has counseled Thomas to stop challenging me. He's sending papal emissaries to patch things up here in England. I tell you, he is mollycoddling a troublemaker and a thorn in my side. When will all this end?"

The king is pacing the length of his receiving room. Not invited to be seated, Geoffrey Ridel stands at one end of the room, waiting for a lull in the king's rant.

"But, Your Majesty, England is at peace. Your countrymen are content. Why are you not also? Permit me to say that your wrath, your indignation, your fury over this matter are vexing you in a way that does not permit your rightful enjoyment of ruling a powerful and prosperous land." Chancellor Ridel concludes his gentle rebuke of the monarch with this stroke of Henry's ego.

"I have a God-given right to be completely happy. Any word, by the way, on our other problem?"

The Chancellor heaves an enormous sigh. Would he not dash to the palace in the middle of the night if he had any news on the "other problem?" Truly he sometimes thinks his king has become unhinged by this matter that he still doesn't want to know about.

❊

"JERRARD! WILLIAM! Look at this letter that Pope Alexander has sent. Tell me if this is not the most unhelpful missive you've ever read. The New Year greeting is the only sentence that is acceptable. He says he has begged the king to allow me to safely return to Canterbury. Allow? Allow?" Thomas bats the letter, newly arrived from Rome, to emphasize his exasperation. "He should be ordering King Henry to beg for my return. Has the Holy Father no spine? And then, look at this paragraph. He advises me not to provoke the monarch any further. He should be advising the monarch not to provoke me. No, he should be telling the king, pure and simple, stop antagonizing the Archbishop, his prelates, his legates or any other churchman in England. Look at me, it is January and I am perspiring with absolute frustration at this matter."

"Thomas, please calm down. We are leaving tomorrow on a most pleasant journey to Fontainebleau. I never thought I'd say this, but I'm glad we're going. You are totally consumed by your battle with Henry. You need a respite from combat, if you will. Maybe the task of making quill pens has overtaxed your delicate system."

"It's only right that I should contribute something to this holy process. But you must admit that such work is hardly fitting a man of my stature and calling."

"Just consider yourself lucky that you don't have Father Silas hovering over you constantly, like this." The young monk jumps up and down, hands flailing at some unseen object. "'Brother William, Brother William, take care, a scraper is not a hatchet. Not an axe. A young parchment is a fragile infant. We must soothe it, caress it, just delicately removing its imperfections.' I tell you, Thomas, sometimes I think he has breathed too many foul fumes in the soaking room. I've decided that this getaway is a good thing. I just must be careful."

"Remember that you are safe because of me. And we have reached an agreeable, hopefully more than temporary, accommodation in our relationship." The Archbishop executes a nod of satisfaction, then changes the subject. "I do sometimes wonder if Henry is still looking for you. That's the only aspect of this whole conflict that entertains me, because my guess is that he is obsessed by you, simply obsessed, and that is likely making him a miserable monarch, which gives me something to be happy about. I am certainly not entertained by cutting slits in the nib end of a goose or swan feather."

"You have been cooped up far too long. You complain about everything. Henry. His appointees. The Pope. His representatives. Quill pens." Jerrard pauses, awaiting an objection, but there is none. "That happens to people who are isolated for a long time, so I hear. Well, you will be at the French court by week's end, and life will become much more exciting for you. Then you will be less testy."

"Promise?"

"I promise."

CHAPTER TWENTY-SEVEN

ALL SEASONS ARE MAGICAL at Fontainebleau. Outside, winter is waning. The days, less cold, are still pale. Inside, the palatial hunting lodge flickers with light, music, lustrous tapestries and the sounds of pleasure, the gratification of a multitude of senses. It's true that the king must attend to affairs of state, but ministers handle most of the day-to-day governing. Without an English war to prosecute, Louis's attention in recent years has been coopted by creature comforts which he shares with an endless stream of visitors, a well-born class of bon vivants and gourmands. He does set aside time for bible study, and daily he retires to his chapel to communicate with a Higher Power. Queen Adele, his wife, oversees the offspring of three marriages, although his daughters with Eleanor are now older and no longer require constant supervision. It is a well-ordered life. But a famous guest is expected, and this king is truly energized by the anticipation of stimulating conversations with his visitor, who is also a contemporary man of fame.

The guest wing chosen for the Archbishop's party faces east. King Louis made this choice. He reasoned that Thomas would prefer his morning prayers warmed by whatever thin rays the winter sun would send through his enormous glass window. The king had received word that the Archbishop of Canterbury's retinue would consist of four monks, all from England. Lavish rooms were prepared for these men dedicated to poverty and prayer; the reasoning was that Thomas should be pampered by his own coterie of religious brothers; therefore, they must be on call at all times and close by. Three of these men are unaccustomed to anything other than small, spare accommodations. For them, the extravagant décor and excessive comforts require additional daily prayers, asking forgiveness for partaking in such immoderate living. Each petition to God includes a caveat: "I am here, Lord, as ordered by His Eminence, the Most Holy Archbishop of Canterbury."

For Jerrard, the lush rooms are certainly a cut above the baronial splendor of Boulton Castle, but the guest chambers boast a feature found in most castles, the garderobe, a small cubicle jutting out from the wall of each bedroom. In the abbeys, monks must use a chamber pot as a receptacle for personal waste. The garderobes at Fontaine-bleau, like those at Boulton, permit the user a seat which opens over a pit at ground level. Yes, the odor sometimes creeps upward on a muggy day, but at least the pampered aristocrats do not have to haul their distasteful discharges to a dumping pit, like the one at the edge of all monastic properties.

"Just like home," exclaims Jerrard, after opening the ornate door to his spacious quarters. He has not had his own garderobe for over three years.

❊

THE FIRST DAY'S DINNER, served mid-afternoon, is a splendid celebration. Thomas dines with the king and queen, their children, an assortment of the local nobility, a few government ministers who happen to be on call and Prince Arnaud with his wife Princess Emma. King Louis has learned that the Archbishop favors a particular wine sauce served with either pheasant or goose. The royal chef has been charged with creating this perfection for the esteemed visitor. The chef, however, has not reached the pinnacle of culinary success by being a mere copier of fine dishes. He has an idea that will ensure his employment at Fontainebleau for years to come. Early in the morning, two kitchen orderlies are sent out to slaughter a colorfully feathered fat young peacock.

While the chef spends the day huddled with his wine sauce attendants, a battalion of kitchen workers carefully separates the skin of the peacock from the meaty torso. It is a painstaking task; the skin cannot be torn, and the feathers, still brilliantly alive with bright pigments, must remain intact. The peacock meat is then chopped, washed and simmered in a broth made from chicken bones. Imported spices are tossed into this brew. Few Frenchmen have access to these savory seasonings from the East, but the royal cooks flavor imperial meals with herbs and condiments that spill into the crown treasury as taxes, customs fees and sometimes ransoms.

When the platter piled with pungent peacock meat is served, there is applause from the royal table. The cooked meat, akin to chicken in taste, is topped with the feathered skin, as if the entire bird, except for the head, had just landed among the diners. Though uncooked, the skin's underside is also coated with exotic spices which drip onto the simmering entrée. The presentation is done while three live male peacocks are led around the dining room, unaware that one day they may adorn the king's table still wearing their fine feathers. This spectacle is part of the dinner entertainment. A single female peacock is tied to a pillar at the end of the room.

The peacock walkers use a straight pole instead of a leash. They know the birds can be unpredictable, especially when mating, and this is the season. The male birds howl, scream, meow, cackle, and groan, often emitting sounds that are simply indescribable. The object of their affections ignores this cacophony of noise and struts triumphantly at the end of her tether. The diners howl, too, at this amusing production, while scooping up the meat from under its blanket of skin and feathers.

The English monks and lesser guests dine in a small but elegant room off of the main dining area. They are served the same dinner;

however, their peacock, served with Thomas's favorite sauce, is absent its feathered canopy.

Jerrard is fascinated by the dessert. It is called Spiced Quince Butter Cake. At least that's what the presenter calls it when questioned by the monks. They have never seen a quince, a bright yellow pear-shaped fruit grown in sunny south France. The cake, flavored with sugar, almonds, cinnamon, nutmeg and cloves, is a true treat. After delighting in a second helping of this delicacy, Jerrard asks to see the raw fruit. Then he tastes it.

"Just like an apple, a pear and an orange. Three in one. Very nice." He wonders if south England, where the Boulton estate is located, could be home to a quince orchard. Then he catches himself, thinking that he is foolish to ponder a future orchard when, as of right now, he no longer possesses any land anywhere. Not likely either is there any-thing left in the Boulton Castle spice room, once a place where one could go just to breathe the intoxicating aromas of faraway lands. It's just not healthy to think about such things. He returns to his quince and finishes it.

During the meal, Jerrard catches bits of conversation and laughter from the king's table, out of sight, but not far away. Thomas is clearly the center of attention. His voice resonates answers, quips, musings, opinions and piety. The king's speaking style is likewise recognizable from their 1163 meeting. Arnaud contributes from time to time; he clearly has not given up the pleasures of fine wine. Jerrard imagines the king's brother taking a third helping of the quince cake, with al-monds tumbling down his magnificent vest.

There are female voices as well, but they are more muted, less easy to identify. Jerrard wonders if he is listening to Emma or the queen or a nameless countess. He remembers Emma's voice; he even re-members her words about being betrothed to someone across the water, about being able to visit her sister Catherine. Hopefully she has been able to do that. He thinks about Gweneth, something he rarely does. There is so little to remember. Does anyone know she is dead?

What about the Sothinghams? Would Henry tell them? It likely depends on how Henry views Lord Bertram. If the king has possibly forgiven him for aiding the Boulton forces, then perhaps he has also divulged the sad news, telling Gweneth's parents how the queen's midwives fought to save their daughter. If there has been no forgiveness, Henry may have told them that Gweneth is just locked up permanently. For the first time since fleeing England, Jerrard wishes he were home so that he could know what was going on in his native land. He excuses himself and makes his way to the Fontainebleau chapel.

Candles and light filtering through richly stained glass windows illuminate the place of prayer for palace inhabitants. Paintings that depict biblical scenes adorn the dark walls. A huge crucifix dominates the altar. The air is heavy with the weight of worship. The chapel is always open. In this late afternoon, a few individuals are scattered throughout the nave. Some sit silently, as if pondering an important question. Others are bent in prayer, knees on the tuffet constructed for supplication, heads bowed, eyes closed, hands clasped. A woman is standing opposite an oil rendering, dark and sad, of the Madonna and Child. She is mumbling, seeking intercession, for something, from Mary and Jesus.

Jerrard chooses a pew near the back, on the right side of the center aisle. He always chooses this location, wherever he prays, and he does not know why. Just like he doesn't understand why he is comforted by his calling, if being drafted into monastic service to avoid capture can be termed a calling. But he has never felt that he is engaging in a deception; he does not view himself as a fraud. Certainly King Henry would call him dishonest, duplicitous, double-dealing; Jerrard is amused as he adds up all the words beginning with the letter D that the king would use to describe him. What is he really then? Co-owner of a treasure? Yes. Man on the run? Yes. Parchment and ink maker? Almost. Former earl-to-be? Sadly. Monk with a mission? Maybe.

He wishes that Thomas could be his mentor and real friend. They have an accommodation, and it is temporarily working. But the archbishop so clearly sees his role regarding what is due the papacy.

Jerrard also wishes he possessed such certainty. He is nearly twenty, and it is time to give up the doubting that interferes with taking possession of one's future. Doubting. Another D word. He must stop this childish word play. It is time for prayer.

"Brother, excuse me." The interjection, in perfect English, penetrates Jerrard's conversation with the Lord. It is a female voice, resonating authority and privilege. It is also, strangely, on his right side. He nearly turns to see who has entered the pew from the outside rather than the aisle, but his head movement is interrupted by a reflex of caution.

"Brother, you are seated in my favorite pew. You must be new here. Everyone knows I like the right side, though, if asked, although I've never been asked...who would do such a thing....I would say that I don't know why I prefer being on the right side, this far back." The voice carries many tones. Softness. Power. Youth. Complete self-assurance. It is remotely familiar.

"Oh, pardon me. I beg forgiveness. I'm part of the Archbishop of Canterbury's retinue, and I'm unaware of chapel protocol. I am embarrassed to admit that I do not know how to address you, since I don't know who you are." Jerrard squirms in his pew, trying to turn a bit to the right to have a better look at the elegant figure seated a few feet away from him. He hears a gentle laugh.

"Then you are the only person in France who doesn't. You are forgiven for that and likewise forgiven for sitting here. I'm feeling very generous today. It must be the peacock dinner and quince pie."

"Oh, you favored that, too? I've never eaten such a delicious dessert. If we could just grow quince in England. You know, have orchards on monastery land. We monks would all be fat."

"I think England is too chilly and foggy to support quince orchards."

"You know England? Your English is perfect, but you are French, right?"

"Yes to both. I am from England, the earldom of Cambridge. And I speak French because I am Emma, princess and wife of Prince Arnaud, brother of the king. That makes me French, too. And who are you?"

In his state of shock, Jerrard almost blurts out his given name. Recovering from that, he is simply dumbstruck. It is Emma. Emma. He had wondered if he would encounter her, but had persuaded himself that such a meeting was unlikely, despite Thomas's suggestion. After all, the friars do not accompany him in his frequent engagements with the royal family. Now, here she is, attired in a voluminous dress, her chestnut hair billowing under a magnificent tiara. He cannot get a good look at her face without revealing his own countenance. She is awaiting an answer, and he is still reaching for the words that elude him.

"You hesitate to make yourself known to me. Are you a fugitive, a false friar eluding the king's law by hiding in his chapel?" The princess's query echoes amusement.

"Your Highness, certainly not. I am overwhelmed by your presence." Jerrard recovers and offers an answer. "I am Brother William, originally from the Wilshire Abbey, then assigned to the Canterbury Cathedral, becoming aide to Archbishop Thomas at Pontigny and now at the Fontainebleau Abbey."

"It is a pleasure, Brother William. You may be seated just over there, in case I have any liturgical questions to ask you." Emma motions to the same row of pews on the left side of the aisle.

As Jerrard obediently slides toward the aisle, he hesitates. A tiny and insignificant question has entered his head, and he feels compelled to ask it.

"Your Highness, uh, Archbishop Thomas mentioned a while back that Prince Arnaud's wife has a sister in the Aquitaine. Have you been able to visit her?"

Emma throws a startled look at the receding friar, who squints to get a glimpse of her face. She is lovely. And serene. That is unexpected. He is relieved that the hood of his cassock renders his own face a shadowy mystery. Why did he have to pique her curiosity with such an ill-considered question? She continues to peer at him, a suggestion of a furrow beginning in her brow.

"Brother William, that strikes me as an odd question, coming from a monastic friar. But I guess you are isolated for much of the time, so perhaps I should think nothing of it. Yes, I have visited my sister Catherine. Or, I should say, she has visited me. Twice. My husband prefers that I remain in France."

※

LATER, THOMAS AND JERRARD sit before the fire in the guest wing receiving room. The Archbishop is regaling his young aide with tales of the dinner and its entertainments. The conversation must, of course, include a detailed description of the peacock parade.

"Jerrard, I've just never seen anything like it, and I thought I had been a witness to many mealtime diversions. They are stunning creatures, but such a racket."

"I know, I heard it."

"What did you think of the presentation of the meal? You know, the feathered covering."

"We didn't get any feathered covering. What are you talking about?"

"I'm surprised that your father didn't serve something like that at one of your banquets. That would have been his style." Thomas is meandering, the visions of the ornamental peacock meal still dancing in his brain.

Jerrard is persistent. "Feathered covering? You had feathers on top of your meat?"

"No, no, the feathers were still in the peacock skin. It was lain atop the cooked meat. Actually, I was told that spices were dripping from the underside of the skin. It added to the flavor. Truly an inventive manner of serving."

"The animal skin wasn't cooked, right?" Jerrard asks this with a grimace.

"I guess not. How could it be cooked with the feathers on?"

"I must say, I am happy that I was not at your table."

"Why is that?"

"When we skin anything – deer, boar, birds, anything – the meat goes to the kitchen and the skin goes to the tanners. Even the peasants don't gnaw the underside of the pellets. If it's not cooked, it's not safe to eat."

"Well now, I will recommend you as an advisor to King Louis's palace chef. You are obviously a culinary expert." Thomas allows himself a touch of sarcasm. Just in fun. The beginning of his palace visit, with an excellent dinner and an evening huddle with the French king, has been something of an ego booster. It is reminiscent of his long-ago stimulating discourses with another monarch.

Jerrard is likewise in the midst of his own thoughts. "I think the French grow different kinds of stomachs, or else they start out with stomachs like ours, but train them differently. Do you know they eat a fungus, out of the ground? It's called a truffle. They use pigs to find them. Of course, the pigs like fungus, too. So do rats. So the French people compete with pigs and rats for fungus."

"Do tell. What else?"

"They spread their breakfast bread with mashed goose liver. Sometimes duck liver, too."

"Jerrard, where do you get this kind of information?"

"It's written down. How's this? They give wine to little children. Daily."

"I had beer as a boy. You know that some of our water is not so good. Alcohol is much safer. Perhaps the French have the same problem. Shall I ask the king?"

"Ha ha. Thomas, I bid you goodnight. And I hope your English stomach survives the spices that dripped from an uncooked bird skin. You might spend the night looking down the hole of your garderobe. See you in the morn."

"Good night, Jerrard."

CHAPTER TWENTY-EIGHT

THE ARCHBISHOP'S VISIT extends from winter into spring. King Louis is delighted to engage in a daily discourse with such a learned churchman. In March, papal legates pay a visit, to bring news from Rome and greetings from Pope Alexander. They also have instructions to discuss, with Thomas, the fractured relationship between the archbishop and King Henry. In his many conversations with the French king, Thomas has learned that the pope's effort to placate Henry stems from a current papal dispute with Frederick, the German emperor. Alexander needs Henry's support to put an end to his own humiliating, if temporary, exiles engineered by Frederick. The legates urge Thomas to petition the king for permission to return to England and, once there, negotiate a settlement. This pandering to Henry, in the mind of the archbishop, is unacceptable. King Louis, always ready to oppose the English monarch, supports Thomas. Letters cross the water, both ways, and the rancor is increasingly notched up.

While the men of power conduct their business, the English friars read and pray. They do eat well. Only Jerrard is privy to the reason that the visit is so long. He retires to the chapel each day, often sitting across from a princess of France. From time to time, she quietly asks a question about a biblical passage or the origin of a prayer. Thomas was absolutely right. Jerrard, dressed as a monk in his brown hooded cassock, simply could not be the same person as an elegantly attired young nobleman. Shedding his fear of discovery, he responds to the princess, leaning into the aisle, muting his answers to avoid offending other worshippers. His tutelage becomes more lengthy, more complex. Emma is curious and inquiring. She is a frequent visitor to the chapel, staying for at least an hour each time she takes possession of her pew. Prince Arnaud never accompanies her. All of this perplexes Jerrard, but he dares not ask any more delicate questions. He simply slips into the role of religious advisor, and he derives much satisfaction from it.

This day in late March has been like the others. The afternoon sun is dipping low as another lavish dinner comes to a close in the royal dining room. Jerrard leaves the other friars and goes to the chapel. The princess is in her regular place.

"Brother William, please sit here." Emma pats the wooden pew on her left side. "I wish to ask some questions, and it would be easier if you were right here." Her voice is friendly. It is a request, not a command. Jerrard moves across the aisle and sits down. Only a few feet separate the friar and the princess.

"Why did you say I was ugly? And fat. With a malformed leg. Bulging eyes. Wart." She taps her chin. "Lisp." Emma's whisper shouts outrage. "Do I sound like I have a lisp?"

Jerrard jumps as if he had been slapped. He rubs his right ear to make sure it is properly affixed to his head. Then he says the only phrase that makes any sense.

"Would your highness care to walk the gardens with me, so that we may breathe the spring air while discussing the New Testament?" The words just roll out, surprising the person who utters them.

Anyone taking a post-dinner garden stroll would spot the contrasting twosome. A royal princess, known to be religious, and a friar, likely a studious man of the cloth giving spiritual instruction. She is English, and he is English. Perhaps some of their conversation is about home. They both look straight ahead, observing all the proprieties.

"Look, I can explain. But first, how did you know it was me?"

"I have known since that first day when you were sitting in my pew. Did you think I was an idiot in addition to being ugly and malformed? With a lisp."

"Thomas assured me that no one would ever recognize me. I really believed that." Jerrard is truly amazed at his unmasking.

"Thomas does not understand the thinking of a young girl about to be kissed. She absorbs the moment and the person who has shared it with her. She does not forget that person." Emma stares at a bare tree.

"Oh." Jerrard's eyes are locked on the same tree.

"My husband was truly surprised when he first saw me. He was prepared to marry and hide. You certainly gave him cause for delight. And I get it. You described me as a toad in order to further your sister's betrothal to Arnaud. Then you took an oath, on the bible, in front of the king, that your description of me was unrelated to that. Shame on you. The king remembers."

"Wait. Let's take this turn and go through that grove of trees. I have something important to tell you. Actually, two things. Related things." Jerrard reaches for Emma's elbow to guide her down a new path, then remembers that protocol denies such a gesture to lowly Brother William. He drops his arm and turns left onto a new path. Emma follows.

They walk into the woods. There is no conversation.

"Alright." Jerrard stops and, for the first time, turns and faces Emma. "I made up all those things about you so that Arnaud wouldn't want you as his bride. How was I to know that he didn't really have any say in the matter?"

"What?"

"This is hard for me to say out loud because I've never really said it at all. I didn't want you to marry Arnaud because I liked you. As you said, you were 'about to be kissed.' That had been my plan that evening we were together. Before everything changed."

"What changed then?"

"That's something I can't talk about. At least now. But here's the second part of what I want to say. My oath, on the bible, in front of

King Louis, and I wish he remembered it correctly, because I do, my oath was that my description of you was in no way related to my father's offer of my sister to be betrothed to Prince Arnaud. So now you know the reason I said what I did."

Her Royal Highness, Princess Emma of France, stands mute.

❋

THE GUEST WING is in a flurry of activity when Jerrard returns. A carriage stands outside the entry. The Archbishop's chests are being loaded. The other friars are busy packing their simple belongings. Jerrard runs into the suite occupied by Thomas.

"What's going on? Are we leaving?"

"Yes, we are. We're returning to the abbey. I've made our proper excuses to King Louis. And our thanks. Get your things together." Thomas is bustling around his spacious quarters, checking all the wardrobes and chests.

"Why? That wasn't the plan this morning." This is truly a day of surprises, not all of them good.

"The pope has sent a message that Henry is provoked that I am luxuriating in such an extended vacation at the French court. Our king and Louis are squabbling again. And, of course, Alexander is pandering to Henry's wishes, so he has ordered me, all of us, to return to the abbey and get down to work, making parchment, ink and quill pens. I've been promoted to copying bibles. Not that I mind doing the Lord's work, but it is truly stimulating to be here."

While his mind spins with the news, another part of Jerrard speaks out. "Perhaps, Thomas, the Holy Father feels that the endless high life here is inappropriate for an archbishop. Maybe he wants you to return to your calling, to be a shepherd of the church."

"Don't preach to me. Remember that I am protecting you. Get your things together."

"Princess Emma knows who I am, and I don't want to leave."

Thomas stops his room inspection and stands motionless. He looks like he has been smacked by an altar boy.

"How did this happen? Did you tell her? Don't you realize how dangerous this can be?"

"First of all, I didn't tell her. She said she knew the first time she encountered me. So much for your theory of losing one's identity behind a hood and cassock."

"If she tells anyone, we are both in a lot of trouble."

"She hasn't told anyone so far. I don't think we need to worry."

"Given this unwanted news, please tell me, please enlighten me on why you would want to stay." Thomas's voice is in a crescendo of anger and astonishment.

Jerrard's lips tighten. He glares at Thomas, but does not answer.

Thomas returns the look, then begins to nod his head in the manner of slowly understanding an unfolding picture. "So that's it. You fancy the princess. How far back does this go? I will say, you've been a busy young man. Marrying the Sothingham girl to secure an army for your father. Now you're a father with a daughter who is, what, three years old. You're an ex earl-to-be, an excellent parchment maker and a religious scholar. I am impressed. You are also a huge threat to our common interest. Get your things and get into the carriage."

CHAPTER TWENTY-NINE

NORMANDY IS IN THE FULL FLUSH of summer. Children play at the edge of the Seine River, where the bank abuts shallow waters and the current is slow. King Henry and the Duke of Normandy are riding along the bank, a part of a day's outing to examine the ducal properties.

"Henry, I want to show you a project that your truce has made possible, even though I know it might not be a permanent truce. But, anyway, I am realizing a dream I've had for decades. You will be pleasantly surprised."

"Cousin, I like surprises. Onward."

Rounding a bend in the lazy river, they come upon a small army of men digging in the bowels of an abandoned canal. An embankment of earth and rock has been constructed to prevent the Seine from washing into the new waterway, measuring about thirty feet across. The duke is giddy from excitement.

"You see, Henry, we're going to follow the route of the old canal back to the castle. Then we'll re-dig the moat. I tell you, the improvements I'm designing are way ahead of their time. First, we will seal up the garderobes. No shit will fall into my moat. The servants can haul it away daily to fertilize their little carrot gardens, or whatever they do with it. Maybe seal the holes in their huts. So I will be surrounded by a lovely pond on all sides. Perhaps I will import colorful fish to swim in it. I've heard that there are pretty fish of a golden hue in the eastern lands. Have you heard of this?"

"I haven't. Would you eat them?"

"Oh, no, they will just be a decoration. I will have little boats made for the grandchildren. The boys can have their version of sea battles. And there's more. You know the people north of us, the Dutch, have these wooden paddles in the air, turned by wind. Very clever. I'm going to import some workers from up there, and they are going to build one or two for me right next to my moat."

"Interesting, my dear duke, but why have air paddles next to the water? Are you going to fan the golden fish?"

"Now Henry, I have a mind suited to subduing nature. The power of the air paddles will turn a wheel in the water. The water will move. Voila! No more standing water. No more summer bugs. Very good for the grandchildren. And," the duke nearly falls off his horse in his enthusiasm, "there will be one larger boat for me and my guests."

"Do you also plan to play in the moat, now that you have de-bugged it?"

"You're amusing yourself at my expense, but when you visit me next, you will take a boat ride with me, from the castle down this canal to the Seine where we will board an even larger craft for a pleasure ride. Tell me, does the king of England have a shit-free moat plus a canal that goes to a major river, with proper sized boats for all three bodies of water?"

Henry scratches his head, searching for a response.

"See, I thought so."

❀

KING HENRY RUMMAGES THROUGH the leather bag which holds the royal pens. Most of the quills are made from goose feathers, a manly grey-brown color. He is looking for another one. It is white, a swan feather, the one whose duty it is to not only express greetings and convey news, but also to seek peace.

"My dearest Eleanor," Henry swipes at a bug with the feather of his quill pen and thinks of the duke's waterwheel. The old man might be on to a useful idea. Of course, if war with the French resumes, always a possibility, the canal, boats, wind paddles and all the rest may go down the garderobe into a dry, smelly moat. Best not to discuss that with the aging duke.

"What a day it has been here at the Normandy castle. My cousin is well and bristling with ideas. He sends his regards. My next stop is Anjou, then the Aquitaine, where I will give your family your affectionate greeting. Some time you must go there with me to renew your acquaintance with your people. I know they would feel so honored with a visit from you.

"Kiss the children for me, starting with our teenagers down to baby John. Remember to hug the little Boulton girl. She is sweet. Must have come from her mother. I would be so happy if you sent me a letter that her father was apprehended in trying to take her from us. Of course, I will be happy to receive any letter from your lovely hand. You see, I remain an optimist, hoping that on my return you will have forgiven my lapse that has caused you so much grief. I am your supplicating husband, Henry."

CHAPTER THIRTY

THE FONTAINEBLEAU ABBEY is exceptional in its location, on the fringe of the French king's vast property, and distinguished in its mission, the production of bibles, but in more time-honored ways, it is like all other abbeys of the Catholic faith. It is a place of quiet reverence, dedication to work and an adherence to an unbroken cadence of life. After their return from the woodland palace, Thomas and Jerrard resume their duties, awaiting the next turn in their respective uncertain futures.

A year passes, slowly. Thomas has mastered the flowery font required for the heavy bibles. Some days he chooses a goose quill; on others he chooses a swan feather. It is a matter of mood. Because he is right-handed, his pens always come from the left side of the fowl; the curvature of the left-side feathers is toward the outside of his right hand, hence also out of his line of sight. In his early training, he had watched these lengthy feathers being expertly shortened to avoid tickling the nose of the writer, then being hollowed, shaped and slit at the opposite end to permit intrusion by ink. Now, when he is not dealing with papal or royal representatives, he sits at a large wooden desk, with a top raised to an agreeable angle, working on the Old Testament, his long-term assignment. It is demanding toil for both hands; in his left he holds a knife which will scrape away any errors before they dry, and he scrapes frequently.

The archbishop is adamant in his refusal to allow the legates from Rome to adjudicate his case with King Henry. He understands papal politics. He will return to England on his terms, excommunicating his enemies, including Gilbert Foliot, the Bishop of London who is handling the archbishop's clerical duties in his absence. He will redefine the relationship between the crown and church, and this time he will have Pope Alexander's support. The reason? He will have delivered the Aureus to its rightful owner. One small problem vexes him in his planning. What will he do about Jerrard's half? He is a man of honor, and he cannot resolve this quandary.

During this interval, Jerrard and the three other English monks continue to establish their usefulness at the abbey. Formerly the geese and swans were plucked for feathers when they were already lifeless, being readied for the dinner table. Swan meat was especially popular because of its duck-like flavor. But the young men had learned that plucking live birds produces stronger pens; each time a bird is de-feathered, it produces hardier writing instruments for the next quill harvest. The monks become shepherds of the flocks, herding the geese and swans into encampments the day prior to plucking, a practice which enables them to deny the birds any food twenty-four hours before the procedure. In this way, the birds do not soil the feathers, and the final product is pristine and ready for final pruning.

Like Thomas, Jerrard considers the options awaiting him. Going back to England is dependent upon the peaceful return of his mentor, the Archbishop of Canterbury. How then will he secure the ownership of his half of the treasure? Can it remain hidden in the cathedral? Will he continue to be safe in his friar persona? There is something else, something that penetrates his thoughts by day and dreams by night. Princess Emma. Nearly a year has passed since their walk through the woods and his revelations to her there. She had turned around and walked away, then stopping to turn back to him.

"You have awakened something in me that I made go away when

I came here and married. It frightens me. I must keep the promise made by my father. But I don't want to."

Then she had turned again and run, in a most unprincess-like way, through the trees.

MEMORIES. THEY BECOME Jerrard's sustenance. He carries out his duties daily, soaking skins in the vat room, stretching and cutting the parchment. He combs the surrounding woods for tree galls and makes dark ink from his acorn-like treasures. The flocks of geese and swans must be tended, and he does this laughing at the antics of his squawking charges. At dusk he retires to the chapel, built and adorned to the specifications of King Louis VII. This place of prayer is unpretentious, but not humble. The wooden pews and kneelers are hand-crafted, but there are no cushions to soften the act of worship. The small stained glass windows have been fashioned by royal work-men, but most of the light comes from candles made at the abbey. The altar is small and stark; behind it rises a magnificent Florentine rendering of the crucifixion. Still, Jerrard feels at home in this chapel; its contradictions reflect the contrast between the two men who re-side within him, the son of privilege and the brother of the church. He wonders, can there be a synthesis between the two? The year passes into another.

CHAPTER THIRTY-ONE

IN THE SPRING OF 1169, the tempo of abbey life is rocked by a proclamation delivered by a single emissary from the French court. The king has decided that he must cleanse his soul by going on a religious retreat. The duties of the monarchy compel him to remain close to Fontainebleau, but the requirements of a retreat dictate that he must sequester himself in a spiritual surrounding. Therefore, he has selected the abbey on the fringe of his royal property to be his abode for one week; he will meditate during the day and sleep at night as a simple friar.

Abbot Germaine is in a full frenzy. The coming days will be filled with the promise of cheery breezes and sunlit afternoons. The nights, however, will be cold, and the monks sleep in cubicles that are warmed solely by their own bodies and thin coverlets. Hopefully the royal party will bring extra blankets. And the king is bringing some of his family! Of course, the abbot is honored by the prospect of Louis's stay, but he will also be accompanied by eleven-year-old Margaret, the third of his five daughters. Oh, dear, a girl. Well, at least he is bringing only one of his children. It could be worse.

The king will also be accompanied by his sister-in-law, Princess Emma. Her husband, Prince Arnaud, has declined the retreat, citing the importance of his position as the monarch's brother and perpetual stand-in for the many court functions that must go on. He intones a blessing on his wife's spiritual inclinations, regretting that he cannot join her in this devout undertaking.

The English delegation is to be moved to the vat and stretching rooms. Temporarily, there will be a hiatus in the production of parchment. The writing rooms will likewise be converted into dormitories. The king will occupy the abbot's quarters; the ladies will occupy Thomas's room. Their courtiers and servants will have to make do in the friars' cubicles; they are accustomed to the occasional inconveniences that come with the backstairs imperial life.

The chapel is scoured clean. The vermin who consider the sanctuary their home must, at least for a short time, find another place to settle. In the abbey kitchen, rodent remains and other unwelcome visitors are swept into pots normally used for cooking and dumped in the area reserved for the daily waste emanating from the building complex.

Throughout all these frenetic preparations, Jerrard is silent, performing his duties as if he were enacting a pantomime. Thomas, however, is fairly undone by the prospect of Princess Emma's visit.

"Jerrard, why don't you go off into the French wilderness for your own retreat? You simply cannot be here when the princess comes. The two of you will give yourselves away. I am sure of it. All these years of sacrifice, of denying ourselves will be for naught. Just find somewhere to go!"

"I'm not leaving. This is something that had to happen. I have been praying on it for a long time."

"You leave the praying to me. And then leave. Period. You hear?"

"Archbishop, you are not the only one who is entitled to speak to God. Look, other matters need your attention. The English church is in a shambles. You said so yourself. Ask Louis to be an intermediary, so that Henry will allow us to go home. I want to move forward, and I want to move forward on English soil."

The archbishop ignores the suggestion. His mind is focused on only one thing. "If you so much as kiss the hand of a French princess,

King Louis will parade your head around the swan and geese pens, letting them peck your eyes out."

"Thomas, you're so eloquent. Do not worry. I will keep my head. King Louis is coming here to retreat from the lavishness of court life and find his way in simplicity and austerity. I will assist his family in doing the same. He will like that. He will not recognize me."

"First I have King Henry to deal with, then the pope and his politicking, then King Louis, who once promised numerous visits to his woodland palace, then Foliot, whom I appointed. And if that's not enough, now I have you to contend with, you whom I saved from sure death. This is my thanks."

"I'm sure there are nights that you exclaim to the heavens, will no one rid me of this contentious friar."

"Nonsense, who would say such a thing?"

THE ROYAL CARRIAGES in the abbey courtyard offer a glittering contrast to the somber buildings beyond and their cassocked inhabitants. The monks have taken a vow of poverty, chastity and obedience to a Higher Power and their superiors in the church. The French monarch is a distinguished guest, but once he sheds the trappings of his regal station, he blends into the daily litany of prayers and meditation. His dutiful daughter Margaret accompanies him throughout most of the day. At times she walks the grounds with her aunt, Princess Emma, to behold the accomplishments of monastic life.

"Aunt Emma, I hear that King Henry is in Normandy. His son Henry is with him. Couldn't we take a trip there when the retreat is finished? Normandy is not so far. I could meet my future husband."

"Why are you asking me? You should ask your father if we can journey there. Anyway, I'm not sure you should see young Henry. What if you don't like him? You will just brood until your marriage. It's better to enjoy the next few years. The wedding will come quickly enough."

"We've been betrothed since I was two years old, part of some truce with the English I was told, but I wasn't curious until recently, and now it's really building up. Everyone says that King Henry is handsome. His son should be handsome, too, shouldn't he?"

"Oh, Margaret, I do wish your mother were alive. She would know, better than I, what to say to her daughter. Queen Adele does want the best for you, but you know, she is preoccupied with raising a future king."

"Did you see Uncle Arnaud before your marriage?"

"No." Emma turns quickly down a path that borders a well-tended vegetable plot. "Look at this wonderful garden. I would say that we will eat nutritious food while we are here, even if it isn't elegant."

"Aunt Emma, what did you say to Uncle Arnaud when you first saw him? I'm thinking a lot about that. I must rehearse something clever to say to Henry."

"I said 'I do.' We were at the altar of Notre Dame, getting married."

"Well, I guess that made it easier. You're right, I suppose. If I wait for the wedding, I won't have to think of anything clever. I will just play the part written for me. Easy."

"Yes, easy."

❁

"FATHER."

"Yes, what is it?" King Henry looks up from his lounge in the king's quarters of Normandy castle. He and his eldest son have just returned from a boat excursion on the now completed canal. As promised, this waterway provides recreation and a means to journey to a larger boat on the Seine River. Today, the duke, King Henry and a small party were rowed to the Seine and back to the castle.

"Father, we could ride your cousin's big boat to Paris and visit King Louis while we're here. I would like to see that city. I also would like to meet the king's family. His wife the queen. The children, too. We're not at war anymore."

"You want to meet children?"

"Well, you know, the one I'm betrothed to. I figure that she's eleven. Margaret, I mean. She must be starting to turn into a woman. I would like to look at her."

"Is this desire infecting other members of your generation? I hope not." The king swats his thigh with an exasperated hand. "Just look at it this way. You could be married to her for, uh, possibly twenty, maybe thirty years. A long enough time to look at her. Concentrate on the young ladies in waiting. Or a scullery maid or two."

"I'm just curious, that's all."

"Save your curiosity for what's under all those skirts." Henry shakes his head. "Kids." Then he has an afterthought. "Anyway, the king and his family are probably not even in Paris. More likely they're at Fontainebleau, greeting archbishops and other hangers on. We have more important things to do."

THE WHITE QUILL IS DIPPED in a blue-tinted ink. Henry hesitates before beginning his letter. He has not seen his wife for months, and he wants to select his words carefully. "My dearest Eleanor, Normandy is taking up too much of my time. The duke, as always, is a charming host. His moat floats an armada of children's boats. His canal is a marvel. He is taking pleasure in his old age and, hence, losing a taste for war. I must work on this. Our conflicts with France are never-ending, and I will surely need his aid sometime soon.

"Our son has expressed a desire to meet his betrothed Margaret. That won't happen. I don't want to pay a social call on King Louis, even if we're at peace this season, and I'm not in favor of the children meeting until right before the wedding. But then I remember our first encounter at the French court. I believe the phrase is *love at first sight*. Our passion stunned the entire continent. We broke all the rules, and

I am still glad we did. Our young Henry would be shocked. Kiss the children for me. Find clemency in your heart and wait for me in your chambers. Your devoted suitor, Henry."

CHAPTER THIRTY-TWO

IT IS MIDWEEK of King Louis's retreat. He moves through the abbey like a ghostly figure, breaking his chapel visits and meditative strolls with brief visits to the dining area. After evening vespers, he returns to the abbot's room for his final prayers before retiring.

Princess Emma and Princess Margaret follow a similar routine, but they spend more time outdoors than the king. Today Princess Emma is alone near the swan and geese pens, now empty because quill plucking has been suspended during the French king's stay. The birds have been relocated to a corner of the monastery property, sparing the monks and their guests the squawking chorus that inevitably accompanies the periodic arrival of the feather providers. Today the area seems desolate. Only one friar is taking a similar stroll.

"Brother William," the Princess calls to the cassocked figure. He turns slightly.

"Brother William, it is I, the chubby, bulgy-eyed, wart-faced princess." Emma pronounces *princess* with a decided lisp. "You remember me?"

Brother William turns the rest of the way around. The cowl of his garment covers his forehead and eyes. His cheeks are buried in the flapping material. Only his nose and mouth can clearly be seen. Emma is looking at a very broad smile.

"I do remember you. My, you've changed." The smile grows larger. Jerrard breaks into a stride that is more Boulton than monastic. He stops in front of the princess. "Tell me why you came on this retreat."

At first Emma says nothing. She turns toward the abbey buildings. Jerrard fears she is going to sprint away, just as she did on their last parting. He is wrong. She stays and holds him in her gaze.

"It has been more than a year since I saw you. You've dominated my thoughts. I know it's wrong. Wrong for more than one reason."

"What do you mean?"

"First, I am married. I've taken vows, and I will not break them. You see, my faith has sustained me since I came here, and I cannot turn my back on that faith because of..." Emma hesitates, searching for the right word, "...because of feelings. And yet I'm here. It's such a contradiction."

"What's the other reason?"

"The obvious. There is no way to change these circumstances. I've devoted a lot of time to thinking about getting from here," Emma points to her delicately stitched footwear and then to a nearby grove of trees, "to there. There is no way." Her words are steady, but there is sorrow in their tone.

Jerrard closes the distance between them, but he does not touch Emma.

"It is possible that I may have a solution. I do have a solution. The details are a challenge, but it can be worked out. That's all I can tell you."

Another voice penetrates the afternoon. It is Thomas, and he is swiftly approaching on the main path.

"Brother William, you are needed at the abbey. Pardon me, Princess Emma, but this is important. Brother William, come now." The voice is a command and not a pleasant one.

"Emma, I will bring you home."

"I TOLD YOU TO stay away from her. What were you thinking?"

"We were discussing her faith, surely an acceptable topic on a retreat."

"You're just like King Henry. Women. Women. Women. Like Eve in the Garden of Eden. Always a temptation. Would that the Almighty had figured out another manner of procreation, we would all be better off." Thomas throws his hands into the air. "I've just had enough on so many fronts that today I have taken some extreme measures. I've excommunicated Bishop Foliot and a number of his followers. The Pope won't like it. Henry won't like it. I don't care. Foliot will complain that he and the others didn't get a fair warning, and I don't care. By this time next year, I plan to be in London, and I don't want to have to resume my duties surrounded by such disloyal and disobedient men."

"Disobedient? I'm surprised you haven't excommunicated me."

"I should, after your performance today. The only problem is that it would call attention to your existence, and that would indeed be a problem. So, you may remain cradled in the arms of the church, though you don't deserve it."

"Thank you, Thomas."

"And stay away from the princess."

"As you wish."

What? The uncharacteristic obedience startles Thomas. Is it possible that Jerrard finally understands the danger posed by his interest in the French princess? Or is his agreeableness just a smokescreen, a ploy to keep Thomas from further meddling in his personal life? The whole situation is deeply troubling, and Thomas understands why. He and Jerrard are not only fellow fugitives and co-owners of the Aureus, they are also spiritual brothers with a shared devotion to church teachings. And they have become something else. Something that he knows is a true gift, as rare as a golden treasure. They have become friends.

Jerrard sequesters himself in the quill outbuilding for the duration of the royal retreat. He has a plan. It will take time, but the plan will work if Thomas can negotiate a return to England. The treasure awaits them, secure in its hiding place for much of the past decade. He is sure of one thing: The king does not know the size of the Aureus; he has never seen it, with the exception of one coin skimmed off the top by an unlucky peasant. Thomas has told him that the legend surrounding its existence is vague about its actual size. This will give him room to maneuver. After Thomas sends his half to Rome, Jerrard will use part of his share to buy back his rightful place in the traditional social fabric of English society. The Archbishop should help him with that; Thomas has never rejected his plea for aid in restoring his baronial rights and property. The church's official position on a divinely blessed social order supports Jerrard's position.

After reclaiming his title, Earl of Boulton, he will take back his daughter, now five years old. Having been gifted with a pile of gold coins, Henry will likely not object; he has many legitimate children plus several bastards, enough in every age group and each sex to marry into all the courts of Europe and their attendant noble families. The rest of Jerrard's gold, still hidden, will have another purpose. For that, he will await the right moment. He will be patient, biding his time until there is an opportunity to accomplish his final goal. He is thinking like a noble of the realm.

And yet, his alter ego, Brother William, ponders his ambition, his end purpose. What has he learned in the past six years? His accidental vocation has given him a certain inner peace. He understands and embraces the tempo of monastic life. What if he didn't own a portion of a bounteous treasure? What if he were like all the other monks, bound to a lifetime of poverty, chastity and obedience? He searches for an honest answer from himself, aware that the temporariness of his position may have always made that life more palatable. At least he is sure of one thing; prayer and meditation have brought more self-awareness than he could have ever imagined. Introspection had never been a desirable asset for young men of the baronial class. Yet daily he gives thanks for the gift of self-examination. And so, his inner dialogue continues.

CHAPTER THIRTY-THREE

"CHANCELLOR RIDEL, I am proceeding with my plan to crown young Henry as junior king of England." Henry holds up his right hand to fend off his chief advisor's expected objection. "Yes, I know, you already told me that it's not a good, what was the term, not a good political move. My great-grandfather would not have had such a phrase in his vocabulary. What have we come to? It's a shame that a monarch must deal with differing points of view, though I guess I'm used to it."

"I hold to my opinion, Your Majesty. If you crown your heir during your lifetime, it may give rise to speculation that you are ill, which can only give comfort to your enemies, make them feel stronger."

"You and I both know that it is to make a point with my other sons. Richard and Geoffrey are rebellious. So is John, even though he is really too young to know what is going on, but nevertheless contributes his fair share to the trouble. A fine lot I am raising. My boys are worse than the barons." He lowers his voice. "Thanks to their mother."

"The other thing, sire, is that traditionally the Archbishop of Canterbury conducts the ceremony. Surely you have thought about that. Don't we already have enough trouble in that area? My emissaries throughout Europe report much distress about the English crown's long-term dispute with its highest churchman, who is essentially in exile."

"I know I must get this matter resolved, but the coronation will proceed without Thomas. The Archbishop of York will preside. Besides, Foliot got his excommunication set aside, with nothing but a little slap on the wrist from the Pope. I'll invite him to attend." Henry allows himself a chuckle. "That will really annoy Thomas. Wish I could be there when he is told that York will preside with Foliot in attendance. Ha ha."

The chancellor shakes his head and takes leave of the king. "Really, Your Majesty, don't you have better things to do than look for ways to nettle Thomas Becket?"

Henry watches Ridel bow and recede. When the chancellor is nearly out of the room, he shouts, "No I don't. It amuses me."

THE SUMMER OF 1170 is warmer than usual. Most of the monks at the Fontainebleau Abbey are toiling in the vegetable gardens, coaxing young plants into maturity with buckets of water carried from a nearby stream. Only Thomas and Jerrard are in the parchment drying room. Thomas is pacing while waving a parchment scroll embossed with the papal seal.

"He thought he was getting away with something. Ha! Crowning young Henry as Junior King of England. Ha! Without my presence. Ha! Well, read this. It's from Pope Alexander, and it gives me the right to put all of England under interdict. See, even the Pope cannot accept such an affront to my position."

"What's an interdict? I've never heard of it."

"It's the act of excommunicating a whole country, a very rare thing. No Englishman can participate in any of the sacraments. No Christian burial in the whole land. All of England will go to hell because of King Henry." Thomas looks out the window at a distant land now delivered to Satan. "I signed the interdict today. A papal envoy is coming from the castle to pick it up."

"Uh, Thomas, we're Englishmen. Are we under interdict too?"

"What?"

"We're English. What about us?"

"Oh, don't worry. This will force Henry to come to terms with me and allow me to return to England as the head of a much stronger church. Then I will lift the interdict. Just don't die any time soon."

"I'll be very careful."

NEWS OF THE INTERDICT shocks Henry, who had assumed Pope Alexander was balancing alliances from the sidelines and would not take sides in the coronation matter. But an interdict had to have a papal sanction. A nation excommunicated! Never has a monarch presided over the denial of salvation to all his countrymen. The king knows this will produce massive unrest throughout the land. The solution is simple: Invite Thomas to return home to England.

The interdict is withdrawn.

BEFORE HIS TRIUMPHANT RETURN to London, Thomas has promised himself a stop in Normandy to present himself to Henry, who is once again visiting his old cousin. Ostensibly his detour is to thank the monarch for ending his six-year confinement on the continent. But Thomas has another final arrow in his quiver, and he cannot resist firing it, even though Henry has sent a personal letter assuring him of a lifetime pension from the king's own vault, a gift of reconciliation.

The archbishop has a final entry in the bible which has occupied most of his last two years at the abbey. He adjusts his writing desk, knife in his left hand and quill in his right. Just a few more words and 2 Kings 25 will be completed. It will be a good place to end his short career as a scribe.

"29 And he changed his prison garments: and he did eat bread continually before him all the days of his life.

30 And his allowance was a continual allowance given him of the king, a daily rate for every day, all the days of his life."

❄

"YOUR MAJESTY." Thomas executes a deep bow.

"Archbishop." Henry returns the bow, not quite as deep.

"This is just a stop, as you know. We must keep moving to the coast. But I wish to acknowledge Your Majesty's largesse in bringing our difficulties to an end and offering such a generous compensation to me for my many years of anguished absence from my homeland." Thomas had rehearsed this short tribute. It sounds good to him as he recites it. He punctuates his words with an engaging smile.

"It's my pleasure to resolve a most unhappy time in our relationship. Now to other matters. Oh, yes, I have a question. I understand that you have been accompanied by four young friars since the beginning. This is most unusual for an archbishop."

Henry stops to gauge the Archbishop's reaction, which is stony silence.

"As I said, most unusual. One personal servant is generally the only aide to our most revered churchman. But you have four young men. Do you like young men?"

Thomas blinks. His smile evaporates.

"I have spoken with three of them. They seem normal enough. The fourth, well I am still looking for him on the castle grounds. How do your monks amuse themselves when they are not in the company of the archbishop?"

"I have no idea. Prayer, I suppose. What is your point?"

"There is from time to time a rumor here and there about priests, bishops, you know, and young men, sometimes young boys. Certainly you have heard such talk."

"I have. This is unspeakable, even by your standards, Henry." Thomas's rage reverberates in a hiss. "We are leaving," He swerves and then stops. "Oh, and one more thing. I almost forgot. I've excommunicated Foliot again and a few others. You will receive their names tomorrow. Good bye."

The archbishop's carriage exits the Normandy castle, crossing the moat with golden fish and tiny watercraft. It is going faster than usual, which is making it a bumpy ride for Jerrard, who is hidden under the driver's bench.

CHAPTER THIRTY-FOUR

THE BELLS OF THE CITY CHURCHES ring endlessly, as if they cannot suppress the joy they are proclaiming. A procession through London, at first comprised solely of the Archbishop and churchmen, grows in size and frenzy. Onlookers cheer, then join the parade of celebrants, all shouting thanks to heaven for the return of Thomas Becket, Man of God and, today, Man of the People. It is a triumphal, hours-long march, past ordinary shops, courtly homes, fetid slums, government buildings, the royal palace, ending at the gates of the city's largest church, St. Paul's Cathedral. Common people reach out to touch the archbishop's flowing robes. The priests and monks who follow him throw coins and small pouches of wool and leather to the crowd. It is a day of victory for one man, who thoughtfully sends church messengers on horseback to ride the kingdom with the announcement that its beloved Archbishop Thomas Becket has returned to do his holy work for the people of England.

The following day, Thomas excommunicates more priests and bishops who participated in the crowning of Henry the Junior King.

By the time the word of the new excommunications reaches Henry, still lounging in Normandy, it is late autumn. Orange leaves float above the golden fish in the moat. The ladies no longer wish to ride the canal boat to the Seine; it is too chilly. The duke, his sons and

King Henry have just completed a fine day's outing on the water. There is a small crowd at the boat dock awaiting them.

"Your Majesty, we have come from London." The speaker is a priest. The Bishop of York stands behind him, nodding. "We came here to beg you to return to England. The Archbishop of Canterbury has excommunicated all of us here. Just because we participated in the coronation of young King Henry. You told us that we would not suffer in any way from Thomas Becket if we took part in that. Now we've all lost our positions, not to mention that we cannot take the sacraments, and if we die...well, it's just terrible. Please come home and fix things."

The cluster of clerics murmurs its agreement with its spokesman. They are clearly agitated. The bishops have had, from time to time, a taste of church politics and court intrigue, but only Foliot, who is not among this throng, has ever known the most severe punishment that the church can levy. The rest of the group, ordinary priests, are frightened and beseech their monarch to save their souls by his intercession.

"Please help us, Your Majesty!"

"I am up to here with this man!" Henry shouts his anger as he bumps his Adam's apple with his right hand. "Do you know that I gave him a lifetime endowment from my own funds? How's that for gratitude? He hands out excommunications like you distribute grain to your peasants, my dear cousin."

THE WINTER SKIES gather over Normandy.

"I cannot relax by day nor sleep at night. This man is a pox on the House of Plantagenet. He sends horsemen throughout England to proclaim his divine return. Next thing you know, he will try to invalidate the coronation of my son. He's up to something. I should never have let him come home to England."

AUREUS

Snow sprinkles the Norman countryside. The castle is ablaze with yule candles. While the duke's large family prepares for Christmas, Henry convenes a council to advise him on reasserting his authority.

"I just want all of you to know that I befriended Thomas Becket when he was a young man without prospects. Intelligent, yes, but no family name to propel him anywhere. But I saw the budding talent, which could have gone either way, and I nourished it and promoted it and gave him a shot at high office. No other monarch would have made a man of such ordinary birth his chancellor, then his archbishop. And this is the thanks I get from a...an upstart clerk. All of you sitting around this table, you who are supposed to be advising me, will none of you rid me of this turbulent priest?"

THE SWAN QUILL IS DIPPED in blue black ink. Henry's hand trembles; he cannot subdue his emotions.

"My dearest Eleanor, Once again you pass the Yuletide season away from me. I hope that the Aquitaine rejoices that its most famous daughter is once again home, but your estrangement from England and me saddens my heart. Is not a great monarch entitled to grand missteps on occasion? Is not a great queen one who bestows grand clemency? Tell the children I miss them, too. Your husband, Henry."

Later that night, four knights of the council ride their favorite horses over the castle drawbridge and out into the cold December night. Their names are William de Tracy, Reginald Fitzurse, Hugh de Morville and Richard le Breton, and their destination is England.

CHAPTER THIRTY-FIVE

"IT'S LIKE WE NEVER LEFT, THOMAS. The coffins, their place-ment and colors. The carvings on the sarcophagi. We could have been taking this walk yesterday, last week."

"The Father who watched all these crypts, I wonder if he is still around. There's so much to catch up on. At least we are sure of one thing, though truly I was never worried about our mutually owned, ah, possession."

"Have you ever thought about what our lives would have been like if the Aureus hadn't made an appearance?"

"I have made it a point to avoid *what ifs*. Anyhow, what is *your* point?"

"Well, think about it now. Here's the irony. We are likely among the richest men in the world, and yet we have lived as wanderers. And I as an outlaw. Without the Aureus, I would now be the young Earl of Boulton, overseer of a grand estate with a place in the crown councils. I would likely be married with a family."

"And perhaps I could even guess the name of your wife, if your father and the Earl of Cambridge had come to terms."

"You likely could. As I was saying, without the treasure, I would be living a most comfortable life, and you, my dear Archbishop, would have commanded Canterbury from its splendid altar all these lost years, maybe even patching up your differences with the king."

"Not sure about that last part, but perhaps these years were meant to be our walk in the wilderness, our path to becoming better men. There, you see, the *what ifs* don't solve our questions about the future. So let me tell you what I am going to do. I've been giving this much thought, but we've had little opportunity to seriously talk since we returned to all this hoopla and merriment surrounding our welcome."

"Shh. Wait. Footsteps."

The two men stand in silence. There is a scurrying sound. It fades away.

"Mice. Rats maybe. Go on, Thomas"

"My life is filled with comfort. King Henry has increased my income with a monthly stipend, probably his guilty conscience working. Anyway, think back to the beginning of our partnership. At that time we both at least considered the idea of denying the other his share of the Aureus, right?"

"Right."

"Yet you told me some time ago that you would not have done that if your father had lived, though I don't know how you could have successfully opposed him."

"I don't either, quite frankly."

"You are, as always, refreshingly truthful. So I must likewise be candid. Because of my position, I was always trying to justify the denial of your share to you. As the defender of the church's interests, I felt an obligation to bring all the Aureus to Rome."

"Something akin to your dispute with Henry, at least at the beginning."

"Exactly. But like you, I could not justify doing such a thing, not to anyone, certainly not to a friend. So, without further ado, I renounce, on behalf of the church, any claim on your share. Take your half and buy your way back into baronial society. Hopefully there's something left of your estate. I will help you any way I can, as soon as my share is safely on its way to Rome."

"Thank you, Thomas. We are moving forward. Our journey, and it has been quite an adventure, has been a real revelation for both of us."

"It's a good thing. I'm getting up there in years."

"Oh, Thomas, you'll be around here for a long time. Canterbury is your milieu. The people love their archbishop."

"I hope you will visit from time to time, when you are Lord Jerrard and running things in Boulton."

"Of course. We will discuss parchment making and peacock dinners. Old times, but you're not rid of me yet."

"I know. I just had a little pang of regret, that's all, losing my long-time companion. But as you say, not for a while. Well, now that Christmas is past, we both need to get completely moved back in and get about our normal routine. Right now I'm going to the chapel to say another prayer of thanks for our homecoming. See you at vespers, Brother William."

THE CATHEDRAL NAVE is empty when Thomas approaches the altar. He is wearing a richly woven robe, his favorite golden cape, to ward off the late December chill. On his head is his ceremonial miter. The decision to wear his headdress was purely last-minute, a desire to recreate the ritual denied to him so many years. For a short time, he stands in front of the mighty cross that dominates the top of the stairs. Then, step by step, he climbs to his place of prayer and drops to his knees.

"Our Father," Thomas begins, then hesitates. There is a clatter behind him. The noise, a cacophony of disrespectful clanking sounds, offends him. He turns to admonish the source of irreverence. There are four men running down the central aisle, swords raised, banging them against their shields. The archbishop rises in anger, raising his hand to put an end to this outrageous intrusion in a House of Worship.

The men are yelling something about arresting the Archbishop. Their words, jumbled angry words, are hard to understand, but Thomas has no interest in their clarification.

"Get out! You offend this cathedral. Get out!"

"You dare to throw us out of here. We represent the king, and you have offended His Majesty King Henry the Second!" Hugh de Morville, in front, charges up the fine red carpet, taking two steps at a time. "You offend the king, so you die!"

The clamor increases as he is joined by three assassins with raised blades.

Above the altar, the painted eyes of angels look down, in anguish, on the bloody scene. Four swords slash and cut, they are pushed in and pulled out, the shields tossed aside to prevent interference with the killing task. The golden robe is splashed with crimson; then the sun color disappears altogether, and the garment glows a wet red. The archbishop sinks slowly, his fall hampered by the jostling of his attackers, his right arm still raised in admonition to the offense committed on this sacred site.

The Norman knights do not hear it, but a choked voice whispers words from a dying heart. "Henry, I forgive you."

THE BELLS OF ENGLAND should be joyfully ringing in the year of 1171. Instead they toll sadly throughout the land. The church's horsemen, who usually transmit papal edicts and news of local appointments, carry a message which stuns barons and peasants alike: Thomas Becket, Archbishop of Canterbury, is murdered in his cathedral by Norman knights.

Never, never has there been a murder of an archbishop in a consecrated church. The populace is stunned, nearly dazed, then angry. This was an unspeakable act. The perpetrators were said to have returned to Normandy, where they were received by the king without punishment. How can that be allowed? King Henry had kept England's highest churchman in exile for six years, and when he returns, he is murdered within a few months. In Bridge Town, the peasant folk remember Henry, the Savior king, and shake their heads. Now he is king with an archbishop's blood on his hands. Feudal superstitions, barely dormant, reemerge. Has Satan taken hold of the monarch?

Monks, priests and bishops begin to use the word *martyr*. King Louis, genuinely appalled at this outrageous event, sees an opportunity to advance his position with the Pope at Henry's expense. All of Christian Europe is exhorted to condemn the English king's involvement with the killing. The largest landholder on the continent is depicted as an ally of the devil.

Ignoring the uproar, Henry travels to Ireland to deal with rebellious local kings. Only a frantic dispatch from his chancellor forces him to confront an unraveling situation and return home to London, where he orders the arrest of de Tracy, Fitzurse, de Morville and de Breton. They are dispatched to Rome where the Pope orders them to serve fourteen years in the North African Crusades to earn forgiveness.

Even news of this so-called punishment, when it is finally dispersed throughout England and the continent, does not improve Henry's stature. He is Europe's most powerful king, and he is despised.

CHAPTER THIRTY-SIX

JERRARD IS ALONE in the Canterbury crypt. The archbishop, in a temporary coffin, lies nearby, just a few feet from the coffin holding the Aureus. Jerrard has come here every day since the murder. He does so because he feels lost everywhere else.

"Oh, Thomas, we three are together again today. You, me and our pot of gold. We've been bound together for a long time." Jerrard rests his forehead on his clasped hands. "I want to send you to Rome, accompanied by your gift, but the church says you must remain here, awaiting canonization. Think about it: Saint Thomas Becket. Saint Thomas. Wow." He pauses, letting sainthood sink into his brain. "In the meantime, I will find among your things, things I've been asked to catalog, a document written by you stating that one of your neighbors down here should be sent to Rome for his final resting place. I've decided who that will be. There've been a lot of candidates to choose from, very deserving candidates, but Father Junius is my favorite. His name is so Roman-sounding anyway."

Jerrard's daily conversation continues. "I like talking to you, Thomas, just like old times. Of course, it was better when you answered, even when your answers were scolding me about something. So, I will tell you of my plan, and you can't interrupt me. Ha ha!" Another pause is punctuated by a muted chuckle. "Remember when you copied the bible at Fontainebleau? Well, I used to read from your script. Every day. It was so well done. Your writing style is indelibly imprinted on my brain. The document about Father Junius will be pure Becket. I wonder if there is a word for copying someone else's handwriting and signing someone else's name. I don't think so, but some day there will be, I'm sure."

The visit is concluded, and Jerrard walks through the crypt to an obscure sarcophagus, now four centuries old. He stops, pats the cold stone and says, "Father Junius, I've chosen you for an important assignment. Don't fail me. Rest well in Rome."

The choice had to be a stone crypt. It would be very heavy and difficult to transport, but the extra weight would not be noticed. Three prelates accompanying Father Junius will also carry a sealed document addressed to Pope Alexander. The document, in Jerrard's hand, but in Thomas's style, will convey an unearthed treasure to the Holy See from the Archbishop of Canterbury. Noting that both men have experienced exile at the hands of a monarch, the "Thomas letter" thanks Alexander for his support during his years away from his post. He closes with a wish to once again see the Pope. A separate parchment in Jerrard's more rugged writing style states that he, Brother William, is carrying out the wishes of the deceased Archbishop. While writing it, Jerrard thinks about his father's long-ago fabricated missives paving the way for his visit to the French court. "Well," he muses, "The creative letter writing trait I inherited from the House of Boulton is now perhaps enabling Brother William to do some good."

Jerrard's two-year-old plan to buy back his heritage has undergone revision. Since the murder, he has, more than ever, prayed for guidance, and he has come to a decision. Though Thomas, in his role of Archbishop, might applaud it, Thomas his friend, Jerrard believes, would caution against it. No matter. Jerrard will honor his mentor and take his chances. Once Father Junius successfully completes his journey, he, the friar appointed to sort out Thomas's personal papers, will find another Becket document, this one addressing the delicate matter of consanguinity in a royal marriage. No wonder Jerrard labors far into the night, quill in his right hand, knife in his left.

"CHANCELLOR, I CANNOT TOLERATE what is happening. There are reports from all over the realm that I am some kind of demon, that I ordered the murder of the archbishop. This is preposterous! I come home to stories about the evil king of England, and those stories are about me. The latest that I've heard is that I murdered Eleanor and the boys. And she won't return from Poitiers to disprove this nonsense. You're my most important advisor. Advise me now. How do I end this? I cannot sleep!"

"Your Majesty," Geoffrey Ridel paces in front of Henry, seated on a kingly chair in his palace meeting room, "The problem begins with your exceedingly hot words uttered to a room full of men, some of whom taking these words to heart as an order, or at least an invitation, to commit a terrible crime. Except for the four culprits, the others, the witnesses, seek to distance themselves from the murder of a man who is becoming a martyr to many Englishmen. They have become quite vocal in extoling the virtuousness of Thomas Becket."

"Oh, don't I know. I guess Thomas's clothing and possessions are in high demand. If you touch his robe, dear Chancellor, you will be rid of red pustules on your face and scabies on your back. Your withered leg will become strong, and death will be snatched away from your glazed eyes and soundless heart. And so on."

"I am informed by the personal representative of Pope Alexander that there is strong support in the church to canonize Thomas. The Pope supports this, and steps toward sainthood are already underway. Sire, pilgrims travel from the faraway corners in our kingdom to pay homage to Thomas's shrine at Canterbury. Your enemies, foreign and domestic, take comfort in this."

"As I said, advise me, Chancellor."

"Yes, well, here is how I see it. Since Thomas's unfortunate death, you have increased your power and land holdings all over the map by artful marriage contracts and excellent diplomacy. Other crowns of Europe are perhaps within your grasp, and there is talk of your becoming the King of Jerusalem." Geoffrey Ridel, having begun his presentation with truthful flattery, now proceeds to the more delicate portion of his plan. "If you can erase this stain on the crown of England, you will be perfectly positioned to take these next steps on the continent."

"I'm listening."

"You may not like what I propose, but I am certain that if you follow my suggestions, you will be able to put all of this unpleasantness behind you."

"I'm still listening."

"You must do penance. You must perform acts of atonement. You must accept guilt for Thomas's murder."

"What? I am the king. Anointed by God. I do not do such things. Such drivel. I pay you for better advice than that."

"With all due respect for your person and your divine right to rule, I strongly urge you to publicly, and frequently, perform acts of penance, beginning with pilgrimages to Thomas's shrine at Canterbury."

"Beginning with?" Henry is astonished. "What else?"

"The public should see their king stripped to the waist and whipped by humble Canterbury monks. This would be an act of contrition wherein you beg for Thomas's forgiveness, and you should do it more than once."

Henry simply glares at his Chancellor.

"This will reunite you with your people and certainly improve your relations with the church."

Henry rises from his chair and walks toward Chancellor Ridel. His right hand is raised to punctuate his words, but his mouth is unable to form them. Silence follows him as he turns to an art-filled wall and fixes his eyes on a painting of cherubs floating above unclad maidens cavorting in a meadow. The Chancellor stares at the vacated chair, hoping that its recent occupant will set aside his stubbornness and take good advice.

Henry is now jabbing a finger at the cherubs, as if to rebuke them for ogling the naked nymphs. Chancellor Ridel holds his breath. The king's internal debate is a favorable sign, but how many times has the chancellor expected an affirmative response only to be surprised by an outburst of petulance and a monarchical veto.

"Birch branches would be alright. I understand that the cuts are mild, and there are no scars."

"Thank you, Your Majesty. You will not regret your decision."

"And the other matter?"

Geoffrey Ridel shakes his head, not only as a response but as a gesture of wonderment. It has been over seven years since King Henry began his search for the young Earl of Boulton. The lad, now a young man in his twenties, is gone. The king seems unable to accept that. Once again, the chancellor thanks the heavens that he is not privy to the contents of this dark secret. Thomas certainly was, and he is dead.

A SINGLE FIGURE IS SEATED in a pew on the right side of the aisle, near the back of the Fontainebleau chapel. It is a young woman wearing a sedate tiara. Her hands are clasped. Her lips move in prayer. She does not hear the figure walking down the center aisle until he slides into the pew, moving close up to her.

"Arnaud! You surprise me. What are you doing here?"

"I came to pray with my wife. Is that not what a good husband does?"

"You haven't done it before, or at least it has been a long time." Emma turns to her husband. No one else is in chapel. She speaks in a normal tone of voice. "So why are you here now?"

"You have been distant. Always. I understand that. But in recent years, more so. Have I offended you in some way? I would like to please you, you know."

The prince is sincere. Emma does know that. Nearly eight years of marriage have taught her that Arnaud is not offensive. Unless, of course, he is engaged in one of his epicurean marathons. She can describe the elaborate dishes served by the food he is wearing on his generous cape. But aside from this distasteful character flaw, her husband has been kind. He has tried to entertain her during their infrequent times spent alone. There have been no children, a situation troubling to Arnaud, but not to Emma. She doesn't know why.

"You have pleased me by joining me here. Let us pray."

CHAPTER THIRTY-SEVEN

THE CAISSON PULLING THE STONE COFFIN leaves the Canterbury Cathedral on a clear cold morning. It is barely sunup, and the dirt roadway still awaits the daily foot traffic. A small grouping of monks waves a send-off to the guardian prelates, one of whom carries another Thomas letter to the Pope.

"First Father Junius. Now Father Ancelus. Soon our crypt will be bare, and all our blessed souls will be sleeping in Rome."

"Oh, we'll never run out of dead saints," Jerrard laughs. "If we all do good works, perhaps we will be rewarded with an eternal hibernation in Canterbury."

"That may be sooner than you think, Brother William. You display much bravado in volunteering to thrash the king here at Canterbury, but he may find a way to punish you later on. Don't whip him too hard. I hear Henry has an unforgiving nature."

"Tell you what. I will allow the other friars to administer a painful flogging, and I will tickle the king's toes with my young birch branches."

"You joke, Brother William, but you'd better hope that King Henry genuinely wishes to do penance." The young friar stops. His lips tighten. He wipes some moisture from his right eye. "How I miss Thomas. He was my beacon. At least *he* will remain here now that we have a beautiful shrine for him."

❈

THE DOVER BARGEMEN GROAN upon sighting the second arrival of a sarcophagus bound for Rome. The first one took days to load upon the strongest boat, but the crossing was easy; now another arrives. True, the summer weather is pleasant, and the waters are calm. But transporting a blessed father of the church is not normal work. The workers pray loudly that they will complete their mission, allowing this second soul to continue its journey to the Holy Father. A sunken boat would be an affront to the Almighty. How many more dead saints must cross the water? Is this somehow related to the murder of the Archbishop? On their knees, they beseech the heavens to grant an uneventful crossing to the continent.

Their prayers are answered.

❈

THE SQUARE FACING the Canterbury Cathedral is filled with peasants and barons, shop keepers and herdsmen, country squires and gentlemen of the court. Some women and children stand at the fringes of the crowd. The word has been spread to the nearby estates and settlements; the king will do penance by being publicly flogged, and his subjects, curious and uneasy, have come to witness this extraordinary event.

It is not the king's first display of public contrition. A month before, he journeyed to Northampton, site of Thomas's unfinished trial, to prostrate himself before local friars who were instructed to whip his bare back in the city's small park. But the onlookers were intimidated by the presence of Henry's personal militia, well-armed and led by Sir Mallory, looking especially fearsome. Most slinked away before the whipping commenced, if one could even call the event a genuine flogging. The friars were timid, and, at the end, the king's back barely revealed a scratch. Chancellor Ridel had attended to critique this dress rehearsal, and he had insisted that the main event at Canterbury should take place without any royal militia in sight.

Dressed simply but wearing his crown, Henry arrives without courtiers or armed guards. He is accompanied solely by his servant Duncan, who will take charge of his horse.

The king dismounts, walks to the center of the square where he removes his shirt. The murmuring of the crowd has diminished to a low hum. Unlike Northampton, the throng is growing larger. Duncan is uneasy as he takes Henry's shirt. He is holding the reins of two horses, and they are skittish.

"Give them an apple from my bag."

"Aye?" Duncan appears not to understand.

"Give each horse an apple from my bag. Take one for yourself, too."

"Oh, yes, yes sire. Sorry." Duncan pulls only two bright red apples from the royal saddlebag. He is not hungry.

"Tell them I am ready."

Duncan nods and takes a breath. He dutifully proclaims his memorized words.

"His Majesty King Henry II of England, founder of the House of Plantagenet, presents himself to his esteemed countrymen to do humble penance for the death of Thomas Becket, the Archbishop of Canterbury."

On cue, four young monks from the Canterbury jurisdiction walk from a cathedral side door to the square's center. Each carries a handful of birch branches. Henry falls to his knees.

The king's words, uttered at ground level, are easily heard by the monks who descend upon his form, flailing their branches as if they are warming up for their task. The onlookers cannot hear, and they press forward. The crowd movement is a static that punctuates the sound of the monarch's repentance: "Dear Lord, I am to blame for the death of Thomas Becket. My thoughtless words, uttered in anger, resulted in his murder. It was a terrible crime against his person, committed in Your sacred house of worship. For this, I am doubly guilty. I beg your forgiveness. Beat me, please!"

The monks comply, and the thrashing begins. The king alternately prays and begs for heavenly absolution. Red marks begin to appear upon his back. Henry throws his head back, shouting submission, pleading for more pain. He appeals to each of his punishers to whip him until he bleeds remorse. He looks squarely at each monk.

"You! You! I would know that face anywhere."

AN ELEGANT CARRIAGE drives through the Fontainebleau gates. Its direction is north, but its occupant's ultimate destination is England. Royal guardsmen ride alongside to escort it to Calais, a port city on the channel.

A dejected figure sits at a palace window, watching the carriage grow smaller and smaller. A single tear blemishes his pristine white vest.

"Oh my dear Emma, I didn't know we were related, but the Pope cannot be wrong. Maybe that's why we never...Better not to think about it. Better to have a grand feast today. Maybe some wine will ease my pain. Perhaps my brother can arrange a union with a Saxony bride. Surely we have no blood ties there. Oh, I am so unhappy. But tomorrow is another day. Tomorrow is another day."

The wetness on the white vest evaporates in the midday sunlight. Arnaud rises. It is time to dine.

CHAPTER THIRTY-EIGHT

"BROTHER WILLIAM, BROTHER WILLIAM!" The young Canterbury friars comb the offices of the cathedral after checking the main nave and finding it empty. They split up to search the grounds and the home of the archbishop. At the gate, the horses bearing the royal militia display their riders' impatience by pawing the bare ground. One of the monks waves and cries out, "We are still looking, but this is a big place. We will find him."

"Somebody go to the crypt. He is known to meditate there." Brother Roland takes charge of the search.

"I didn't know that. Why? It's such a cold place."

"Just go. The soldiers are making me nervous." Roland glances at the horsemen.

"You nervous? Wait until Brother William sees that they are here for him. He's the one who will be nervous. And rightly so. I told him not to be so enthusiastic about the flogging. But no, he wouldn't listen. And now look, King Henry's personal militia."

"Just go, I said."

"Why don't *you* go down there and look for him?"

"I'm superstitious. All those dead eyes staring at me." Roland tilts his head and points his glassy gaze upward. "Don't tell anybody, but the crypt gives me the creeps. Creepy crypt. Crappy creepy crypt. Ha ha."

"Oh, no, another brother who thinks he is a comedian. Where do you get that stuff?"

The two young men laugh, but a shout from Sir Mallory ends their merriment.

"Okay, I'm used to going down there. Roland, you stay here and keep the troops entertained.

"Brother William, there you are. We've been looking all over for you."

"I come here to meditate. The silence soothes me."

"Well, this news is not so soothing. King Henry's personal militia is at our gate. They have a summons for you from the king. Also, a horse to carry you to the palace. Dear brother, I fear for you."

"Don't worry, I'm happy to have a visit with our monarch. I've been expecting this invitation."

THE ELEGANT CARRIAGE comes to a halt near the water's edge at the port of Calais. A watercraft bearing the French king's royal insignia is waiting for its single passenger. Several trunks are dragged from a small surrey behind the coach and loaded onto the boat. Finally it is time for departure. Emma boards the sturdy cog, its sails already flapping in anticipation of the voyage, and turns her face to the south, to Fontainebleau.

"Good bye, France. It has been an education. Now I am going home."

SIR MALLORY LEADS JERRARD into an austere room occupied by a small throne and little else. The king is talking with his chancellor and a few councilors.

"Here he is, Your Majesty." Mallory gives the young monk a small push forward.

Jerrard stumbles, then regains his footing and begins a deep bow. The king waves his hand at the small circle of men surrounding him.

"Out, out, everybody out." As one, the assembly follows Mallory to the heavy door. "No wait, Chancellor, you stay."

"Uh, Your Majesty, I do not wish to intrude upon your private visit with this Canterbury friar. I'll just wait in the visitors' hall. Not far, if you need me for anything."

The chancellor's exit is blocked by the king's arm and voice.

"No, you stay. And you," pointing to Jerrard who is completing his bow, "You can terminate this insincere display of respect and stand up straight."

The heavy door closes, leaving the king with two men, one reluctant and the other at the desired end of a long journey. Silence. Candle flames lap at the heavy air, but the near noiselessness is not tranquil. The chamber vibrates with tension, anger and hope.

King Henry speaks. "Chancellor Ridel, you have grown tired of my asking the same question for eight years. Well, no more. I will ask no more. No need."

Geoffrey Ridel says nothing. He has a feeling that he is going to be let in on a well-kept secret, and this is not his personal preference.

"You see before you young Lord Jerrard, once the up-and-coming Earl of Boulton, going by the name of Brother William. Ah, the irony, adopting your father's name as a monk of the holy church. Are you proud of that, Brother William?"

"Yes, I am. It is the only thing belonging to my father that I have." Jerrard nods. The chancellor simply stares at this unfolding story. The king is barely listening. He is preparing to unleash a full scale tirade.

"Well then, Brother William Jerrard of Boulton, imposter and collaborator against your king, I once considered charging you with treason as well as your father. Maybe I'll do that now. And you will be found guilty." The king's voice rises as years of pent-up frustration come to the surface. His natural ruddy skin tone deepens to a ruby red. "And you will be condemned to death. It won't be a pretty death either." A royal index finger pokes at the air in front of Jerrard. "It will be ugly. And painful. The rack maybe. We'll use yours. Or burning you at the stake."

King Henry is now shouting. "You will forfeit your life. Understand? Understand?" Suddenly there is silence. The only sound in the room is the king's heavy breathing, now being brought under control. His next words are much softer. "But first, where is the Aureus?"

"Your Majesty, this is all too confusing. The Aureus? That is just folklore, is it not?" The chancellor finally speaks, shaking his head in bafflement.

"I will make it easy." Jerrard steps into the dialogue, and King Henry does not object. "It is a real treasure of gold coins, Roman coins, found on our property by our workers. My father took it, and…"

"By murder," Henry interjects. His face is still damp with anger.

"Correct. He took it, by murder, and you found out. So, chancellor, the charge of treason was just a reason to make war on Boulton. To get the Aureus. The king attacked my father to win a treasure, not to punish him for a crime against the crown. Are you following?"

"I am." Geoffrey Ridel remembers his tiny doubts about whether the Boulton betrothal offer could fit a legal definition of treason, the doubts he pushed to the back of his mind as he completed the royal writ so many years ago.

"Thomas learned of the treasure and sought out my father, offering to hide the Aureus, just in case. They were going to split the treasure, though each wanted it all for himself. Actually, Thomas wanted all of it for the church."

"Just like him. Church. Church. Church. Once upon a time, he was a reasonable man. Entertaining, too." Henry's face is crimson once again. He beats one fist into an open palm. "And when your father was killed, you became half owner of the Aureus. Tell me, how did you two rogues work that out? I'll bet neither of you dared turn your back on the other."

"Actually Thomas was my mentor, my protector and my friend, a true friend during all his years in exile. Though I could never take your place, King Henry. But, back to the treasure. Thomas, the church actually, got it all. I own only the cassock on my back."

"What?" Henry, rarely flustered, raises his hands in disbelief. "No. You are lying. Thomas is dead. You have the Aureus, but not for long."

"The Aureus is in Rome. All of it."

"What?" This time Henry has no other words.

"In two installments, but gone from Canterbury, where it resided for many years in a sarcophagus. It was transported in crypts bearing dead saints to their final resting place in Rome. You can verify their journeys. So, you see, the church won the Boulton/Plantagenet War, and it wasn't even a combatant. I simply carried out Thomas's wishes, and one wish of my own. Now I am here at your mercy."

Henry stands silently, processing this information. The color in his face is receding to an unnatural pallor, as if the Aureus were the life-blood being sucked from his body. He takes one, then two, steps backward, recoiling from this unwelcome news.

"You gave it away." It is a statement, not a question. "You just gave it away. Just gave it away."

"Well, yes, though I did ask one small personal favor, one which only the Pope could grant. But I remain what I was to Thomas, a poor Canterbury friar, an instructor of church liturgy."

King Henry scrutinizes the young man whose actions he cannot comprehend. His mind is reaching for royal words to summarize this bewildering situation, and they do not come to him. Twice he begins to speak, but all that follows is a continuation of the monarch's heavy breathing.

The silence is finally broken by the chancellor's voice. His tone has changed. His confusion has evaporated. "You wanted to atone for Thomas's death, Your Majesty. Here is your opportunity. Give back to this young man the birthright he lost so many years ago. He was Thomas's friend during his years in exile. You could honor the archbishop that way."

Henry blinks. He blinks a second time, then finally speaks. "Excellent idea, Chancellor. I was thinking of doing that very thing. I tell you, you are quite an artful politician. Are you sure you don't want to be archbishop? Young Boulton here could conduct your religious studies."

CHAPTER THIRTY-NINE

MANY VESSELS ROUTINELY ARRIVE at the English port of Dover. But on this day, a crowd has gathered for the landing of an unusual vessel, sighted in late morning. It is flying the distinctive French royal coat of arms, a golden fleur de lis on a blue background, and many Dover inhabitants have never seen a French boat.

On a nearby stretch of shoreline, a tastefully clad rider watches the royal cog sail into the harbor. He has come to this place every day for a week. Behind him, a sizeable coach flying the Boulton ensign sits atop a grassy dune. Two men relax on the driver's bench behind a team of horses. A single steed bearing a woman's saddle is tethered to the back of the buggy.

"Sire!" One of the drivers, a man known as Ethan, points to the approaching boat. "Is that it? It's French, like you described."

The rider nods yes and motions the drivers to follow him to the docking area. As they approach, the crowd splits, making room for the rider and his coach. There is much chatter about the rider and the boat's passengers. Or perhaps there is only one passenger. Who could it be? And who is the young man who commands the carriage with the Boulton insignia? Everyone from this seaside city, where gossip is a much traded commodity, knows that the House of Boulton was defeated in a battle regarding treasonous activities. The stories of dead men flying like projectiles into the castle are still told in the waterside ale houses. Some retired warriors, warm with beer, remember seeing the corpses flapping their arms like wings. It was quite a sight. The king certainly knew how to entertain his troops. A fine commander, that man Henry. Too bad the stain of an archbishop's murder lay on his crown.

And so, the crowd parts, then presses forward, anxious to see who the French king would send to English shores. There is much conversation about the emblem on the blue flag. A man announces that he has traveled across the water many times, and he can speak with authority about the golden design. It is a flower. A French flower. Others disagree. No flower looks like that. England is home to a variety of flowers, and none that are gold resemble the one stitched onto the blue cloth.

The discussion stops. A plank is thrown across the small opening between the boat and the wooden dock. Boatmen and dockworkers hold lines taut to lessen the unsteady rocking of this short board. A woman appears from the small canopied area in the middle of the cog. She walks to the plank and skips across it to the pier. Following her, burly men carry trunks that display the curious flower on a blue background.

Emma is home.

Jerrard, one hand behind his back, steps through the crowd, now dancing with anticipation. When he reaches Emma, the hand produces a bouquet of blue forget-me-nots. Cheering begins. Many note that proper English flowers are far superior to the French kind. Emma is not listening. Nor is Jerrard.

"Many years ago, we were rudely interrupted. Not this time."

The kiss that waited nearly nine years will not be rushed. For many bystanders, this is their first introduction to pure joy. Bards and minstrels sing of these fabled moments, but here, by the dock, it is really happening. The cheering is boisterous, infectious, and uplifting. It lasts as long as the kiss.

❈

"I BROUGHT A HORSE FOR YOU, if you'd like to ride with me. I've heard you are a good rider, and I've much to tell you."

"Very thoughtful. All I need is a lift of this foot." Emma offers her left leg to Jerrard, and she is in the saddle.

In a few minutes, the tiny caravan begins its westward journey. Lord Jerrard and Lady Emma are in front, followed by the carriage, now laden with trunks packed at the French court.

"We're going to my castle. No, wait, our castle. You won't be impressed. It's run down by disuse, but I've got my workers back, so, in time, it will look like it did before. My mother, brother and sisters are there. So is my daughter. Gweneth, same name as her mother. She's nearly eight now. Her other grandparents, the Sothinghams, are dead. Likely from a broken heart. Is this too much information at once?"

"No. I've been waiting for this for a long time."

"Alright. Are you easy to shock?"

Emma pulls back on her reins. Is the beautiful moment in time already passing?

"Again, no. But I prefer pleasant surprises."

"I hope this is one of them. You, with your experience, may very well agree with me."

"I'm waiting."

"Here it is. I'm planning to allow Gweneth, when she's older, to say yes or no to a marriage agreement. Maybe even give some weight to her own preferences. And if we have daughters, and I hope we do, the same for them. Pretty radical, wouldn't you say?"

"I would say."

"What if you had said to your own father, who, by the way, is coming with your family to our castle, what if you had said that you fancied Jerrard of Boulton, and he then arranged a marriage with me, and we wouldn't have wasted all this time? Think about it."

"You are a revolutionary. Off with your head." Emma laughs and punctuates her remark with a toss of her chestnut curls. "I don't think this idea will catch on, even though I personally like it."

"It will take a while, but I predict that sometime in the far-off future, maybe centuries into the future, people will marry whom they choose."

"Okay, but then, how else will great families be joined? Alliances made? Borders secured?" The chestnut curls are bouncing sideways as Emma's head shakes in bewilderment. "We found each other, but how would most people find a suitable mate?"

"Very challenging, I admit. I think I will just be happy that we are finally together."

"Will people be more contented?" Emma persists in the novel suggestion.

"Probably not. But it will be different. You are sure a questioner, but I knew that from my brief but enjoyable time as your religious instructor. Part of your charm."

"Then, what I want you to tell me is exactly how my divorce was arranged, how you reconciled with the king. There is so much I want to know."

"Plenty of time for that. Just now, ride closer to me. I want to share something else with you."

Jerrard's right leg now touches Emma's billowing skirt.

"See, you have returned to two men, Brother William, the monk, and Jerrard, Earl of Boulton. They've learned to coexist within me. I hope you will love both of us."

"Two men. My. So if I tire of one, I can turn to the other?"

"Something like that."

The two riders are very close now. Their conversation is a murmur, interrupted by shared laughter. To the drivers, they appear to be one. Ethan grins.

"I hear he told the Holy Father in Rome about the marriage being unclean, that Lady Emma was related to the French Prince. It's called consanguinity." He stumbles over this last word and says it again.

"Con-san-guin-i-ty. Means they're blood relations. It was a sin that they slept in the same bed. You know what I'm talking about." He summarizes with a knowing nod.

The driver named Gunner is puzzled. His frown follows his head, as it shakes slowly from side to side. "Didn't she know they were related when they got married?"

"You would think so. You would certainly think so."

EPILOGUE

IN THE FOLLOWING YEARS, King Henry added to his domains through war, diplomacy and marital matchmaking. He was the most powerful monarch in Europe. During this time he also had to face rebellions by each of his four sons, egged on by their mother, Eleanor, and aided by the king of France. Until the end of his life, Henry alternately fought and forgave his ungrateful children.

At the time of Thomas Becket's murder, Eleanor was living apart from Henry, in Poitiers, her childhood home in the Aquitaine. Their separation lasted nearly five years. In 1173, she agreed to return to England where she was immediately imprisoned by the king. From then until Henry's death, she was confined in various castles or closely supervised when she lived with her husband.

King Henry II of England died on July 6, 1189. He was fifty-six years old. His queen was immediately freed from all royal restraints. Eleanor lived to see two of her sons, Richard the Lionheart and John, rule England. She died in 1204, at the age of eighty-two.